SKELTON'S GUIDE TO BLAZING CORPSES

By David Stafford

Skelton's Guide to Domestic Poisons
Skelton's Guide to Suitcase Murders
Skelton's Guide to Blazing Corpses

SKELTON'S GUIDE TO BLAZING CORPSES

David Stafford

Allison & Busby Limited
11 Wardour Mews
London W1F 8AN
allisonandbusby.com

First published in Great Britain by Allison & Busby in 2022.

A CIP catalogue record for this book is available from
the British Library.

10 9 8 7 6 5 4 3 2 1

ISBN 978-0-7490-2724-7

Typeset in 11.5/16.5 pt Adobe Garamond Pro by
Typo•glyphix, Burton-on-Trent DE14 3HE.

The paper used for this Allison & Busby publication
has been produced from trees that have been legally sourced
from well-managed and credibly certified forests.

Printed and bound by
CPI Group (UK) Ltd, Croydon, CR0 4YY

In memory of
Marc Beeby

PROLOGUE

Guy Fawkes' Night,
Wednesday, 5th November 1930

When the Spanish Armada was defeated in 1588, the news was spread around the country by beacon fires blazing on prominent hilltops. Dunworth Beacon, just outside Great Dunworth, boasted the biggest and brightest of all the fires. That's what Mr Glazier said, anyway, and because he was Chairman of the Parish Council, and because nobody else had ever bothered to give the matter much thought, it was generally accepted as true.

To commemorate the event, every year on 29th June Mr Glazier lit the fire again, bright enough to be seen from Biggleswade in the east and Clophill in the west. He also lit fires to celebrate the King's birthday, the birth of a royal baby,

Empire Day, Trafalgar Day, Christmas, New Year, Easter and the birthday of William Pitt the Elder who, he claimed, spuriously, had some connection with the village.

Mr Glazier liked fires. And he didn't think any fire was complete without fireworks. He made these himself to his own recipes. They banged more loudly, flew higher and whizzed more fiercely than anything you could buy in the shops.

Guy Fawkes Night, 5th November, was always his greatest triumph. For weeks he would have the lads of the village carrying fissionable materials up the hill, where they would be scientifically arranged with reference to draught, ashfall and pyrolysis. The lads did as they were told because Mr Glazier was such a commanding presence. Some of the younger ones found him terrifying. A head taller than anybody they'd ever seen; he wore spectacles with one lens made of black metal instead of glass and extending down towards his mouth to conceal an empty eye socket and unsightly scarring. His left hand was a hook, which he used with great speed and dexterity, manipulating a log, for instance, then smacking the point of the hook into it to hoist it into the air, shaking it off, catching it and twisting it into its required position.

The injuries had been sustained during the war, in which he had served gleefully in the Royal Engineers, blowing up bridges, buildings, tanks, hills and forests, and generally having a fine old time.

But tonight, Guy Fawkes Night, though the bonfire had been built higher than ever before and though he had devised many new fireworks that, he hoped, would be heard in several counties and possibly cause light structural damage to nearby property, a gloom had descended. It was raining. The fire was soaked and there was a grave danger that his rockets and Roman candles would all end up damp squibs.

Nevertheless, at 7.30 he decided for the sake of tradition to brave the weather and light the damn thing anyway – give the villagers something cheery to see out of their windows. So, in sturdy boots, trench coat and sou'wester, a gallon can of petrol in his hand, a second gallon dangling from his hook, he made the ascent of Dunmore Beacon.

He removed some of the outer material so as to gain access to the inside of the fire, where the petrol would be most effective at drying out the whole. It caught with an audible 'whoosh'. So entranced was he by the movement and growth of the flames that it was several minutes before he noticed that it had stopped raining. The sky was clear, and there were people, with electric torches and hurricane lanterns, braving the mud and coming up the hill. They'd expect a show.

George Sonning was the first to arrive.

'I didn't bring the fireworks, George,' Mr Glazier said. 'Thought it'd be too wet. I should pop back and get them, I suppose. Tell everybody there will be a short delay, would you?'

Geoffrey Spencer had finished his homework by half past six. His dad had looked it over and criticised him for underlining freehand rather than doing it properly with a ruler.

'Nobody underlines with a ruler. Not even the teachers.'

'It doesn't matter what other people do, though, does it? If they want to produce sloppy work, that's up to them. But at Carter and Royal's we always use rulers.' Carter and Royal's was the insurance company where Dad worked.

It soured the atmosphere in the house already slightly soured by the fact that it was far too wet for any bonfires or fireworks. Mrs Spencer tried to ease the tension, but mostly they ate their baked potatoes and sausages in silence.

After supper, though, Geoffrey saw that the rain had stopped, and Mr Glazier had lit the fire after all.

'Shall we go up and have a look?' Geoffrey asked.

'No, it'll be muddy.'

Geoffrey watched the blaze from the window.

'I think I might go up,' he said. He was nearly sixteen. 'I'll put my wellies on.'

Mum looked at Dad, who rolled his eyes. It was up to her.

'All right, then. But be back by ten. Keep your scarf wrapped round your mouth so you don't breathe in the smoke. And don't get too close. You know what happened to Jeremy Fleming.'

Every bonfire night the name of Jeremy Fleming – Three Fingers Fleming – was invoked as a reminder of what happens to those who use Catherine wheels incautiously.

On the corner of Keeper's Lane, Geoffrey ran into Jeannie Crowson. This was all right. He'd had his eye on Jeannie

Crowson ever since the cricket match when she'd helped with the teas and said his face looked very brown against the white of his shirt.

Both of them had electric torches, but halfway up Keeper's Lane, Jeannie's torch flickered and died, so Geoffrey pretended his had bust, too. Then he made ghost noises and Jeannie pretended she was scared, so he put his arm round her, and she didn't seem to mind that at all.

Just ahead of them, around a bend in the lane, there was a whooshing sound and a great sheet of flame shot into the sky.

'Blimey, that's a big 'un,' Geoffrey said. 'What is it? Roman Candle?'

They ran towards it.

'Somebody's done their bonfire in the middle of the road,' Jeannie said. But even before she'd finished speaking they could see it wasn't a bonfire. Somebody had set a car alight.

'I bet it's them kids from Clophill,' Geoffrey said, trying not to sound scared. He was petrified of the kids from Clophill. Beyond the flames, they could see somebody running away. 'I wouldn't get too close if I were you, Jeannie. It might explode or something.'

But in fact, after the initial whoosh, the flames seemed to have died down.

Jeannie screamed. 'Oh, my God,' she said. 'There's somebody in it.'

Geoffrey moved closer. There was a figure, almost unrecognisable as human, behind the wheel. The skin had already blackened.

Once, Geoffrey's dad had burnt a pile of leaves. He didn't know there were frogs hiding in it. As the frogs burnt, their legs had slowly extended and stiffened. The driver's arms were doing the same, moving slowly upwards, away from the wheel.

Jeannie, hovering now near the edge of the flames, stuck out an arm to see how close she could get, then pulled it back fast and edged away.

'We should try and get him out, Geoffrey. He might still be alive.' This was a stupid thing to say, and she knew it. 'Or get some water, pull him out with a stick.'

'We can't do nothing,' Geoffrey said. 'I'm going up The Bell to get help.'

Rather than trying to get round the car, he climbed over the fence and took a straight line to the pub, stumbling across a ploughed field, with Jeannie following. He tripped and hit his head on something hard but got straight back up and kept running.

The rain started again.

On Stubbs Lane, they could see a group of blokes running towards the pub to get out of the rain. A couple of them had already noticed the light of the flames over the hedgerows.

Geoffrey shouted, 'There's a car on fire up Keeper's and there's somebody in it.'

A couple of the blokes ran into the pub to raise the alarm. There was confusion among the others because some of them had lights and some of them didn't, and some went the Stubbs Lane way, and some came over the gate into the field and went that way.

Geoffrey bent over, breathing heavily.

Jeannie came up behind him and put her arm around him.

'You all right?' she asked.

'I hurt myself a bit,' he said.

Jeannie helped him into the pub and sat him down.

'You're bleeding on your head,' she said.

She took her hankie out, spat on it, and dabbed at the blood, then held the hankie tight against the cut to stop the bleeding, keeping the other arm tight round his shoulder.

Geoffrey put both his arms round her waist and held on tight.

They'd seen the face. That was the trouble. It was grinning and there were flames coming out the top of the head.

Monday, 10th November 1930

Arthur Skelton, barrister-at-law, 39-years-old, pebble-glasses, face like a pantomime horse, wing-collar, grey homburg, thick overcoat against the chill, woollen scarf his mum in Leeds had knitted wrapped three times around his neck, gave some thought to the stone pier at the bottom of the steps outside Marylebone Police Court. He knew that sitting on cold stone was supposed to give you piles. Then there was the actual act of sitting down and getting up again to consider. He was six foot three, most of it spidery leg, and had been born with a displaced hip which still gave him trouble.

On the other hand, he needed somewhere to smoke and brood for a few minutes, so, throwing caution to the winds, he sat down, filled his pipe and read the advertisements on the passing buses.

Dewar's Whisky. Aaah, Bisto. Player's Weights. *Daily Graphic* for the BEST pictures.

He was fed up.

Usually, winning a case would be cause for at least a bit of a spring in the step and a glow to the complexion, but the morning's proceedings had left a nasty taste.

On the previous Saturday, Giles Gordon Ewers, 19, a student up at Oxford, having just scored the winning try in a college rugby match, was driving back to London in his AC two-seater. Drink had been taken. Feeling boisterous, he had dangled a walking stick, the sort with a duck's-head handle, out of the side of the car, in the manner of a polo mallet, and knocked down a lamp and the guard rails around some roadworks.

Two cyclists on a tandem, riding close behind, unable to stop, had collided with the guard rails and overturned. One of them sustained a head injury that left him momentarily unconscious, the other a leg injury, which had required twelve stitches.

Mr Ewers, though clearly aware of the accident, failed to stop and instead accelerated away.

All of this was observed by a motorcyclist who, having ascertained that other passers-by were attending to the injured cyclists, had given chase. Further along the road he stopped a police constable, who had jumped on the pillion. After giving chase for a couple of miles or so, they caught up with Mr Ewers, who stopped when ordered to by the constable and allowed himself to be taken into custody. He had spent the rest of the weekend in a police cell.

On the Sunday morning, the boy's father, General Sir James Ewers, had disturbed the leisurely breakfast being enjoyed by his solicitor, Aubrey Duncan, and insisted he get the best barrister available down to the police court first thing on Monday to make sure the boy was released, ideally with an apology from the police for making such a 'fuss' about a 'boyish prank'.

Since the General, a litigious man, was one of the solicitor's more lucrative clients, Duncan had disturbed the leisurely lunch of Arthur Skelton. And since Skelton and Duncan had worked together on many cases in the past, and since Skelton's chambers were practically next door to Duncan's offices, and since the fee being offered was breathtaking, arrangements were made.

A weekend in police custody usually left people looking seedy and unwashed. Giles Ewers seemed shiny, well-breakfasted and smiling.

'Lord bless us,' Ewer said, adopting the fake cockney accent favoured by bright young things, 'The guvnor's sent a proper brief. What's it going to be? Five quid and a wigging from the beak followed by a worse wigging from the guvnor?'

Young people of a certain class, Skelton had come to realise, had too often had their understanding of criminal law guided by the works of Mr P. G. Wodehouse, whose hero, Bertie Wooster, often told tales of having to pay a fiver to a magistrate for knocking off a policeman's helmet on New Year's Eve, or getting a 'wigging' from some dowager aunt for burgling her house.

He glanced at the charge sheet that had been handed to him on his way in. There were several.

'I'm afraid the first charge alone,' he said, 'that of dangerous driving, could attract a two-year sentence.'

The boy smiled, 'But surely …?' He leant slightly to one side, as if the thought of prison had literally sent him off balance. 'You haven't got a cigarette, have you? I ran out.' He held up his empty cigarette case and let one of the sides flap down.

'Pipe man, I'm afraid.'

'Could you perhaps send one of the chaps out to get some?'

'Court ushers are not employed to run errands for the accused.'

The boy sat up and sulked.

'Shall we get on with it?' Skelton said. 'Now, first of all I would advise against pleading guilty. Given the nature and number of the charges, the magistrates would have little option other than to send you to prison. You have already admitted to taking drink after the rugby match.'

'Yes, but, only a couple of pints.'

'Mild?'

'Bitter.'

'And in your experience, after a couple of pints, are you a competent driver?'

'Sharp as a knife.'

'But on this occasion, you seem to have driven erratically, not to say recklessly.'

The boy was silent.

'Do you have a mechanic who takes care of your car?'

'The guvnor's chauffeur usually has a look at it when I'm in town.'

'And is it in generally good condition, brakes, steering, tyres and so on?'

'He said it was making a bit of a racket, but I said I like it like that.'

'A problem with the silencer, perhaps?'

'She's a rust bucket, but I do love the old dear.'

Skelton remembered a case from a couple of years earlier – not one of his – in which the defence had claimed that the driver appeared to be drunk but was actually suffering from inhalation of fumes, which were escaping into the car from a defective exhaust. There was obviously no time to get expert testimony and mechanical inspections before the trial today, but it might be enough to secure an adjournment. It was something, anyway.

He told the boy how to behave himself in court. Head down, look ashamed, no smiling, speak when you're spoken to, answer the questions with one-word answers if possible. Then he provided him with pen and paper and dictated a letter he could send to the couple on the tandem, expressing his heartfelt apologies and offering them, by way of compensation, twenty-five pounds to cover repairs to the bicycle and medical expenses. This meant that in court, to further demonstrate the boy's contrition, Skelton could say, without perjuring himself, 'Mr Ewers has already written to …'

On the way into the court, he saw Charlie Perry, one of the ushers, and stopped for a word.

'What happened about Fulham?' Skelton asked. The last time they'd spoken, some weeks earlier, Charlie had told him that his son, Bert, had been invited to try out for the Fulham boys' team.

'He's played, three games,' Charlie said. 'Hasn't exactly shone in any of them but he keeps his end up and they haven't sacked him yet.'

'You get down to see him?'

'Wild horses wouldn't keep me away, Mr Skelton,' Charlie said. 'You doing the Ewers boy?'

Skelton nodded glumly.

'I wouldn't have thought you've got much to worry about. Mr Mariner served under the General at Cambrai.' Mariner was the Chairman of the Magistrates.

Skelton sighed. To claim that the link would compromise Mariner's eligibility to have anything to do with the case was, he knew, pointless. Half a million men served under General Ewers at Cambrai. The fact that Mariner – a senior officer, no doubt – would most likely have messed with him, passed him the port and met his good lady wife, would be considered irrelevant. And besides, whenever a representative of the wealthy and privileged classes came to court it was inevitable that the accused and whoever was on the bench, if they didn't have a school, college, regiment or club in common, would be married to each other's cousins, would have met weekending at Binkie and Gloria Shoebridge's, or would have attended their respective daughters' coming-out balls.

In court, the first time Mariner used first the phrase 'this regrettable example of youthful exuberance' then 'ebullient high spirits' Skelton knew he was wasting his time. Whatever he or anybody else said in court, the result, just as the boy had predicted, would be five pounds and a wigging.

And so it was.

Charlie came out onto the steps and saw Skelton sitting on the pier. 'All right, Mr Skelton?'

Skelton said something vaguely cheerful, but Charlie could tell by his face that he was not all right at all and had a shrewd idea of why he wasn't all right. He stood in front of Skelton and held up his left hand to show that he was missing the first joint of his little finger.

'See that?' he said.

'Oh, dear.'

'Russian revolution.'

'You were in Russia?'

'No. Black Lion Yard, off the Whitechapel Road. This was the '05 revolution, not the '17 one. Lot of Russians live down that way, and when the news came through about the Tsar's troops shooting people, there was a degree of upset, some people saying one thing and some saying another, mostly in

Russian, so I couldn't follow a word of it. Then fights broke out and I got knocked over. Fell against a cart, caught a nasty splinter in there. It went septic and in the end they had to amputate.'

'Does it hurt?'

'I like to think of it as an injury sustained fighting for a noble cause.'

'Which side were …?'

'Bolsheviks?'

'Do you still …?'

'Card carrying.'

Skelton had his pipe going nicely now. 'Is that allowed? Working here?' he asked.

'I'm undercover.'

'Not now you've told me, you're not.'

'You can be trusted, though, Mr Skelton. I don't know nothing about your politics, but I know you're an honest man. You can be trusted.'

'It's very nice of you to say so, Charlie.'

'And I can promise you, when it comes – the revolution – General Sir James Ewers will be first up against the wall.'

'Sounds a bit extreme.'

Charlie grinned. The clock on St Mary's church struck the hour and Skelton tried with difficulty to stand. Charlie gave him a hand, which turned into a warm handshake.

'Give my best to your lad,' Skelton said.

* * *

There were no cabs to be had on Marylebone Road, so Skelton took the underground to Charing Cross, looking forward to a walk along the Victoria Embankment.

Curiously, as he came out of the Tube station, he found himself flanked by crowds of people, all moving in the same direction. He asked a woman with a fox fur and a child grasped firmly by the hand where everybody was going.

'It's the Lord Mayor's Show,' she replied, as if to a lunatic.

Of course it was. He'd been reading about it in *The Times* on the train into town that morning. To avoid it, he tried turning up Savoy Street, but the crowds up there seemed even thicker. At Temple Gardens, he gave in and decided he might as well watch the procession along with everybody else, standing five or six deep now, on either side of the road.

Skelton, a head taller than most other people, placed himself at the back so as not to impede anybody's view and found himself next to a man, almost as tall as himself, with a boy of seven or eight sitting astride his shoulders. They exchanged a friendly nod.

Behind them, a boat on the river hooted. Somebody nearby shouted, 'Better out than in.' People laughed. Then they stiffened as, in the distance, they heard the first notes of a military band. First just the drums, then the brass and woodwind.

The players, on horseback, came into view, the drummer in the lead pounding two kettle drums, one on either side of his horse, with great flourishes of his sticks, followed by tubas or something like it, then saxophones and trumpets.

Skelton had seen pictures of mounted bands before and had wondered, but, in the flesh, the full absurdity of the phenomenon came clear. Playing a musical instrument was difficult at the best of times. Playing a musical instrument with both hands, while simultaneously controlling a horse with the reins wrapped around one arm seemed unnecessarily complicated, like underwater clock repair or surgeons on skates. Why do it? Why not, say, put them in carts pulled by horses, so that they could concentrate on doing one thing really well.

The lad on his dad's shoulders seemed to be thinking along the same lines.

'Are those men soldiers, Dad?'

'Yes, son.'

'Where are their guns?'

'I think they must have left them at home, son.'

The band was followed by more soldiers on horses who seemed to have neither guns nor musical instruments, which made them more pointless still.

Then came various lorries decorated to represent this and that. One that was, according to the banner that preceded it, something to do with St Bartholomew's Hospital, was done up like a mediaeval castle with people dressed as characters from Robin Hood standing on the battlements. They waved.

'What's that, Dad?'

'Dunno, son.'

'When will the exciting stuff happen?'

Another, promoting Australian imports, had a chef stirring a huge pudding bowl. This provoked no comment from the lad at all. Skelton checked to see whether he might have gone to sleep.

After a moment's hiatus, the boy started bouncing and his dad had to hold his feet tight to stop him falling off.

'I CAN SEE ELEPHANTS!'

This was the exciting stuff he'd come for.

Skelton could see them, too. Four real elephants were lumbering down the road, attended by mahouts with canes and feathered turbans. The front two, side by side, had howdahs on their backs. They were followed by two more in single file, the one bringing up the rear holding the next one's tail in his trunk.

'Dad, can you see the elephants? Dad, they're real elephants. Dad, they're elephants. Elephants, Dad. Dad, look, look, it's elephants!'

Something was wrong.

The elephants seemed alarmed. The front ones veered off course. The others followed. They hurtled into the crowd. Some people fell, others tried to rush away. There was a crush. Skelton, the man and the boy fell, with Skelton breaking the boy's fall. His hat and glasses went flying. A bony woman fell on top of him, their faces uncompromisingly close. He couldn't breathe, not just because the woman's hat was covering his face and nose but because there was too much pressure on his chest, and something sharp digging into his ribs. Something hit his leg and turned his foot back.

The pain eased gradually as those who were still standing managed to move away and those who had fallen began to stand. The sound was different. Where a few moments earlier there had been cheering and chatter, now there was silence broken by groans and, somewhere up the line, a scream of pain.

The thin woman managed to stand. She muttered a few words of apology. Skelton was about to ask whether she was all right, but she'd gone. His head hurt, his foot hurt, his ribs hurt. Worst of all was his leg. He'd spent his childhood in and out of hospital, enduring operations, manipulations, one sort of brace after another trying to sort out the displaced hip he'd been born with. Nothing had ever worked. Still he walked with a limp. Now it hurt more than it had for years.

'No, I'm fine, Dad,' the lad was saying. 'I fell on that man and he had his hand over my head so nobody could fall on me.'

The boy's dad, who was standing, apparently unharmed, stood over Skelton and said, 'Do you need some help?'

Skelton accepted the man's offer and allowed himself to be pulled to his feet. He could stand. Nothing appeared to be broken, but the hip was agony.

'Are these yours, mister?' the boy asked holding out his glasses.

One of the arms was a little bent, but mercifully the lenses were intact.

The elephants were nowhere to be seen. Further up the

line, police, Boy Scouts and the St John's Ambulance Brigade were attending to the wounded.

'Shall I ask one of them to come down and have a look at you?' the man said.

'No, I'll be fine,' Skelton said. The boy picked up his briefcase and umbrella, which lay near. 'I wonder …?' Skelton nodded towards his hat, which was rolling in the wind a little way off. The boy raced off to retrieve it.

'I'm Arthur Skelton, by the way.'

'Cyril Monkhouse,' the man said, 'and this is Howard.'

'Thank you both very much for your help. What exactly happened?'

'Some lads, I think,' Cyril said. 'Ran out and frightened the elephants.'

'Ah, yes. A regrettable example of youthful exuberance, I expect,' Skelton said.

'Eh?'

'A phrase I heard used earlier today.'

'Well …' Cyril said.

It was a strangely awkward moment. The three of them, Skelton, Cyril and Howard had shared a moment of peril and they were now to part. On the other hand, to say 'Shall we go and get a drink somewhere', seemed presumptuous.

'Well, thank you again, Cyril,' Skelton said and wondered why he felt so emotional. Almost weepy. Shock, probably.

'Well, thank you for looking after the boy,' Cyril said. His voice was cracking, too.

They shook hands with far more grip and enthusiasm than

either of them intended, and thought but did not say, you are now embarking on the great journey of the rest of your life and may your health be robust, your fortunes prosper and your hopes fulfilled.

Tuesday, 11th November 1930

Skelton drained the soggy bits of stray biscuit, the residue from dunking, from the bottom of his cup and started filling his pipe. He and his clerk Edgar, a dapper man with broad hips and tiny feet, were having their regular morning meeting, in chambers at 8 Foxton Row. To the oak panelling, formidable desk and leather-bound books common to most barrister's rooms, Skelton had added two easy chairs, the sort with wooden arms, and a low table. He'd never been comfortable at a desk. Sometimes, if he had a lot of hard reading to do and wasn't expecting any visitors, he would lie on the Turkish carpet.

Today, he felt a particular need for soft furnishings. He was still in pain from the previous day's misfortunes, stuck liberally with plasters and smelling of Germolene, but he had his pipe, there was tea, there were biscuits, and the fire in the grate had reached that comforting stage when the drama of the flames had given way to a sensible glow.

Edgar poured a third cup, moved the tea tray from the low table to the desk and replaced it with the pile of paperwork that needed attention.

'Do you have curtains?' he asked.

'What?'

'In your house? Do you have curtains at the windows?'

'Yes.'

'What are they like?'

'Green, I think. Or red. One or the other.'

Edgar frowned impatiently. 'No, I mean what are they made of?'

'Cloth, I'd imagine.'

'Velvet? Brocade?'

'Possibly. Or … is there such a thing as just ordinary cloth?'

Over the previous weeks, Edgar had frequently raised questions of interior decoration. Having lived in boarding houses of one sort or another practically all his life, now, at the age of forty-six, he had acquired a flat of his own, in a mansion block in Belsize Park, and had engaged an excellent housekeeper to cook and clean.

'I don't think I can have curtains,' he said.

'No?'

'I mean, I have curtains at the moment. They came with

the flat. A sort of jacquard damask with a floral pattern in washed teal and a royal blue.'

'Oh,' Skelton said, slightly alarmed, the way you would be if somebody suddenly and for no reason began speaking in the language of the Iroquois people.

'They're very ugly. And I know I have to replace them with something, and I look at this fabric and that fabric, and they all seem equally unpleasant. There are one or two Eloise Bourgeois very angular geometric designs that just about pass muster, but I am tempted to go the way of Le Corbusier, dispense with curtains altogether and have shutters installed. Or would that be too austere, do you think?'

Skelton sat back and smoked his pipe happily, enjoying the way Edgar made a meal of the nonsense syllables – 'jacquard damask', 'Eloise Bourgeois', 'Le Corbusier'.

Edgar, like Skelton, was not top drawer by birth. As a boy he'd lived an almost feral life with a mother and a varying number of brothers and sisters – some of whom may have been strays taken in from other families – in a series of hovels, usually in the Bethnal Green or Stepney areas of London. Somewhere along the line he had acquired the habit of reading – anything from a discarded sardine tin to Plato's *Republic* – and, under the tutelage of Tyser Knapp, a career criminal, had learnt the art of the snakesman as well as dipping, parlour-jumping, and flying the blue pigeon. He would, like Tyser, almost certainly have ended up dying young of prison fever were it not for an enlightened magistrate who, impressed by the boy's carefully argued rebuttal of the charges against him (he cited Blackstone twice), instead of sending him for a whipping and a lagging, secured him a position as errand boy at a chambers in Chancery Lane where Edgar had learnt his lessons as quickly as he had done under Tyser Knapp. Within six months he had acquired beautifully legible handwriting and absorbed the rules of punctuality, politeness, spickness and spanness, as well as a good grounding in the workings of the legal professions. He had also acquired the voice he had possessed ever since and would be the first to admit that he might have overdone it. Hard work rounding the vowels and sharpening the consonants had resulted in, rather than the timbres of gravelly *gravitas* he had hoped for, the shriek of an outraged duchess. Over the years he had learnt to control both the volume and pitch of the shriek so that it was bearable at all times, and now and then pleasant to listen to, even musical. In the space of a single sentence he could run from a *dolcemente basso profundo* to Wagnerian *soprano* and the elastic eyebrows always followed the pitch.

'You need space, though, don't you?' he said, 'for shutters. To allow freedom of movement when they open and close.' He mimed the opening and closing, first with arms out and eyebrows up, then arms in and eyebrows down. 'Although, sometimes in old houses you see shutters in two or three hinged sections, don't you? I wonder if Ernest could run something up for me.'

He'd mentioned Ernest before, a man in a mews who made things from wood and metal. Edgar swore by Ernest.

'What do you think?'

'I think …' Skelton said, and, after a long pause, decided to leave it there.

It had never occurred to him that what Edgar called 'interior design' could be a topic of interest. He remembered, a long while ago, when he and his wife Mila had first moved into their house in Lambourn, going to a shop in Reading that seemed to sell ordinary-looking furniture and ordering a houseful of it, and then choosing, from sample books, whatever seemed the least offensive wallpaper and curtains. Neither of them had taken any real interest in the proceedings. Pictures had proved a little more difficult until they discovered that people were often only too happy to let you have their unwanted ones, often nicely framed. So, they'd hung some of those here and there wherever the walls seemed bare. Fruit and views, mostly.

Edgar took a Gold Flake from his cigarette case and lit it thoughtfully, then, deciding they should get on, picked up the pile of papers and started sorting them.

'Letters from all over the place about the Abrasives business,' he said.

Romero and Gaines versus Anglo-American Abrasives was a case that had been going on, in one form or another, for months. Sometimes it reared its head as *Anglo-American Abrasives versus Thomas, Briggs and Studely-Hogg*, and sometimes as *Thomas and Briggs versus Studely-Hogg*. Skelton had yet another meeting about the matter later in the morning and picked through the correspondence to see if anything might require his immediate attention. He had practically lost track of exactly who was suing whom and had long ago ceased to care one way or the other, but he persisted if only because Edgar's share of the majestic fees provided him with the means to go the way of Le Corbusier and keep Ernest-in-the-mews gainfully employed.

Edgar untied the ribbons on a new brief and announced, '*Rex versus Denison Beck*.'

Skelton already knew something of the case. It had come in from Aubrey Duncan, the solicitor who'd been shanghaied by General Ewers to summon a barrister, and with whom Skelton and Edgar had worked so frequently in the past that he was almost family.

Denison Beck was a 'medical electrician' with premises in Wimpole Street who, according to his advertisements, claimed to be able to cure, with his Frankenstein apparatus, anything from 'incapacity for exertion' to 'disrelish for food' to 'spermatorrhoea'. Skelton could only guess the nature of 'spermatorrhoea'.

Beck's 'cures' had become quite the thing among the smart set, who hoped they might alleviate their permanent hangovers thus enabling them to drink more, and among old fogeys who wanted neither to be old nor fogeys.

Mrs Edith Roberts was a former Gaiety Girl whose dancing career had been brought to a tragic end when, while executing a particularly difficult manoeuvre during a song entitled 'A Lot of Funny Folks One Sees at Ladies' Universities', she collided at speed with a canvas horse and sustained some injury to her back that forced her into retirement from the musical stage.

Luckily, she subsequently made a good marriage with a wine and spirits dealer three times her age, who died soon after the wedding leaving her comfortably off.

The bad back had never got better and at times gave her great pain. According to friends and her maid, though she had searched high and low, she had never been able to find a medical practitioner who could form an accurate diagnosis, never mind suggest an effective cure. Until, that is, she encountered Denison Beck. She made frequent visits to Beck's consulting rooms, sometimes twice or three times a week. Over the course of a year, the back was considerably improved.

Then poor Mrs Roberts had suffered a heart attack and died. She was a forty-two-year-old woman, healthy apart from her bad back, with no history of heart disease. The coroner smelt a rat. Suspicion fell on Beck's treatments. Experts inspected his electrical equipment and concluded that mechanical fault or human error could easily have fatal consequences.

Beck was arrested on a charge of manslaughter.

Skelton picked up the brief and glanced at the first page. 'And the prosecution think they can make this stick?'

'Apparently so.'

Skelton wrinkled his nose sceptically. 'Manslaughter by negligence?'

'It is indeed the slimmest of cases. I'd imagine the defence would simply be a matter of repeating the arguments that were used in the Bateman appeal.'

They were both aware of *Rex versus Bateman*, in which a doctor who had botched the delivery of a baby, killing both the mother and the child, was found guilty of 'gross negligence manslaughter' but subsequently had the verdict quashed when the appeal judge ruled that *mens rea* – criminal intent – had not been proven.

'Except there is a difference,' Skelton said. 'Does Beck have any formal qualifications?'

'There might be a certificate from a Peruvian university, but nothing that's recognised by the British Medical Association.'

'So, if the prosecution argues that Beck has no recognised medical qualifications and that therefore the entire enterprise is fraudulent, they'll have their "criminal intent" and *Rex versus Bateman* won't apply. Is Beck in Brixton?' Skelton asked.

'He got bail.'

'Really?'

'Marylebone Police Court,'

'Mariner on the bench?'

'I'd assume so.'

'That man really does work on the assumption that anyone with a posh voice and an income of more than £800 a year is innocent and everybody else is guilty. Can we arrange a meeting with Beck, perhaps later this week?'

Edgar stood up to get the appointments book from

Skelton's desk. As he did so, Skelton's attention was drawn to his trousers. They had the most impeccable creases he had ever seen. Brand-new trousers, fresh from the tailor, were never creased so perfectly. And the sides, between the creases, were smooth as glass. Skelton looked down at his own trousers, which looked, as they always did, as if they'd recently seen service for potato storage.

'I can see you're admiring my trousers,' Edgar said, smiling. 'All the work of the redoubtable Mrs Stewart, my housekeeper. I think I may have already mentioned that her cleaning is of a standard rarely met in operating theatres, but that is far from being the greatest of her arts. If wars could be settled on the ironing board Mrs Stewart could conquer the world.'

'Does she have some special trick?'

'Several, I think, the most noticeable being the use of pins.'

'Pins?'

'She pins the trousers to the board so they're practically rigid and you don't get all that unexpected rumpling.'

'Don't the pins make holes?'

Edgar put one foot on the low table to get a closer look.

'None that I can see. Perhaps she's very careful to pin through the weave. Or perhaps you can get special pins. Very thin ones.'

Skelton began to notice other details. Edgar had always been nicely turned out but today his shirt looked like something in a book about angels, his shoes, which were the ones specially made for Edgar's difficult feet, looked brand new even though they were at least a year old, and his waistcoat, that most difficult of all garments, sat tight and seemed to move with him like a second skin. He decided to contact his old Cambridge college and suggest they institute a degree in Domestic Management and Maintenance with Mrs Stewart as Senior Professor.

He was on his way to the Anglo-American Abrasives meeting in Chancery Lane when the clocks struck the eleventh hour of the eleventh day of the eleventh month. The city came to a standstill. Trams stopped. Horses snorted. Women clutched prams and bowed their heads as if at an altar rail. A sandwich board man, advertising two-shilling permanent waves, stood rigidly to attention.

In the two minutes' silence, Skelton thought of the snapshot, taken when he was at Cambridge, of him and four other students posed in what they had hoped was a dignified manner in the quad at Pembroke. It stood, framed, on the mantlepiece at his parents' house in Leeds. He was the only survivor of that group of five. Both of his brothers had come through it, thank God, but he'd lost cousins and schoolfriends. Edgar had lost two brothers and had another brother who, shell-shocked, took his own life in '21. And everywhere, twelve years after it was all over, you saw men with a leg, an arm or half a face missing, men still trying to cough the gas out of their lungs, men and women who at the going down of the sun and in the morning could not unknow what they knew and could not unsee what they had seen.

The American Abrasives meeting was as tedious as mumps. The room was overheated by steam radiators. One of the Romero and Gaines people spoke for forty-five minutes in an unchanging drone about the *ultra vires* rule and the principle of vicarious liability until Skelton was digging fingernails into his thighs in an effort to stay awake.

It was, therefore, with a sense of half-holiday relief that, just before six, he found himself picking a way through the rotten fruit and cabbage stalks left over from the Leather Lane market for an early dinner.

Mila, his wife, had, for years, taken part in a discussion group in Maidenhead. They chose a topic a week. Mila thrived on a robust political discussion. She had caused outrage among the more staid members of the group by her support for Bolshevism, but, more recently, appalled by Stalin's treatment of Trotsky, she had veered away from Bolshevism and towards the collectivist anarchism advocated by Mikhail Bakunin and Peter Kropotkin. This, of course, outraged the staid members even more. There was talk of banning her lest she brought the bombs they were sure she must possess to meetings.

Often the Maidenhead group would invite guest speakers, one of whom, Gillian McPhail, a lecturer in French literature at Birkbeck College in London, gave a talk on French symbolist poetry and its legacy.

Afterwards, Mrs McPhail and Mila had fallen into conversation about Proudhon, the anarchist philosopher and Gillian had suggested that Mila should come along to an informal course that she was planning at Birkbeck called 'Trends in Modern Thought' and Mila had thought it would suit her down to the ground. She'd been looking for a new challenge. Earlier that year she had learnt to fly an aeroplane, but had found it was an expensive hobby and, in light of the various aeronautical disasters that seemed to crop up on a weekly basis, most notably the crash of the R101 airship in the previous month, possibly too perilous for a woman with a husband and two children. So, she gave it up not long after getting her licence. Though her understanding of politics could put most cabinet ministers to shame, she had never had much in the way of formal education. Her girls' school, while giving students a firm grounding in the need to play up and play the game, regarded more scholarly matters as men's business. So, Gillian's course seemed just the thing.

Before the seven o'clock class (Gillian preferred to call them 'meetings') she and Skelton had got into the habit of taking an early dinner together in a little cafe she'd found not far from the college on Leather Lane.

The cafe's Victorian sign had faded, leaving only the letters 'Mel Hy' visible. Nobody could remember what was there before the cafe came into existence. Reg, the current proprietor's theory – that it was the 'Melton Mowbray Hygienic Pork-Pie Company' – was probably as good as anybody's, but Skelton preferred to believe that it was once the premises of a violin-playing mesmerist who traded as 'The Melodious Hypnotist', while Mila went with an ice-sculpture workshop specialising in flowers called 'Melting Hydrangeas'.

The people who worked in the market never called it anything except 'Smelly Melly's'.

The menu, based on various kinds of stodge, suited them. Though they both enjoyed French cuisine when they were in France, in England the folderol that usually came with it in posh restaurants didn't suit them at all. Their mistrust of anything fancy – Mila was a Socialist, Skelton was from Leeds – like their penchant for the smell of boot polish and their aversion to satin, was a key ingredient in the cement that bound them together.

Skelton saw his wife through the steamy window, deeply absorbed in one of the several newspapers she read each day. She had a pencil in her hand which meant that she was either marking up stories which, for one reason or another, particularly outraged her – she was fond of outrage – or she was doing the crossword.

'It was all started by some students, apparently, from King's College,' Mila said, as soon as she saw him enter. This was par for the course. She rarely bothered with formalities, preambles and preliminaries, preferring to jump straight to the middle of a conversation and keep going until her husband caught up.

She picked up the *Daily Graphic* and read aloud, '"They

were waiting with the college mascot representing a lion. The mascot was waved, and fireworks discharged".'

Skelton twigged. The elephants at the Lord Mayor's Show.

'I don't remember hearing any fireworks,' he said. He eased his bad leg out to one side. It would present a tripping hazard for an inexperienced waiter bearing a tray of badly stacked glasses, but Reg, he knew, was canny.

'Perhaps they were the ones that fizz without banging.'

Skelton nodded and Mila continued, '"The elephants decided that they had had enough and charged the students. One of them was chased around a tree but escaped. Other people who had nothing to do with the escapade were knocked over and trampled on by the crowd".'

'Was anybody actually killed?' Skelton asked.

'"Eleven persons were treated at Charing Cross Hospital for slight injuries",' Mila read, '"but no one was detained. Mr Race Power, of Brixton Hill, manager of Power's Dancing Elephants, said tonight: 'The four elephants, which belong to my wife, are all about thirty years old. This is the first time in our whole experience that they have been involved in anything of the kind. They are four big pets, and they are as good as little children.'" "Colour slightly".'

'What?'

'Crossword clue. Five letters. "Colour slightly".'

'Paint.'

'Ends in an E.'

'Rouge.'

'Second letter I.'

'Filne.'

'That's not a word.'

'You're so fussy.'

The food came. Both had ordered pie with spuds, greens and gravy. Once, a customer, a city type, had asked Reg what kind of pie it was.

'Meat,' Reg had replied.

'What kind of meat?' the gent had asked, and Reg had laughed all the way back to the kitchen.

'Poachers do rabbits.'

'What?'

'Twelve across. Something something S something something something E.'

'Poachers do rabbits?'

'That's what it says.'

'Shouldn't it be "Poachers do this to rabbits"? Trap, shoot, eat, kill, snare.'

'Snare would fit at the end, but it's only five letters. There's another two on the front.'

'Resnare, unsnare. Is "ensnare" a word?'

'More of a word than "filne".' Mila wrote it in.

The pie came. The crust was exactly the right consistency to soak up gravy without getting soggy.

'Did you finish your homework?' Skelton asked.

'It's not homework. It's recommended reading.' Mila passed him a book called *Russian Poetry, An Anthology*. Skelton turned a couple of pages. It didn't look promising.

'And Gillian gave us some cyclostyled notes.' Skelton sniffed the notes. Sometimes cyclostyles smelt interesting. These didn't.

'Pushkin,' he said.

'What about him?'

'He was a Russian poet. I can't think of any others.'

'Gillian is very keen on the revolutionary ones, Mayakovsky and Esenin.'

'Are they good?'

'It depends what you mean by "good".'

'Like Longfellow.' At school, Skelton had learnt chunks of Longfellow's *The Wreck of the Hesperus*, Tennyson's *The Charge of the Light Brigade* and Wordsworth's *Daffodils*. He liked the Hesperus best, so considered Longfellow his favourite poet.

'Not much like Longfellow, no.'

'Are they old or young?' Young poets, he knew, were often feckless recent graduates pretending to be poets. The old ones had at least stuck at it.

'Fairly young, I think. But dead.'

'Famine?'

'Suicide.'

'How?'

'Esenin hanged himself, Mayakovsky shot himself.'

'Where?'

'I don't know. Moscow, I expect.'

'No, I mean … in the head?'

'What difference would it make?'

44

'It would make all the difference in the world. You remember that chap I defended six or seven years ago. Shot himself in the heart, missed, hit a rib and a lung, had an awful time getting better, then got sent to prison for attempted suicide. Shooting yourself in the head is fast and certain. Bang. Anywhere else, in the heart or what have you, you've no idea how long it's going to take, have you?'

'Freezing to death is supposed to be a lot more pleasant than is often imagined,' Mila said.

'Who says?'

'Polar explorers. Apparently, you get cold. Then you get very cold. Then you start feeling warm and sleepy. Then you go to sleep and you never wake up again.'

'The warm and sleepy is probably not too bad but the very cold might be irksome.'

'Better than burning, though. Did you see the man in the paper?'

Skelton had. 'In the car in …'

'Bedfordshire. He had debts, apparently, and was facing a bigamy charge and God knows what else. All the same, pouring petrol over yourself and lighting a match …'

Mila cleaned her plate. Skelton had two spuds left so she stole one of them. 'What time is it?' she asked.

Skelton looked at his wristwatch.

'Twenty to. Are you going to have a pudding?'

'I thought I might just have some more pie with spuds, greens and gravy.'

'Excellent idea. "Tinge"?'

'What?'
'Colour slightly.'
Mila wrote it in.

Wednesday, 12th November 1930

The taxi arrived at Wimpole Street.

'Denison Beck – Medical Electrician' was one of four brass plates on the door, the others belonging to an ophthalmic surgeon, an aural surgeon and an F. C. Motherwell who offered 'American dentistry'.

The door was answered by a porter dressed in a maroon Eton jacket and bow tie. He didn't look well. There was a film of sweat on his forehead and a haunted look in his eyes.

He asked them their business and ushered them in, staggering slightly as he walked towards the staircase.

'Are you all right?" Skelton asked, wondering if he was just very drunk, as porters often are, even in Shakespeare. 'Do you want me to get you a doctor?'

It seemed a foolish thing to say. Like standing in the Champs-Élysées and saying, 'Would you like me to get you a Frenchman?' There were probably forty or fifty doctors in Wimpole Street and another hundred around the corner in Harley Street.

'I'm fine, thank you very much for asking,' the porter said but, all the same, looked up at the staircase in the way that Whymper might have considered the Matterhorn.

'I'm sure we can find our own way,' Skelton said.

The porter looked grateful. 'Just at the top of the stairs,' he said, 'first door on the right.'

The door was opened automatically with some sort of buzzer. They moved from the lino of the hallway to a carpet so thick you could turn an ankle. A woman, dressed, coiffed and be-rouged to look like a waxwork introduced herself as Miss Alison. She sat at a spindly writing desk before a display of buttons and a telephone. Selecting a green button, she purred into the telephone.

'Mr Beck is expecting you,' she said. Another green button caused the door opposite magically and silently to open.

Beck's consulting room would have met with Marie Antoinette's approval; a precise shambles of pastel colours, gold bits, plaster and woodwork carved into ribbons and flowers, and more gold bits. Beck himself sat on a throne behind a desk that was the size of a spare bedroom. It had more gold curly bits attached. None of the electrical apparatus he used for his 'treatments' was in evidence, but his desk was blessed with at least four times as many buttons as Miss Alison's. Skelton guessed that some of them were to do with the telephones of which there were three, some of them to make doors open, some of them to make lights come on and go off. Others possibly made the moon come out or fomented revolution in Istanbul.

Introductions were made. Beck stood and padded silently towards them, the carpet visibly bouncing beneath his patent leather shoes like ancient peat, and pressed a button on the wall. A panel slid silently to one side revealing a mirror-backed drinks cabinet. Some of the drinks were yellow. Two were blue. Like the desk, the chairs and the walls, all the glasses and decanters had gold curly bits on them.

'Drink?' Beck asked. His voice, like that of Miss Alison, was the purr of a cat set loose in Billingsgate.

'I wouldn't say no to a cup of tea,' Skelton said.

'What about you, Mr Haynes?'

'Hobbes,' Edgar said. 'Yes, please. Tea with a spot of milk and no sugar.'

Beck flicked a red switch on his desk, picked up one of his telephones and ordered tea for three. He ushered Skelton and Edgar into satin chairs and arranged himself in front of a bookshelf, his dove grey suit flowing over him like water, his silk shirt the palest yellow, with tie in a contrasting lavender. Skelton found himself wondering how he got his hair to do that – to remain soft and blonde and apparently brilliantine-free but still all in one place except for one lock at the front, which fell over his unlined forehead.

He was a fraud. Skelton had known men like him at Cambridge – all absinthe and quails' eggs and girlfriends. Rarely out of a punt. Never clever enough to notice they were dim. Did no work then crammed in the week before finals just enough to scrape a degree, an achievement that, often as not, coincided with Dad endowing a new wing for the library or filling the Master's cellar with the '96 Graham's Quinta dos Malvedos.

'I'm sure you're very busy, Mr Beck.'

'No,' Beck said. 'I'm not busy at all. The police have insisted we shut down the practice until all this business is settled.'

'Well, the sooner we can get it settled, the better.'

Edgar passed Skelton a sheet of paper on which he'd scribbled some reminders and took out his own fountain pen and notebook. Beck sought sanctuary on the throne behind his desk. Skelton stood and paced.

'Now, I'm sure I don't have to point out to you the seriousness of the charge that's been brought against you. Manslaughter can attract a sentence of life imprisonment. You're in fact very lucky you've been let out on bail now.'

Beck adopted an expression of apprehensive concern and Skelton, astonished at how little of the man was remotely genuine, turned away in case an involuntary sneer of contempt should infect his lips.

'The 1861 Offences Against the Person Act is somewhat open to interpretation and offers certain ambiguities that could be turned to our advantage.'

He spoke for a quarter of an hour, mostly about Lord Hewart's learned observations on *Rex versus Bateman,* with special reference to *mens rea* and *animus nocendi,* and added some thoughts on the police's *fumus boni iuris.*

When he had finished, Beck let a few seconds go before saying, 'I have many influential friends. To be honest, I doubt whether there'll be a trial at all.'

Skelton sighed. Of course he had. And their intervention would more than likely secure a miscarriage of justice, just as it already seemed to have led to his presently sitting on his throne rather than being locked up in a Brixton remand cell.

Skelton nodded slowly as if considering the proposition. 'And while it is earnestly to be hoped that their influence will indeed procure the desired effect, I think, perhaps, as a fall-back position, we should proceed on the assumption that there will be a trial and, unless we construct a robust defence, you will be sent to prison for a very long time.'

Beck examined his manicured fingernails and adjusted a marble ornament on his desk. In prison, there would be no manicures. No marble ornaments.

'Several lines of defence suggest themselves,' Skelton said. 'The police, I believe, have already brought in medical and electrical experts to examine the equipment you use in your treatments. Their reports, inasmuch as I can understand them, seem to suggest that it could very easily induce a fatal heart attack.'

'In the hands of an incompetent, of course it could. Just

as medicines can kill if misprescribed. Just as the surgeon's scalpel can kill more easily than it can cure. But I am not a bungler, Mr Skelton. See.'

Beck flicked one of the buttons on his desk. A buzzer sounded and a green light came on above a door.

'If you'd care to come this way, Mr Skelton, Mr Holmes.'

'Hobbes,' Edgar said.

Beck led the way into the treatment room.

It was a disappointment. A year or so earlier, Skelton and Mila had been to see a German film called *Metropolis* at the Vaudeville in Reading. They hadn't liked the film. Too long and too silly. The plot had involved a mad scientist who made a robot woman in a room filled with huge, complicated electrical things, some of which exuded lightning. Skelton, in his mind's eye, had conjured something similar for Beck's treatment room. There was a chair with some wires connected to copper hoops – possibly armbands or headbands – which in turn were connected to a small wooden box that housed switches and a dial; and a sort of bed or couch, similarly equipped with copper hoops and wires. It was nowhere near big enough or fancy enough to make a robot woman although, according to the brief, experts who examined it were sure it was enough to kill a real one.

Aubrey had said he could get experts prepared to say the opposite, but pitting experts against experts, Skelton knew, was never a good idea. The jury gets confused and reverts to prejudice and instinct. If they took a dislike to Beck, and there was no reason to think they wouldn't because Skelton certainly had within a few seconds of meeting him, he'd get life.

The best bet, under the circumstances, would be to counter the jury's instinct with snobbery. If Beck could persuade some of his 'influential clients' – lords, bishops, statesmen – to stand up in court and swear that he was the finest of men who put the safety of his clients above all else and whose treatments had magically cured their lifelong ailments, they'd be home and dry. It went against the grain, of course, and would be a travesty of justice akin to young Ewers walking away with a wigging and a fiver, but, as was the case with Ewers, if Beck walked free he would have done his duty as defence barrister.

The 'influential clients' would have to be selected with care. No chequered pasts, no Sunday paper scandals, no skeletons in cupboards allowed.

When they were back drinking tea among the gold curly bits in the Marie Antoinette room, Skelton asked if Beck could furnish them with a client list.

'I am afraid that won't be remotely possible,' Beck said.

'No?'

'I work here under conditions of the strictest confidentiality. Many of my patients have personal health issues which they would prefer their own wives and husbands not to know about. The idea that they might discuss them in a court, have them reported in the press and bandied about as servants' gossip is unthinkable, not to say a despicable and professionally ruinous betrayal on my part. If any of them are to be approached in relation to this matter, then I shall approach them.'

'Has it occurred to you, Mr Beck, that there is a lot more than a professional setback at stake here?'

Beck sat very upright, 'And as a man of my word and a man of honour, let me tell you, Mr Skelton, that a life spent in the world's filthiest dungeon would be preferable to a betrayal of trust.'

'He's probably worried that his clients would be queuing up to denounce him as a fraud,' Edgar said, in the taxi back to Foxton Row. 'That's why he doesn't want to give us the names.'

Skelton chuckled. 'The police will have gone through his papers, anyway, won't they?'

'One would have thought so.'

'There'll be a client list in there, I shouldn't wonder. Or an appointments book or some such. Ask Aubrey to get hold of it. If we pick out a few with more socially acceptable complaints than spermatorrhoea, I'm sure we can sort something out.'

Back at Foxton Row, the post had brought Skelton's weekly letter from his Welsh cousin, Alan.

He had two Welsh cousins, twins, Alan and Norah. Their mum was Mabel, Skelton's mum's sister, who came from Leeds, but their dad, George, was from Rhyl, where he now managed the Pavilion Theatre.

There was a strong possibility that cousin Alan was touched in the head, not least because, in puberty, the time when many boys begin to show an interest in girls, Alan got interested in angels. They appeared to him. They spoke to him and told him to do God's work.

It took him a while to work out what this meant – doing God's work – but after a certain amount of experimentation, trying one thing and another, he came to realise that it was touring the country in a caravan, preaching, singing and playing the banjo. He'd been doing this ever since.

His sister, Norah, for the want of anything better to do, had joined him. She sang better than Alan and played the accordion to a very high standard and the two of them lived in an Eccles De Luxe Four Berth caravan drawn by a Morris Oxford saloon, both bearing signs saying, 'The Joy of Jesus Mission'.

There aren't many people in this world who relish being sung at by evangelists, but Alan and Norah had the good sense to lay more stress on the 'Joy' than the 'Jesus', and lightened the load of 'The Old Rugged Cross' and 'Love Divine All Loves Excelling' with comic, novelty and music hall favourites. At the moment, everybody wanted to hear 'Yes, We Have No Bananas', but 'Make Yourself a Happiness Pie' was also popular, as was the perennial favourite 'When Father Papered the Parlour You Couldn't See Pa for Paste'. They had a good repertoire of more sentimental songs, too. Their special version of 'I Ain't 'Alf Proud of My Old Mum and She Ain't 'Alf Proud of Me' was always met with a warm round of applause and wet sniffles of appreciation.

Earlier in the year, while in Scotland, they had learnt to dance the tango and had decided that that dance, as long as you avoided any of the unwholesomeness that infected the movements when Argentinians and Rudolph Valentino did it, was in no whit at odds with the teachings of Our Lord. So now, as well as the preaching (which some have said was more like a comic monologue than a sermon) and the singing, they liked to get their congregations up and dancing to the strict *chum chum chum chum* rhythms of Norah's accordion.

Their meanderings – where they directed the Morris Oxford and where they decided to stay – were driven by perceived need. Wherever they heard of a spot that had been beset by fire, flood, disease or disaster, that was where, they knew, they would find people most in need of the Joy of Jesus.

Cousin Arthur Skelton, the famous barrister, of course, always knew where the worst crimes of murder and mayhem were to be found, so often they allowed their footsteps to be guided by him. And sometimes they were able to unearth nuggets of information that were useful to their cousin's pursuit of justice – most notably a couple of years earlier in the case of Mary Dutton, the so-called Collingford Poisoner. Alan saw nothing untoward in acting as a sort of informal detective for his cousin. As far as he was concerned the three of them, himself, Norah and Arthur, were united in their devotion to a common cause – bringing honesty, truth, fairness, virtue and joy to a naughty world.

In return for their nuggets, Arthur's financial support of their mission had, down the years, never been less than generous.

Alan usually wrote a letter a week and, more often than not, Arthur's replies would come wrapped around a postal order or cheque.

c/o The Newport Street Congregational Church, Newport Street, Burnley, Lancashire.

Monday, 10th November 1930

My dear cousin Arthur,

I hope that this letter finds you in good health and that little Elizabeth had a lovely birthday. Did our card and present arrive on time?

It is Norah who always remembers these things. I am so hopeless that sometimes I cannot even remember my own birthday never mind those of friends and relatives, but Norah is quite meticulous about such matters.

I hope the book is not too old for her. Norah said that she remembered reading *The Children of the New Forest* when she was a girl, so she knew that it was a sensible and wholesome book. What worries me, though, is that Norah would have been eleven or twelve when she read it and Elizabeth, correct me if I am wrong, is just nine. Then again, I expect Elizabeth is a good bit more advanced in her reading than Norah was when she was that age. Norah has always been very clever, but the school we went to did not cohere to the same educational standards as schools do nowadays. There were only two teachers for all the ages. One of them hit you all the time and the other fell asleep, so all we really learnt was how to keep quiet.

I was never much of a reader at any age except for the Bible.

Our big news is that we are now Moral Hygienists – if that is a word. Should it be 'hygienist' or 'hygiener' or perhaps some other variation? Anyway, that is what we are, and I expect a bit of an explanation is in order.

You remember when we were in Scotland, our friends there, Beryl and Jack, very kindly taught us how to dance the tango. I am sure I told you about that. Anyway, since leaving Scotland, during our time in Liverpool and Darlington and Burnley we have been incorporating the tango dancing into our meetings, along with the singing and the preaching. And very popular it has been, too. So popular, in fact, that we have enhanced it with other dances – the foxtrot, the one-step, the lancers, the slow waltz and even the quickstep, which seems to be all the rage at the moment with the youngsters.

Well, gradually the dancing seems to have become the main attraction. Indeed, it is more popular than the singing ever was and a good bit more popular than the preaching. It has allowed us to invite a bigger congregation and, perhaps more significantly, a *younger* crowd, to share the joy of Jesus.

Here in Burnley we have recruited a happy group of local musicians – trumpet, clarinet, and a trap-drummer – to augment Norah's accordion and my banjo. Both the trumpeter, Clifford, and the clarinettist, Ronald, can improvise in the 'hot' style. It is instructive to observe the way in which their wails and trills put 'pep' – which is, I would like to point out, another word for 'joy' – into the dancers' feet. It makes me wonder whether the usual po-faced understanding of what the music of angelic hosts sounds like is all wrong. Is it possible, I wonder, when Gabriel blows his horn, that what comes out bears more similarity to Paul Whiteman than it does to J. S. Bach? Paul Whiteman is an American bandleader, by the way. Clifford, the trumpet player, has many of his gramophone records.

Sometimes the music seems to infect the dancers so that, even if they are 'sitting this one out', they find themselves dancing all by themselves in a style they call 'jazzing'.

The Joy of Jesus finds expression in many different ways: Shakers shake, Quakers quake and the young people of Burnley jazz.

Anyway, at last Wednesday's meeting, towards the end of the evening, when I had said the final prayer and led the singing on 'Whiter than Snow', three rather official-looking people, two ladies and a gentleman, all dressed very severely in black, brown and navy, turned up and stood waiting at the back of the room.

This made me a little apprehensive because, from their manner and appearance I assumed that they had come to tell me off about something. We are, at the moment, based in a hall attached to a Congregational church. Traditionally, the Congregationalists take a dim view of joy, and particularly of dancing. Though some allege that their views on such matters have relaxed a little since the seventeenth century you can never be sure, so it would not have surprised me one jot or tittle to hear that some fusty church elders or suchlike had got wind of our cavortings and sent a deputation to put a stop to them.

Mercifully, I was wrong, and when I approached the stern-looking trio, they introduced themselves as representatives of the Chaundler Fund for the Promotion of Moral Hygiene.

Norah and I knew of their work. You probably do, too. You sometimes see their representatives at railway stations. They wear brass badges announcing their affiliation, keep an eye out for unaccompanied young women and take them to one side for a friendly word.

By coincidence, not long ago we had chatted to one of these representatives at Lime Street station in

Liverpool. She said that you get a lot of Welsh girls coming there on trains from the valleys of South Wales and the small towns of North Wales, filled with hope that the big city will offer something better than a constant struggle to put food on the table and a husband scarred from working in the pit or at the furnace.

The Chaundler ladies offer advice about where the young women can stay and what places and people they should avoid. And they give them a leaflet with the address of their headquarters where they can go in the event that they find themselves in trouble of any sort. They also keep an eye out for men – who loiter in railway stations looking for unaccompanied young women, but with less innocent intent – and, if necessary, report them to the police as procurers or white slavers.

The rivers of temptation that sweep young women into the mire of prostitution run deep and run wide.

The two rather severe ladies who arrived at our meeting were sisters, Miss Price and Mrs Brandon and the gentleman was Mrs Brandon's husband. They told us that their particular concern at the moment is the generation of girls, just coming into womanhood, who were made fatherless by the war and have been brought up by widows. These are girls many of whom, with no proper breadwinner in the family, have been denied decent food, never mind clothes and luxuries all their lives. At fifteen, sixteen or seventeen, they make the dangerous discovery that there is a certain kind of man who will happily pay their entrance to the films or dance halls, who will buy them chocolates and even frocks if they want them, who will perhaps take them for rides in motor cars, and the ways in which they can repay these men cost them nothing except their moral hygiene, an attribute upon which they have probably never learnt to place much value.

Miss Price and Mr and Mrs Brandon had heard from other volunteers working in the area about our meetings in the Congregational hall and had learnt of their popularity with young women.

This is true. As I say, before we introduced the dancing, most of our meetings were conducted in a sea of white hair and creaking ailments. Now we find ourselves assailed by giggling youngsters.

There are always more girls than boys, perhaps because they like dancing more, or perhaps because boys have more places they can go, billiard halls, boxing clubs – or you see groups of them on waste ground, whatever the weather, playing pitch and toss for farthings and ha'pennies.

Girls do not seem to mind dancing with each other, – or, as I mentioned earlier, 'jazzing' on their own. In fact, they might even prefer another girl as a partner because she is more likely to know the steps and be able to execute them without risk of injury. And they can be sure that there will be no funny business going on, or expectations made of them.

Anyway, Miss Price and Mr and Mrs Brandon could see the way in which our mission – to introduce people of all ages to the joy of Jesus – could be combined with their mission – to protect young women from the serpentine enticements by which they are so often beset.

They also pointed out that, although it cost as much as a shilling to get into a commercial dance hall, our 'dances' are absolutely free and are accompanied by a certain amount of religious and moral instruction. We have always seen the dancing – this must be stressed – as an *addition to* and never a *replacement for* – the preaching and singing. It is very gratifying to note the enthusiasm with which the young women, half-drunk with the joy of dancing, will, at the end of the evening, join in with 'The Old Rugged Cross' or 'I Am H.A.P.P.Y.'.

So, Miss Price and Mr and Mrs Brandon put a proposition to us. They intend to put us on a circuit, like a variety circuit, through the towns of Lancashire, Cheshire and Shropshire, then up through Staffordshire, Derbyshire and Nottinghamshire, and thence back through Yorkshire to Lancashire again.

We will spend three or four nights in each place. They will arrange the halls and put advertisements in the newspapers to herald our arrival. This will be a great blessing. Usually, upon arriving in a town, we have to spend a good two or three days tramping around looking for a suitable hall that will have us, then perhaps a week or so building a decent sized congregation.

In addition, they have offered to pay for all of our petrol and provide us with an allowance (very generous, too, at 45s a week) to cover our food and other living expenses.

All we have to do in return is to gear the preaching towards the aims and purposes of the charity, distribute their pamphlets, and work with local volunteers to keep an eye out for the girls and women in greatest danger, with a view to steering them towards the advice and, if need be, financial assistance that is available.

To this we have readily and happily agreed. It will be a completely new adventure for us, and we have no doubt that having everything so organised cannot but be of great assistance to our mission.

Well, I shall sign off now because I can hear Norah calling. I got beetroot juice on my knitted waistcoat yesterday and she says that it will never wash out. I do not see what is wrong with having a bit of beetroot juice on your knitted waistcoat, but she says that people will think I am dying of a fatal wound. There is a chap in the market here who sells woollens at very reasonable prices. I would not vouch for the quality but as long as it is grey and covers the fraying on my shirt front, I am not fussy.

I am ever yours faithfully in the joy of Jesus,
Alan.

Monday, 17th November, 1930

'*Rex versus Prosser*,' Edgar announced, when he'd had enough tea, biscuits and cigarettes to consider the day begun.

'Is this the burning car one?' Skelton asked. 'Bradford, is it?'

'Bedford. Actually, more like Biggleswade.'

The 'Blazing Car Mystery' had dominated the headlines for a week. Initially, it was assumed that the deceased, Harold Musgrave, a vacuum cleaner salesman, bankrupt and facing charges of bigamy, had taken his own life in a particularly grisly act of self-immolation. Then, the post-mortem had revealed that Mr Musgrave had died from a blow to the back of the head *before* the fire was lit. This was no suicide. Poor Mr Musgrave had been murdered, and the corpse and car no doubt burnt to destroy any evidence left by his killer.

Soon afterwards, the Bedfordshire police had arrested Tommy Prosser, a local bad man who'd done time in the past for robbery, violence and drunkenness. The evidence against him was compelling, but less than conclusive. Earlier in the day, Mr Musgrave had withdrawn £1,250 from a bank in Biggleswade. Tommy Prosser happened to be in the bank at the time, so, the police claimed, knew that Musgrave had the money on him. Later in the day, Prosser bought a two-gallon can of petrol from a garage just outside Biggleswade. He could provide the police with no plausible or verifiable reason for buying the petrol and neither could he give adequate account of his movements at the time the murder took place. And, when the police searched his house, they found a bloodstained starter handle. Analysis indicated that the blood was human. Prosser couldn't give a good account of that, either, so it was assumed that it was the murder weapon.

But the police had not been able to find any trace of the £1,250 either in Prosser's house or, as ashes, in the car or fluttering about nearby.

Edgar stood and brushed biscuit crumbs from his trousers. 'The police think that, having learnt that Musgrave had the money on him, Prosser either cadged a lift in town, or flagged the car down later, perhaps faking some sort of emergency.'

'Any witnesses?'

'Nobody saw him near the car or in the area prior to the murder, although the people who first discovered the burning car say they did see a man running away who may have fitted Prosser's description, but only inasmuch as he was medium-build, medium-height and wearing a dark coat.'

'So, could have been you, for instance. Or Aubrey, or any one of ten million men. Were they even sure it was a man?'

Edgar turned the pages of the brief. 'I think a general assumption was made.'

'So, all the police have is conjecture and circumstantial evidence. Do you know, I think we could win this one standing on our heads, Edgar.'

'There is a slight problem,' Edgar said.

'Yes?'

'It's on one of these Poor Persons' Defence Act Certificates. Maximum fee fifteen guineas. If you'd rather not, I could easily pass it on. You have got your plate rather full at the moment.'

A week earlier, Skelton's fee for turning up at Marylebone Police Court for Giles Ewers, the smirking boy with the general for a dad, had been nearly forty times that. He was earning obscene amounts of money from the Anglo-American Abrasives business, a case he barely understood. He liked to think of himself as a man of principle whose sole master was blind justice. The travesty of the smirking boy and the pointlessness of the Abrasives had compromised his ideals. A fifteen-guinea job for a hard-done-by pauper would provide a cleansing restitution.

Skelton checked the name of the solicitor on the first page of the brief.

'F. E. Holland? Do you know anything about him?'

'Nothing at all. Chancing his arm, if you ask me. Offering you a fifteen-guinea brief.'

'The fee is immaterial. I think we should do it.'

Edgar pulled a face. If people found out that his chief would work for fifteen guineas, he feared, they'd both be in the poorhouse by Christmas.

'Perhaps you should read the brief first,' he said. 'I'm not sure it's quite as straightforward as you assume.'

Edgar left him to it.

Skelton eased himself into one of the low chairs, got his pipe going and settled down to read.

Holland, the solicitor, had provided a lively summary of events, based mostly on the pedestrian testimony of PC Myatt, Great Dunworth's senior and only policeman, and a somewhat racier account provided by Chester Monroe, a journalist working for the *Bedford Weekly Illustrated*.

Holland had also provided a useful map, showing Great Dunworth and the next-door village of Lower Dunworth, Keeper's Lane, between the two, where the murder had taken place as well as other places mentioned in the account – Dunmore Beacon, the Bell Inn, the parish church and so on.

The fire had been discovered by two sixteen-year-olds, a boy and a girl, who had seen a figure, supposedly Tommy

Prosser, running away from the scene. They had raised the alarm at The Bell, and someone called Ernie Robinson had offered to cycle to the police house in Great Dunworth to report the incident.

At the police house, PC Myatt was not in the best of tempers. He was supposed to have dined on a baked potato cooked in the ashes of a neighbour's bonfire, together with sausages toasted on sticks, but rain had put paid to that. Consequently, he had had no supper at all when Ernie Robinson showed up to report the terrible fire on Keeper's Lane.

PC Myatt told Ernie to cycle up to the doctor's house, then, still supperless, had put on his uniform and waterproofs and cycled down to Keeper's Lane. The rain, which an hour earlier seemed to have eased off, had started again.

The constable's first task on arriving at the scene had been to clear the gawpers away. A fair old crowd had gathered. He was helped in this by Mr Glazier, Chairman of the Parish Council, who had been attending to the bonfire at the top of Beacon Hill and come down to help, and Sid Hatch, president of the cricket club. A Mr Bracken, who lived in a cottage nearby, had brought out a couple of Tilley lights so they could see what they were doing, and Mr Glazier had a hurricane lantern.

Then Jed Stubbs from Stubbs Farm turned up in his tractor and suggested he tow the burnt-out car into an adjacent field to get it off the main carriageway because people would be wanting to come up and down Keeper's Lane in the morning. There was a question, however, regarding the corpse and whether it should be left in the car or removed, and, if it were to be removed, how they would go about it. It was little more than a charred shape, still approximately upright even though the seat it had been sitting on was almost burnt away. Nobody present had had experience of dealing with charred corpses and there was some doubt as to whether it could be removed at all. Might it crumble at a touch?

Sid Hatch pointed out that children would be passing in the morning on their way to school. No matter how far the car was towed off the road, they'd be curious, and you wouldn't want them seeing a thing like this. But PC Myatt suggested that the correct procedure, as he understood it, was to leave the body where it was so that in the morning the Bedford coroner's people could inspect it properly.

Dr Norman had arrived by this time in his car. He reminded PC Myatt that the coroner's office and the mortuary in Bedford were temporarily closed for renovations during which time cadavers were being taken to Northampton to be dealt with there.

This changed matters. PC Myatt didn't know anything about Northampton. It was an entirely different police force over there with different arrangements. It would take time just to get in touch with them and it might be days before they could send somebody out. He asked whether Dr Norman would mind keeping the body at his house for the time being. The doctor said he didn't think this was a very good idea. Other than the cupboard under the stairs, which was full of golf clubs and cricket bats, he had nowhere to put it. He wouldn't want it in the private parts of the house because he had children of his own and his charlady tended to arrive before six. Can you imagine? And obviously the effect on patients, were he to put it in the surgery or waiting room could be devastating.

Then Mr Bracken, the man from the nearby cottage who'd brought the Tilley lamps, said they could put it in his shed if they wanted. It was dry and he could lock it safe from the eyes of gawpers and children.

So, the constable and the doctor helped by one or two of the others managed to extract the corpse from the car. Although it did not, as some had feared, crumble at a touch, one or two bits did break off. Both the constable and the doctor were sure that this wasn't their fault and reckoned that even if the most professional undertakers or mortuary assistants had done the job, the bits would still have come away. It couldn't have come out otherwise.

While Jed Stubbs towed the car into the field, PC Myatt, Dr Norman, Mr Glazier and Mr Bracken carried the corpse, wrapped in a tarpaulin that Mr Bracken had provided, to the shed. Then Mrs Bracken invited them all into her kitchen and kindly made hot cocoa with rum in it.

The following morning, PC Myatt tried to phone the coroner in Bedford, but the telephone, which had not long been put in, had gone wrong again. So, he got Mr Stephens, the baker, who was going up that way in his van to take a message to the main police station in Bedford explaining the situation and got on with his normal day's work. Stephens came back later the same day with a note from the sergeant in Bedford, saying that the Bedford mortuary was closed, and PC Myatt should get in touch with the coroner in Northampton. This, of course, Myatt already knew. He had hoped that the sergeant or somebody else at the station would take charge of the matter and contact the Northamptonshire people themselves. The Bedford people had cars, after all, and telephones that worked.

He was thinking about cadging a lift from somebody either into Clophill, where they might have a telephone that worked, or all the way to Northampton, when a cheeky young chap on a motorcycle turned up, introduced himself as Chester Monroe, and said he was from the *Bedford Weekly Illustrated* and had found out about the suicide and fire and wanted all the details. He had a camera with him. He said he'd already taken photographs of the burnt car and had discovered that the body was being kept in Mr Bracken's shed. He wanted to take photographs of that, too, but Mr Bracken was unwilling to do so without specific permission. PC Myatt didn't think that would be respectful.

Chester Monroe said that if PC Myatt was having so much trouble getting in touch with Northampton, he could either ride back to his office in Bedford and telephone from there, or if he fancied it, give him a lift on his pillion all the way to Northampton. PC Myatt told him it wouldn't be right for him to go to Northampton himself because he had his duties to attend to but said that if Mr Monroe would be good enough to take a message for him, he would be very grateful. The journalist said he'd be glad to. So, Myatt wrote out a message and Mr Monroe rode off to deliver it.

The people from Northampton came on the Friday morning.

The brief also contained clippings from the *Bedford Weekly Illustrated*, which came out on the Saturday.

There were good photographs of the car and what looked like a studio portrait of the dead man, Harold Musgrave.

Chester Monroe must have worked hard and fast to put the story together. Skelton had no idea what the deadline would be on a paper like the *Bedford Weekly Illustrated*, but he'd imagine that with plates to be made for the pictures and so on, it would be some time on the Friday, possibly Friday lunchtime, so it was quite remarkable that between the Thursday and the deadline, Mr Monroe had somehow been able to discover the supposed suicide's name, Harold Musgrave, that he was a commercial traveller for the Auto-Vac-It vacuum cleaner company, that his home address and the Auto-Vac-It factory were both in Coventry, that, because of his success as a salesman, the company had awarded Mr Musgrave the two most lucrative 'patches' – the Midlands and the South-East, including London – and that despite this success he was heavily in debt and was facing a bigamy charge and several paternity suits. And he'd even been able to get hold of the photograph of the dead man, presumably from one of the wives or the Auto-Vac-It offices. And all in time for the Saturday edition.

The story had made it to the national newspapers on the Monday, by which time the body had been conveyed to Northampton, where the autopsy had discovered the crushing of the skull at the back of the head and concluded that this was no suicide but murder and the police had picked up Prosser within a couple of days – clearly their chief suspect for any crime committed in the area, regardless of evidence.

Edgar came back with tea.

'The prosecution case is built on quicksand,' Skelton said. 'We'll have it demolished in half an hour.'

'If you're sure …'

'We should go and see Holland and Prosser. He's in Bedford Prison. Bedford's what … an hour on the train?'

'Ooh, could be longer. I believe they're repairing the line or improving it or something.'

'Bring a book, then.'

Edgar joined the tips of his fingers in a gesture that, on another man, might have appeared thoughtful but on Edgar, who was not in the habit of joining the tips of his fingers, appeared odd. Out of character. Possibly sly. 'I was wondering,' he said, 'if perhaps you might like to drive.'

'Drive? To Bedford?'

'I'm sure it would be much quicker and easier than going on the train.'

'You get sick in cars.'

'Yes, but I was talking to Mrs Stewart about that and she told me about these powders that were apparently used to great effect by Napoleon's Camel Corps to cure sickness induced by the constant bouncing up and down.'

'And the remarkable Mrs Stewart has some of these powders?'

'The camel powders, yes.'

'And do they work?'

'They worked miraculously well for Small Michael.'

'Who …?'

'Mrs Stewart has two nephews both called Michael. Small Michael and Big Michael. Small Michael, after several dolorous years of unemployment, found a job as a coalman, but almost had to give it up because of bilious attacks in the delivery lorry. He took the camel powders and is now in line for promotion.'

'You can get promotion as a coalman? There's a hierarchy of them?'

'I believe so.'

'Have you tried these camel powders?'

'Not yet, no.'

'So, the trip to Bedford would be by way of an experiment?'

'Mrs Stewart assures me that—'

'I still think the train …'

'The other thing is … Luton is on the way to Bedford, isn't it?'

'General direction.'

'I was wondering whether we could pick up a cocktail cabinet?'

'A what?'

'I've bought a small cocktail cabinet.'

'Do you drink cocktails?'

'I plan to. It's second-hand, in perfect condition and very beautiful. See …'

Edgar showed Skelton a picture in a catalogue. The cocktail cabinet resembled a child's puzzle in which various wooden pieces, mostly triangles, have to be assembled to form a perfect square – except it had been assembled all wrong so that the triangles stuck out at odd angles threatening to put somebody's eye out.

'It's Czech,' Edgar said. 'A beautiful example of Czech cubist design.'

Skelton looked for hints of gingham or plaid then realised he meant the country not the pattern. He knew what cubism was. He'd read an article in a magazine about a French artist called Braque who went in for that sort of thing before the war. He wondered whether he should boast about being so *au fait* with artistic trends, but then realised he didn't know whether 'Braque' was pronounced 'Brack', 'Brake', 'Braykew', 'Brack-way' or something even more outlandish, so, rather than make a fool of himself, kept his cakehole shut.

'I was wondering whether, on the way to Bedford, we could stop off in Luton and pick it up,' Edgar said.

'In the car?'

'It's quite small. I'm sure it would fit nicely on the back seat of your Bentley.'

Skelton imagined the pointy bits piercing his upholstery and looked doubtful.

'I'm fairly sure,' Edgar continued, 'it's designed either by Pavel Janák or Josef Gočár.'

'Are they men?'

'Cubist furniture designers.'

'There's two of them?'

'We could go tomorrow.'

'I thought I was in court all day tomorrow.'

'Somebody fell ill or died. The trial's been postponed indefinitely. And I could rearrange the meeting with Buscott.'

'Who's Buscott?'

'A man you had a meeting with tomorrow, but I can easily rearrange it. I'll get in touch with F. E. Holland, the solicitor in Bedford, to make sure he can see us in the morning, and I'll arrange with the prison to see Tommy Prosser. So, if we had an early start, we could pick up the cocktail cabinet first thing and still have a full day ahead of us.'

Skelton sucked thoughtfully on his pipe. The *fait* it would appear, was *accompli*. This, then, would be his penance for compromising his ideals by being an accessory to the smirking Ewers boy and the Abrasives people. He would be defence counsel for a pauper and removal man for his clerk. All for fifteen guineas. More than enough, surely, to give anybody's conscience a good scrub.

Tuesday, 18th November 1930

Skelton left home in the Bentley just after five-thirty in the morning and picked up his clerk from Belsize Park at seven.

In the car, Edgar chatted happily. Following Mrs Stewart's instructions, he had enjoyed an ample breakfast of sausages, eggs and toast before taking the camel powders. He had every confidence that, for the first time in his life, he would be able to endure a car journey without fear of what he'd once heard described in court as 'digestive disemboguement'.

Not long after Jack Straw's Castle in Hampstead, he stopped chatting.

'I think those pills have made me a little light-headed,' he said, and lapsed for a while into silence.

Skelton, worried that the camel powders hadn't worked at all, readied himself for an emergency stop. Then, at Stag Lane Aerodrome, Edgar began to talk again, and the talk was strange. Too fast, too animated, too loud.

'The chap is selling it at less than half what you'd usually pay for a cubist cocktail cabinet,' he said. 'Ooh, look that horse is pure black, I wonder whether he sometimes pulls a hearse. So, I wrote to him asking how he'd come by it and he told me that, excitingly, it has a rather glamorous provenance. Margot Fitzsimmons – you've heard of Margot Fitzsimmons, haven't you? You must have heard of Margot Fitzsimmons. She was involved in that terrible scandal in Chelmsford then pretended to live in a tethered dirigible for a while. Anyway, Margot Fitzsimmons turned her hand to interior design and one of her ex-lovers, possibly the King of somewhere, gave her, as a goodbye present, Cottisham House and Park in Buckinghamshire, which he had reputedly won in a game of backgammon from Sashy Bax Molyneux, the last true Lord of Nogent. And Margot came up with the idea of turning Cottisham House into an ultra-stylish health resort, so she added a sort of Mies Van Der Rohe sunroom at the back, and had all the rooms and bathrooms done out in this rather severe Djo Bourgeois manner with painted aluminium and edges so sharp that some people cut themselves getting out of bed. Those cows are all standing in a line as if they're queuing for the cinema. Then poor Margot discovered that people didn't want to be healthy. Or perhaps they were happy to drink

82

the lemon juice and have their livers nurtured, but not if it meant losing a leg on the bedroom fittings. Anyway, nobody came to Margot's health resort, so she sold it to a Hungarian arms manufacturer and this chap in Luton bought up all the fixtures and fittings, including the Czech cubist cocktail cabinet, and advertised them in *Modern Design* magazine. And I didn't want to have it delivered in case it got damaged, and it really is very good of you to offer it the safety and comfort of your Bentley. You should give it a name. Some people give their cars names. You should give your car a name. Oh, look, there's a farmer. Is that his den, do you think? I wonder if he wants a wife?'

He continued in this vein until, just before St Albans, he fell asleep, with his head slumped against the window, which his breath quickly fogged.

Skelton found the address he'd been given. It was on the outskirts of Luton, and an unprepossessing dirty brick warehouse with a dilapidated sign announcing it to be 'Gillet's Quality'.

He nudged Edgar awake.

'Is this it?' Skelton asked.

Edgar slowly came to, blinked and looked around.

'Gillet's,' he read. 'That is the name I was given.'

'Quality what? Is the rest of the sign missing or is that it?'

'Perhaps it's a double-barrelled name, Gillets-Quality, like Bowes-Lyon or Clarendon-Gow.'

They got out of the car, found a small door up a couple of steps around the side of the building and knocked. It was opened immediately, as if their arrival had been eagerly anticipated, by a wispy young woman who looked about seventeen-years-old. She wore a man's dungarees and was so tiny she had to bend backward to look up at them. She seemed very afraid.

'My name is Hobbes,' Edgar said. 'I arranged to collect a cocktail cabinet.'

The young woman made no indication that she had heard, or, if she had heard, that she understood the nature of language. There was a hiatus.

Edgar was just about to say, 'I wonder if I could speak to your father,' when, in a distant sing-song voice such as one might hear at a séance, she said, 'Yes, I'm Mrs Gillet. You've come about the Czech cubist cocktail cabinet.'

She seemed to be looking not at Edgar or Skelton, but at somebody standing behind them at some distance, and this impression was so vivid that Edgar glanced over his shoulder just to make sure.

After another short silence, she abruptly turned, said, 'Follow me,' and set off down a long corridor, galloping like a fawn.

Skelton and Edgar had almost to run to keep up.

The corridor smelled like the inside of a neglected shoe.

Mrs Gillet turned left, cantered a few more paces, then pushed open a wide door that gave access to the main warehouse.

It was a vaulted room big enough for three or four trains to find a home and was piled high with every kind of furniture, both domestic and commercial. A grand piano lay on its back across two roll-top desks. A marble mantlepiece stood between a ringer and a brass bedstead.

Skelton looked suspiciously up at a mahogany dining table, some way above his head, balanced on four dining chairs, which in turn were balanced on a sofa. He was sure he saw it teeter.

He and Edgar edged their way, being very careful not to touch anything, but Mrs Gillet scampered off down a colonnade fashioned from rolls of linoleum.

Skelton and Edgar followed. She turned left. They reached the turning just in time to see her turn right and realised that unless they got a move on, they would lose her and thus lose themselves in the maze of wardrobes and tallboys. They scampered.

Eventually she stopped and turned to face them.

'It's up there,' she said, and pointed.

There were two partner desks, an oak one standing on a mahogany one. These were piled with a ramshackle jumble of dining chairs, their legs intertwined in a way that may have made them as secure as the Forth Bridge but didn't look like it. Then, balanced on top of the chairs was the Czech cubist cocktail cabinet.

'Should we get a ladder?' Edgar asked.

'No need,' Mrs Gillet said, in a half-whispered sing-song. She put one foot on the mahogany desk, then, like Mallory making his doomed ascent of the North Col, began to mount the chairs. Skelton and Edgar took a few paces to the side hoping that, if the chairs came down, they would not bring the adjacent wardrobes and sideboards with them.

Miraculously, she reached the top without dying. Once there, she sat astride two of the more secure looking chairs, took a length of rope from the pocket of her dungarees, tied one end to the cocktail cabinet, and lowered it to their waiting hands below.

Mrs Gillet's descent, as is so often the case, was more perilous than the ascent.

Skelton couldn't bear to watch and instead examined the cabinet. It was, if anything, pointier than the picture had promised, with misshapen wooden tetrahedrons sticking out at odd angles, interrupted by facets of glass and Bakelite. It had doors, but the layout of shelves the inside might conceal didn't bear thinking about, so there was no temptation to open them. Anyway, his first instinct, that it had been designed with the specific intention of having somebody's eye out, was confirmed and he wondered whether there was a big glass eye industry in Czechoslovakia that needed a boost.

He didn't say anything, though, because when he looked up, he saw that Edgar was gently touching the Bakelite. There was love in his eyes. Mrs Gillet slipped off the mahogany desk and stood with them, the three of them in silent reverence.

'It has a weight to it,' she said, in the same sing-song voice, 'but not as much weight as you might think it has and certainly not as much as you couldn't carry it.'

'Of course,' Edgar said. And picked it up.

Mrs Gillet cleared her throat. 'It was, I believe,' she said, 'to be a cash transaction.'

Edgar put the cabinet down again and took an envelope from his pocket into which he had already counted out the money. Skelton wondered how much but there was no telling from the shape of the envelope whether it was 2s or £20.

Again, they lifted the cabinet and walked a few paces. Then the same thought struck both of them at the same time and they put it down.

'I'm afraid you're going to have to show us the way out,' Skelton said.

Mrs Gillet nodded and cantered off. Skelton and Edgar grabbed the cabinet and gave chase.

Outside, Edgar carefully wrapped the thing in the tartan rugs that Skelton kept in the car and laid it on the back seat, packing it with more blankets to be sure it wouldn't roll or fly into the air should the car suddenly stop.

'How old do you think she was?' Skelton asked, when they were on the road again.

'Mrs Gillet? Hard to say,' Edgar said. 'Sixteen, seventeen. I can't believe she's more than twenty-one.'

'Do you think Mr Gillet's a cradle-snatcher, then, or are they two extraordinarily resourceful youngsters?'

'Perhaps they inherited it from his father.'

'Could be,' Skelton said. 'I can't think life expectancy in a place like that is much to write home about. The father's probably in there still, buried under a mound of gas cookers.'

Skelton drove off.

By the time they got to Streatley, Edgar was asleep again.

F. E. Holland's office was in a street too narrow for the Bentley. Skelton parked where he could, and nudged Edgar awake.

'It's just up there,' he said.

Again, it was a moment before Edgar regained full consciousness.

He got out of the car. 'Will it be all right, do you think?' he asked.

'What, the car?'

'The cabinet. It'd only take a moment for a thief to—'

'Because every man, woman and child in Bedford is ever watchful for an opportunity to steal a Czech cubist cocktail cabinet.'

Edgar looked up and down the street to make sure that his chief's sarcasm was not misplaced.

They found the office in a shabby building up two flights of stairs covered in torn lino. Holland greeted them at the door. A young man – under thirty, anyway – he looked as if he could do with several decent dinners, custard puddings to follow and something for his nerves. His pale hands fluttered.

'Excuse the mess,' he said and gestured helplessly at the papers, files, books, cups, plates and ashtrays that covered every surface. 'Mrs Roebuck usually keeps things orderly, but she's had something wrong with her womb since the beginning of September, so I'm having to manage myself. Or rather, I'm failing to manage.'

He began to clear off a couple of chairs but glanced at one of the files he was moving and was immediately absorbed in its contents. A good while went by before he remembered that he was not alone.

'Sorry, sorry,' he said. He put the file in a prominent position on his desk so as not to forget it and carried on clearing. 'One of my Wednesday evening cases. I do a Poor Man's Lawyer stint up at the settlement two evenings a week.'

Skelton knew about the Bedford Settlement. It was a place where local teachers, lawyers and other adepts of one sort or another offered free evening classes and dispensed advice for those who asked. Skelton had worked in a similar place in Manchester during his pupillage. On Tuesday nights he did a weekly 'surgery', sitting in a cramped little office with a long line of supplicants queued outside: wounded soldiers and war widows having trouble getting their pensions, industrial compensation claims, rent disputes, domestic ding-dongs – all sorts. Skelton had found his weekly dive into the great pool of human misery exhausting and couldn't imagine the strain it must put on Holland, who seemed a good bit less resilient than he'd ever been.

When Skelton and Edgar were sat down in approximately clutter-free comfort, Holland returned to his desk but found himself unable to resist another peep into the file he'd left there.

'Sorry,' he said. 'Bailiffs are coming for Mr and Mrs Willis this afternoon. Was sure it was later in the week. Can't have them homeless. You couldn't lend me three pounds, could you?'

'Er ...'

'Only, I've left it a bit last minute, so the only thing I can do for now is pay their rent for them and I won't have time to get to the bank. It's ...' Holland referred to the file, 'three pounds fifteen and six they owe, so ...' He turned, took a cash box from a shelf behind him and opened it. 'Yes, I can do the fifteen and six.' He lifted the tray out of the cash box. 'Oh, as you were. There's a small fortune down here. Riches beyond the dreams of avarice. Must be ...' he counted some notes, 'seven pounds. And Johnny shall have a new ribbon to tie up his bonnie brown hair. Right, where were we? Yes, of course, Tommy Prosser.' He fumbled through the mess on his desk looking for the file, found it, scraped the jam off it, ate the jam and licked his fingers clean. 'You're seeing him at, when is it, eleven? Well, good luck with that.'

'Is he a difficult man to deal with?' Skelton asked.

'The sad truth of the matter, Mr Skelton, is that Tommy Prosser got stuck with me as his solicitor because all the halfway decent Bedford solicitors refused to have anything to do with him. He's not a very pleasant man at the best of times, but then, at the worst of times he is prone to these outbursts.'

'Outbursts?'

'Outbursts. Of rage. Usually violent rage and often very violent rage, indeed. And, I'm sorry to say that, in the past, when he's found himself in trouble with the police, his rage has been directed against those who are trying to help him as much if not more than his enemies. He seems to nurture a particular dislike for solicitors.'

'He attacked his solicitor?'

'Over the years he's attacked three solicitors, putting one in hospital.'

'Has he attacked you?'

'Not yet, no. But I'm sure it's only a matter of time. Now, you should be all right seeing him in prison because if they know what they're doing they'll have him heavily restrained. They'll most likely have put something in his tea as well. A splash of bromide can be wonderfully soothing.'

'How is he in court?'

'Atrocious. Surly, angry, obstructive. And then, you have to take into account the poor man's physical appearance. Did you ever read *Great Expectations?* No, neither did I, but there's supposed to be a terrifying convict in it called Magwitch. People have said that Tommy Prosser makes Magwitch look like Little Lord Fauntleroy. It's why I approached you, Mr Skelton. And why I thank you from the bottom of my heart for taking on the case. The jury will be very much inclined to start climbing out of the box screaming "guilty" as soon as Prosser's brought into court and it will not be easy to change their minds even though, as I'm sure you'll agree, the prosecution case is nonsense. They will need persuasive argument delivered with compelling authority with the oratorical skills of Lloyd George or Abe Lincoln – the kind of thing you're a dab hand at, Mr Skelton. And, the main thing is, you see, that Tommy Prosser is a horrible, horrible person, but I don't believe for a moment that he killed Harold Musgrave.'

'How can you be so sure?'

'Speak to him. You'll see.'

A young man was standing by the Bentley, looking this way and that.

Edgar, convinced he had designs on the Czech cabinet, almost ran towards him.

The young man looked up, stamped on his cigarette end and smiled.

'Mr Skelton, Mr Hobbes,' he said. 'Chester Monroe, *Bedford Weekly Illustrated*.'

He was what Skelton's mother would call a 'tyke' and his father 'a cheeky little bugger'. Fresh open face, wide-spaced eyes, froth of red-gold curls, waistcoat with lapels and pearl buttons, double Albert watch-chain, garish tie.

Skelton, a little warily, shook his hand.

'Aah,' he said, 'you're the chap who got the body identified before the coroner had even seen it.'

'All in a day's work,' Monroe said. 'You're due up the prison at eleven, yes? See Tommy Prosser.'

'Yes.'

'Got time for a cup of tea and a bun first? My treat.'

Skelton exchanged a look with Edgar. It was a quarter past ten and both were starving.

Monroe took them to a tea room on the high street, swapping hellos with six or seven people along the way. The waitress greeted him with a giggle. There was a history of flirtation.

Tea and toasted teacakes were ordered.

'So, how did you do it?' Skelton asked.

'Do what?'

'Get all that information about Musgrave so fast?'

'Very straightforward, Mr Skelton. First I heard was when Myatt – the copper at Great Dunworth – sends a message to the Bedford Police station and I gets a tip off from a pal of mine who works there. So, I gets down there on my Triumph. The car had been dragged just off the road into a field. Easy enough to find and the number plate had an AC prefix, so I knew it was a Warwickshire reg and I could get the owner's name off that but, as it turned out, I didn't need to, 'cos in the back of the car I found some vacuum cleaner bits, all burnt up, but you could still see the name, Auto-Vac-It, Coventry. So, after I'd finished delivering Myatt's message to Northampton, I rode up to the Auto-Vac-It factory and had a chat with a chap called Milner who said it had to be Musgrave's car. He was actually quite put out by the poor man killing himself – as we thought he'd done then – but he wasn't surprised. And he told me about the bigamy charge, and the debts and fixed me up with a photo. Bob's your uncle.'

'It's a very impressive piece of work,' Skelton said.

'The journalist will always be first with the story if he follows some simple rules: get all the news; don't stop with half of it; run down every clue; work rapidly; don't putter but persevere until you get what you were sent for; don't come back empty-handed; above all, be resourceful in devising ways and means of getting news.'

'Is that what your editor tells you?'

'Nah. All he ever says is, "Here's a shilling. Take the bottle down to Hector's for a refill." He practically lives on pints of port out the barrel. Nah. It's from my Bible. *Writing for Newspapers* by John Spencer Meyer of the University of South Dakota. The Americans are miles ahead of us in the newspaper business. English newspapers report the news *they* think is important. That's not going to sell papers, is it? What you have to print is the news *the reader* thinks is important. You have to think about the things ordinary people want to read about. "Always get the human-interest angle. Never forget, people like a good fight, whether it's in politics, business or sport. Petty disagreements make them yawn. Don't neglect children in the news; though small, they make a big appeal. Keep on the lookout for good stories of animals."'

Through the window they could see workmen with ladders removing bunting from lamp posts.

'There's an example. Last Friday, the prime minister came here. Spoke at the Corn Exchange. *Times* sent a bloke up, *Herald*, all of them. Did he *say* anything ordinary people would want to read about? No, he did not. Did he *do* anything ordinary people would want to read about? No, he did not. Was it really worth sending them blokes from *The Times* and the *Herald* all the way from London? No, it was not. He'll lose the next election.'

'MacDonald?'

'Course he will. Mussolini, Hitler, they've got the right idea. You get people saying Mussolini's just a dumb big bruiser and Hitler's a noisier version of Charlie Chaplin, but that's the point, isn't it? They are recognisable characters, like Felix the Cat or who's that woman does the banana dance in Paris?'

'Josephine Baker,' Edgar said.

'That's the one. Mussolini and Hitler, they *do* things and they *say* things ordinary people want to read about, but more important than that, they are the sort of *characters* ordinary people want to read about. And that's why they're in the papers all the time, isn't it? Not just the Italian and the German papers, neither. In the *Mail* and the *Express* and *The Times*.'

The tea arrived. Edgar poured. Monroe waited until he'd finished, then, ignoring the tea, leant back in his chair and said, in a voice loud enough to turn heads, 'So, Tommy Prosser, is he going to swing?'

'I'm afraid it would be most unethical of me to make any comment on the case at all,' Skelton said.

'You don't think he did it, then?'

'As I say, for me to make a comment—'

'So, you *do* think he did it, then. What's it like defending a man you think is guilty?'

Skelton smiled. 'I'm not sure your line of questioning would be allowed in court, but you could have been a hero of the Spanish Inquisition.'

Monroe took this as a compliment and buttered his teacake with a flourish. 'You know it's the first story I got in the nationals, don't you?'

'What, the burning car? No, I didn't. Congratulations.'

'Frank Chettle's offered me a job.'

'Who's Frank Chettle?'

Monroe rolled his eyes – the ignorance of some people. 'Frank Chettle,' he said, 'editor of the *Daily Graphic*. Third biggest circulation. Be the top now I'm working for 'em.' Monroe grinned at his own immodesty. 'Frank's giving me a trial. I'm to keep running with the burning car story. Come up with a new angle every day. So, obviously, you're gonna be the star of the show.'

'What?'

Skelton felt the way he did at school when Dennis Lawley's gang was looking for people to give his special Chinese burn and saw him hiding behind the bins.

'Well, co-star, anyway. There's Musgrave, the bigamist, up to his ears in debt and lord knows what else. Plenty of human interest, there. But he's dead. Then there's Tommy Prosser – not sure whether he's the dastardly villain or the victim of cruel injustice. And then there's you, solid family man, guardian of the truth, saviour of Mary Dutton and

Ibrahim Aziz. But can the "Conjuror of the Courtroom" do the same for Tommy Prosser? "Conjuror of the Courtroom" isn't my best, I'll come up with something better. Maybe do an interview with your wife. Mila, is it? And don't neglect the children, photo of you playing with Lawrence and Elizabeth. "The family man". Have you got a dog?'

Skelton swallowed his teacake. 'I …' a moment's choking. 'How do you even know I have a wife and children?'

'Press cuttings. Couple of years ago when you were the "Latter Day Galahad" doing the Hannah Dryden case.'

Two years earlier, Skelton had been involved in a libel case, the so-called 'Scandal of The Decade', brought by Hannah Dryden, a society hostess, against her ex-husband. The case gave him his first taste of the headlines when, to his embarrassment tinged with secret and guilty delight, he had found himself as famous, according to Edgar, as Dolores del Rio. Journalists on the *Express* and *Mail* had spared no effort in ferreting details, mostly erroneous, about his wife, children, parents and school. It was Hannah Dryden herself who had christened him, 'The Latter Day Galahad'. He had hoped that, with the passage of time, it would all have been forgotten.

'One has to …' he said, 'I don't think I can stress this too emphatically … one has a duty when called to the bar to uphold the dignity of the legal profession and of the law in general.'

'Of course, of course, of course, of course,' Monroe said. 'And I am not and would never suggest anything that might compromise that dignity. Take it from me, Mr Skelton, I have more respect for the law and for its officers than any man on earth.'

Monroe saw, out of the window, a young woman walking past. He gave her a wave and her friendly wave back made him smile, almost blush. Then he turned back to Skelton and tried to pick up the threads.

'So,' he said, 'have you got a dog? A dog's always better than a cat, isn't it? They do tricks sometimes. Although having said that, I did once know a cat who could jump up on the wall and work the door knocker when he wanted to be let in.' He saw from the expression on Skelton's face that good stories about animals would not be forthcoming. 'Listen, I can see you've got your apprehensions about being the star of the show, but I promise you can trust me always to put you in a good light.'

Skelton was still frowning.

'The other thing you have to think about is the jury,' Monroe went on. 'They will, believe me, take a lot more notice of things said by somebody with a bit of zip whose picture they've seen in the paper than they would of somebody they've never heard of, like John Sankey or Gordon Hewart.'

John Sankey was Lord Chancellor. Gordon Hewart was Lord Chief Justice. Both were distinguished and scholarly gents, but neither possessed an iota of zip. Monroe certainly knew his stuff.

Edgar offered his Gold Flake. Monroe refused and took, from his waistcoat pocket, a packet of Lucky Strike,

American cigarettes in a soft packet. Tapping the top of the pack magically made a single cigarette pop up. He took it in his mouth and lit it with an American lighter. An exotic smell filled the cafe, not like Turkish or French tobacco, a smell all of its own.

Edgar wrinkled his nose with a sour expression.

'It's toasted,' Monroe said.

'What?' Edgar said.

'It's what it says on the advertisements. "It's toasted".'

'What is?'

'The tobacco. I think.'

'I've heard they often like to put butter and marmalade on it, too,' Edgar said.

Monroe looked at his cigarette. There was a precious moment before he realised that Edgar was pulling his leg.

'I didn't like him,' Edgar said, as they approached the prison gates.

'I gathered that,' Skelton said.

'Did you?'

'A little bit bumptious, perhaps.' He was about to add 'But harmless enough' but thought better of it.

Their entry into the prison was the usual procession of register signing, document showings and interminable unlockings and relockings, with the coalhouse smell of the outside of the prison being gradually replaced by the smell of recently disinfected lavatories the nearer to the cells you came.

The warder told them that he would stay with them in the cell while they interviewed Prosser, that they weren't to get too close and there would be nowhere for them to sit. Chairs, he explained, could be used as weapons and might present an obstacle if they needed to leave the cell in a hurry.

The sense of danger seemed to rouse Edgar from his camel powder drowsiness.

'Is he really that dangerous?' he asked.

'Worse,' the warder replied.

It was the gloomiest cell Skelton had ever seen. Though it was moderately bright outdoors, in here the colours were faded to grey and there was a chill in the air as if a storm was brewing.

One look at Prosser was enough to tell you that no jury would acquit. Skelton did not know the derivation of the phrase 'plug-ugly' but was fairly convinced that the 'plug' – whatever it was – must have resembled Tommy Prosser. There was nothing inherently evil there. In repose, the expression could almost have been described as benign, but it was so rarely in repose. Mostly it bore an expression of suspicious rage, pinched, the brows drawn together, the mouth tight closed, the eyes black darting dots. He had the frame of a welterweight wrestler just on the verge of going to seed. The strength was still there, but the muscles had acquired a layer of fat.

Most of all, he put Skelton in mind of photographs he'd seen of John Daniel, the gorilla owned, ten years or so earlier, by a Miss Alyse Cunningham. The beast had, apparently, lived in her house, slept in a proper bed, washed itself in the bathroom and played nicely with local children. An old Africa hand he'd met at some do, however, had told him that if there was a shred of truth in Miss Cunningham's tales, she was a very lucky woman. The gorilla is indeed the gentlest of animals until it is riled. Then it will tear you limb from limb. The difficulty is that they're unpredictable buggers. You can never be quite sure what might make them angry. All the great apes are the same. The Africa hand had once known a chimpanzee who was essentially civilised but would severely injure anybody who wore squeaky shoes. Hated the sound.

Prosser looked up when the door was opened but looked down again when he saw that no food was being brought and stared at his boots. Grey, unpolished boots with no laces, the leather wrapped around the shackles that held his ankles. Heavy chain held his wrists, too.

'Good morning, Mr Prosser,' Skelton said, brightly. 'My name is Arthur Skelton. I'm the barrister who will be representing you in court and this is my clerk, Edgar Hobbes.'

Prosser snorted quietly to himself without looking up.

Edgar took out his notebook and fountain pen, then put it away, worried that the nib could be used to stab, and took out a blunt pencil instead. 'Mr Skelton is here to help you in court,' he said. 'In order to do that, he needs to ask you some questions.'

Prosser shifted his weight. The warder, suspicious of any

movement, advanced a little, brandishing his truncheon. Prosser sat back and stared at his boots.

'There are just a few matters I'd like to clear up,' Skelton said, 'a few questions, and it would be a great help to your case if you would answer them as honestly as possible.'

Without looking up, Prosser said, 'They take your bootlaces.'

Skelton said, 'Yes,' and waited for Prosser to say something else. He didn't. 'You were in the bank changing a five-pound note into notes and coins of smaller denomination.'

No answer.

'Can you tell me how you came by the five-pound note?'

No answer.

'In your statement to the police, you said that you got the five-pound note by selling a car that you had stolen. But you refused to reveal the make of the car or where you stole it from?'

Prosser stared at his boots.

'I'm sure you're aware, Mr Prosser, that if we're to make a case in court, the more evidence we can produce to prove you're telling the truth, the more likely it is that you'll be acquitted of this terrible charge and set free.'

Silence.

'Then you said that you bought the two-gallon can of petrol because you had stolen another car but that it had run out of petrol and you needed to deliver it to the man who'd bought it. But, again, you refused to give the name of the person who bought the car.'

'I'm not a nark.'

'You must realise, Mr Prosser, that though this man you refuse to name would face a charge of receiving stolen goods, it is a charge that might well be dismissed. And even if your purchaser were to be so charged and found guilty, the sentence would probably be no more than a small fine. Whereas ... I'm sure I don't need to spell out the gravity of the charge you face.'

Skelton waited a full minute. Eventually Prosser looked up, perhaps to see if they were still there.

'Could we talk about the starter handle?' Skelton said.

The chains rattled as Prosser shifted his feet. The warder tensed.

'A man came to see me,' Prosser said. 'We had a set-to. I had to see him off.'

'You struck him with the starter handle? Who was this man?'

Prosser's body tensed and his breathing quickened. An outburst seemed imminent. The warder checked that the cell door was still open, ready for a speedy exit, and held his truncheon in the 'I am about to strike' position.

'Did you kill Harold Musgrave?' Skelton asked.

Prosser stared at his boots again. Skelton waited another full minute in silence, then nodded to the warder. They were done.

He and Edgar stood, and the warder began to usher them out. Then Skelton turned back and, dropping the barrister act said, 'I don't think they'd let you have a bottle of Scotch, but I could do you twenty fags.'

Prosser looked up. Edgar took out a twenty pack of Gold Flake and started to hand them over, but the warder stopped him, took the cigarettes and threw them for Prosser to catch.

'Can he have matches?' Skelton asked.

'I can give him a light if he wants one.'

Prosser peeled the cellophane from the cigarette packet and said, 'Can I ask a question?'

Skelton wished he could sit down or at least draw a little closer. 'Of course.'

'I know I've had it. Nobody's going to believe nothing I say, so, what I say is best get it over quick. If I just say I done it, if I just tell you I done it, now, and tell the screws and the governor, would that be it? Can they just take me out and hang me? Just here. Take me outside and hang me?'

'I'm afraid you'd still have to go to court.'

'In court, then, if I say I done it, would they just take me out and hang me? I'd just as soon get it done with.'

'Listen,' Skelton said. 'There's a good chance, if you behave yourself in court, if you answer the questions properly – not like you've just been doing – there's a good chance I can get you off. You can go free.'

'Never going to happen. They'll have me, whatever.'

'I'll come and see you again before the trial. All right?'

Prosser managed to manipulate a cigarette into his mouth and gestured to the warder to give him a light.

It's always impossible to know how things can happen so quickly. In less than half a heartbeat, Prosser had his chain wrapped around the warder's neck and had somehow taken possession of the truncheon.

'Don't do nothing,' he said. 'Or I'll pull his head off.'

The warder was choking, red in the face. Prosser picked him up and made for the door. Skelton and Edgar stepped back to let him pass, but not quite fast enough. Prosser pushed and Skelton fell, half-sitting, against the iron bed.

Edgar helped him up. They looked out into the corridor. Prosser had the warder on the floor, next to another door. With his free hand he was banging on the door with the warder's truncheon. Prosser shouted, 'Open it or I pull his head off.' An electric alarm bell began to ring.

The door opened and six or seven warders appeared all armed with truncheons. They beat the prisoner on the head, the neck, about the waist and the legs. He dropped the warder and fought back, spitting and screaming obscenities. More warders appeared. He was hopelessly outnumbered, but still it took a good two minutes to bring him down and even then the warders did not let up, smashing their truncheons against the backs of his knees to make sure he didn't get up again. They pulled his arms tight behind his back, the chain biting into his belly and got handcuffs on.

Prosser, still conscious, looked back at Skelton. The anger had gone out of him and instead his face wore an expression of terrible, pleading despair. His eye caught one of his boots, which had come off in the struggle. He tried to wriggle towards it, to reach it, perhaps with his mouth. One of the warders put a foot on his chest to hold him still.

A man in a suit, possibly an assistant governor, arrived, saw Skelton and Edgar, apologised profusely that they had been subjected to such a dreadful misadventure and hurried them out of the prison.

In contrast to the gloom, the pale November sun felt like midsummer in Nice.

'Are you sure you're all right, old chap?' Edgar said. 'You took a nasty tumble.'

'You're talking to a man who has recently been trampled by elephants.'

They sat on a bench built into a churchyard wall. Edgar took out his cigarettes. Skelton filled his pipe.

'Can you remember, was there anything in the brief about Prosser having a family?' Skelton asked.

'Not as I remember.'

'What about his house? Is it a cottage or a hovel or what?'

'Is it important?'

'D'you think anybody's ever shown him a scrap of kindness or friendship?'

'Oh, lor',' Edgar said.

'What?'

'I've warned you about caring so many times. It's unprofessional. Worse than that, doing it for fifteen guineas is downright indecent. But Honest Arthur from Leeds doesn't see it like that, does he?' Edgar looked at his chief. Had he gone too far? It is customary for clerks to afford a certain respect to those they serve. 'Honest Arthur from Leeds,' was bordering on insolence. Skelton smiled. Flattered.

Edgar continued. 'I'll admit that in some circumstances it is difficult not to care, but Tommy Prosser's a brute. He's been in trouble with the police ever since he was seven years old.'

'Well, so were you for that matter.'

'Ah, but I reformed,' Edgar said.

'Because somebody cared.'

They smoked for a while in silence.

'I wonder if he's ever had anything he could care for.'

'He seems quite fond of his boots,' Edgar said.

They got back to the car.

'Are the camel powders still working, do you think?' Skelton asked.

'I think so,' Edgar said. 'I should be all right. As long as I don't get too dozy again.'

They drove off. Skelton wondered aloud what would happen to Prosser if he was acquitted and guessed that it would only be a matter of time before the police took him in for some other crime and kept doing it until they found one that would stick and either put him away for a long time or send him to the gallows. But Edgar, before they reached the outskirts of town, was snoring.

Tuesday, 18th November 1930, afternoon

Edgar woke to find himself in the large market square of some town he didn't recognise. He looked around, saw a pub called The Swan, another called The Rose and an imposing building that could have been a town hall.

'Where are we?' he asked.

'Biggleswade.'

'I thought we were going back to London. Did we get lost?'

'I thought I'd come the scenic route.'

'Could we have lunch?'

'That's what I was thinking.'

Edgar got out of the car and stretched as if greeting the dawn after a blissful eight hours.

Skelton joined him. 'Just need to pop into the bank,' he said.

There was a lunchtime crowd in the bank, but eventually Skelton managed to get a word with Cartwright, the manager, who introduced him to Mr Trickett, the cashier who'd served Prosser, and Mr Feltersham who'd counted out the £1,250 for Musgrave.

'It's a huge sum of money. Did it cause much of a stir?' Skelton asked.

'I think Mr Cartwright would have had words to say if it had,' Feltersham said. 'It's bank policy never to cause a "stir". I had to go in the back, of course, to get the notes, but then I counted them out sort of to the side, like this, so that nobody but Mr Musgrave could see unless they were specially looking.'

'But Prosser would have seen?'

'To be honest, I don't see how,' Trickett said. 'He was down here with me and Musgrave was right up there with Mr Feltersham. And Mr Prosser was much too worried about his own business to have been looking anywhere else.' Trickett, a young man of about twenty, had a trace of hair on his upper lip, which he stroked as if it was a luxuriant handlebar. 'He was changing a five-pound note, you see, and wanted four ten-shilling notes and the rest in silver, and he kept wanting me to count it again. He seemed very doubtful that there are eight half-crowns in a pound.'

'Did you tell the police this?'

'They never asked.'

* * *

At a big cafe in the square, Skelton and Edgar both ordered the crumbed lamb cutlets followed by the steamed lemon pudding for Skelton and the Bramley apple tart for Edgar, then coffee and a smoke, and more coffee, then some treacle toffees, sherbet lemons, buttermints and summer refreshers because Skelton fell into conversation with a man at the next table who turned out to be a traveller for Trebor, the confectionery people, and had bags loaded with free samples.

A little way south of Biggleswade, Skelton took a right turn and followed a winding country lane, through Great Dunworth and Lower Dunworth, and past a pub called The Bell. He pulled up just after that and took out the map that Holland had provided with the brief. After studying it for a moment, he drove slowly on until he found the turning for Keeper's Lane.

Edgar woke up.

'Where are we?'

'Lower Dunworth.'

'Oh, there.'

Skelton got out of the car. Edgar found a packet of sherbet lemons in his pocket, popped one in his mouth and followed him.

Musgrave's car had been towed away, but you could see where it had burnt. The hedge was black and withered and, even though there'd been a lot of rain, the tarmac was discoloured. And you could see the footpath across the field that Geoffrey Spencer and Jeannie Crowson would have taken to raise the alarm at The Bell.

They got back in the Bentley and drove past a couple of cottages and an impressive pair of gates with 'The Grange' worked into the wrought iron. It all seemed to be fields after that, so Skelton turned around at the first crossroads and drove back to The Bell.

It was nearly dark by this time. On a patch of grass next to the pub, a gaunt man was raking up leaves and feeding them into a bonfire in a bin.

'We're closed,' he said, when he saw them getting out of the car.

'We just wanted a word. I'm Arthur Skelton, I'm defending Tommy Prosser in court.'

'Course you are,' the man said, 'I read your name in the paper. I won't shake your hand 'cos I'm filthy. You're going to have your work cut out with that one, I can tell you.'

'Do you like buttermints?' Skelton asked and produced a bag from his coat pocket.

The landlord was taken aback but peered into the bag, 'Ar, all right, then.'

He took a sweet.

'Here, have the whole bag,' Skelton said. 'We've got loads, haven't we, Edgar?'

Edgar smiled and produced two bags from his own pockets. 'We met a man in Biggleswade,' he said. 'Very liberal with his free samples.'

'This is Edgar, my clerk.' Skelton said. The landlord was

eyeing the bag. 'Go on. Have you got kids?'

'I've got nieces and nephews.'

'There you are, then.'

'Well, if you're sure.'

He took the bag. 'You can come in and have a drink if you like.'

'I thought you were closed.'

'Not to bona fide travellers. Anyway, the only copper's up in Great Dunworth and his bike's got a puncture.'

'This'd be Constable Myatt?'

'You've met him?'

'I've read about him.'

The landlord, who introduced himself as Wal, led the way through a storeroom into the pub, a functional sort of place with not a trace of horse brasses, ancient settles or sawdust, where they found – opening and closing times clearly being seen as no more than loose guidelines – another customer, immediately recognisable by his face patch and hook hand as Mr Glazier, firework-fiend and Chairman of the Parish Council, nursing a large Scotch and reading *The Times*.

The landlord made introductions and explained that Skelton was defending Tommy Prosser. This Glazier already knew.

'Let me get you a drink,' Skelton said.

Glazier ordered another large Scotch. Edgar, worried about mixing alcohol with his camel powders, had barley water and Skelton a brandy to sharpen him up for the drive back to London. Wal did the honours.

'Have a seat.' Glazier said.

Skelton, eased himself carefully into a chair, keeping the leg straight.

Glazier noticed. 'France?' he asked.

'No, no. Nothing so honourable,' Skelton said. 'I was born with a displaced hip. Never gone right. Kept me out. You were in the Royal Engineers, I believe.'

'Yes, indeed.' Glazier brandished his hook. 'But I don't want you thinking the enemy did this to me. I probably killed thousands of them but never once sustained injury at their hands. Not so much as a bruise. No, all this is self-inflicted. Tricky things, explosives. One is generally advised to treat them with the utmost caution but they're not nearly so much fun if you do.'

He grinned lopsidedly. The scarring had left him with only half a working smile. 'Have you ever blown anything up?'

'No,' Skelton said. 'I'm afraid not.'

Glazier turned to Edgar. 'You?'

'I once had an antique pistol explode in my hand,' Edgar said.

Skelton looked at him, sideways. There was a great deal he didn't know about Edgar's misspent youth.

'Lose any fingers?' Glazier said.

Edgar held out his hands to show they were intact.

'Good for you.'

Edgar took one of the Trebor packets from his pocket. 'Would you like a treacle toffee?'

'Don't mind if I do.' Glazier took one and dunked it in his whisky.

Wal brought the drinks and sat with them, sipping half a mild. 'If you got any questions about that night,' he said, 'Mr Glazier's the man to ask.'

'Have you met Tommy Prosser?' Glazier asked.

'Just been to see him in Bedford gaol,' Skelton said.

'How is he?'

'He tried to kill a warder and pushed me over.'

Glazier did his one-sided grin again. 'Wonderful spirit.'

'You like him?'

'He dug my cesspit. Just him with a pick and a spade. Two days, five shillings a day, working from dawn till dusk without a break. Clay. My God, he got cross with that hole. Went for it, cursing. He didn't do it, by the way.'

'The murder?'

'He didn't do it.'

'You know this?'

'I can easily imagine him bashing the back of a man's head in for – what was it? – twelve hundred and fifty. More money than a chap like that'll see in his lifetime. But the rest of it, buying the petrol, setting fire to the car to destroy the evidence, that takes planning. Did he strike you as a man who plans anything more than one jump ahead?'

'The thought had occurred to me,' Skelton said.

'No. Tommy Prosser's a man of impulse. He sees something – unlocked cars are his speciality – he takes it, and he knows a chap he can flog them to.'

'The chap he flogs the cars to, you don't by any chance know who that is, do you?' Skelton asked.

''Fraid not. Tell you one thing, though. Going on the evidence, I'd say there's far more likelihood that I did it than Tommy Prosser.'

'In what way?'

'I have a long history of involvement with fires and explosives. I was around and about walking past Keeper's Lane at the time of "the incident", sometimes with a can of petrol in my hand.'

'But you didn't know that Musgrave had a huge amount of money in the car.'

'Of course I did. I'd had lunch with Cartwright.'

'The bank manager?'

'Business lunch. He told me all about the chap who came in for £1,250, even pointed him out in the square, getting into his car. You see, if anything, I'd say the evidence against me is a good bit more convincing than it is against Tommy Prosser, but I'm Chairman of the Parish Council with an honourable service record and he's a ne'er-do-well. So, he's the first man the coppers finger when anything's amiss and I'm "Mr Glazier, sir". And it's not as if a thousand or so wouldn't come in useful. There's a great pile of Victorian nonsense, not a house, a what-d'you-call-it, a folly, belongs to Billy bloody Gutteridge – *Sir* Billy bloody Gutteridge – just over the way. Blocks my view something terrible. If I could persuade Billy to part with it for, say, two or three hundred – might have to run to a thousand if he turned stubborn bastard on me, which he's more than likely to do – bit of deftly positioned gelignite, go up lovely, and I reckon on a good day I'd be able see all the way to Sharpenhoe Clappers.'

Wal drained his half of mild. 'I've got to get the new dartboard up,' he said. Skelton had noticed the dartboard, leaning against the wall in the corner, a London board with the folding blackboards.

'I've already drilled and filled the holes in the wall. Just need somebody to hold it in place for me.'

Skelton and Edgar volunteered and, when it was screwed fast, they had to try it out. Mr Glazier joined them. Wal fancied himself and massacred Skelton, who still had 125 on the board when Wal went out with a double 16. Glazier wasn't much better, but Edgar scored 180 with his first three darts and went out with a double 18 on his first try.

While they played, Skelton and Glazier discussed a fairly well-established defence tactic called 'the alternative hypothesis', which can be summarised as saying 'The evidence against the accused could equally apply to this man or this man'. No end of people knew Musgrave had the money on him. On bonfire night, hundreds of people probably bought cans of petrol.

'Would it help if I were to show my face in court?' Glazier asked.

'It's certainly a thought.'

'Might be fun. Standing up there and practically confessing. I am right, aren't I? The evidence to say that I did it is actually more compelling than it is for Tommy Prosser.'

'I'm sure a case could be made. And possibly convince a jury.'

Glazier let out a single bark. 'Ha!' And, in a voice loud enough to be heard all the way from Sharpenhoe Clappers, said, 'Japes!'

It was pitch-black by the time they were back in the car.

'You don't think he could actually have done it, do you?' Edgar said.

'I wouldn't be in the least bit surprised. A man who delights in risk. What could be more thrilling than standing up in court, confessing to murder, knowing there's a very strong chance you'll get away with it, but still, it would be a terrific gamble?'

'I'll have a word with Holland. Perhaps the police should have a word with Mr Glazier.'

They drove on a little way.

'Is your proficiency at darts another sign of your wasted youth?' Skelton asked.

'I suppose so. In those days, though, we never had a dartboard.'

'So …?'

'Hats, front doors, market produce and arses,' Edgar said. 'Mostly arses.'

Wednesday, 19th November 1930

Skelton had known Stanley Cotterell since school. He was a year younger and had a weak heart, something to do with scarlet fever. Along with Skelton and a few others, he'd been excluded from PE and some of the more rigorous sports, instead sitting in what was delicately called 'cripples corner' where, while the more able boys chased a ball around a muddy field or jumped over a vaulting horse, they were supposed to play chess (not draughts) or read an improving book.

Cotterell had gone on to become a solicitor with a practice in Camden Town three doors away from a chop house that worked such magic with a saddle of lamb that people found the taste and texture haunting their dreams. Old men on their deathbeds had been known to say, 'I married a good woman, had seven healthy children,' then, pausing to give due weight to the capstone of this life well lived, added, 'and I had lunch at the Camden Town chop house. Twice.'

'I was wondering if I might pick your brains,' Cotterell said when they'd put in their orders and been provided with sherry.

'A legal matter or a personal one?' Skelton asked. 'Because I should warn you that I'm no good at personal. Particularly if it involves feelings.'

'No, it's legal. Well, sort of. A divorce.'

'You're getting divorced?'

'No, no. Gwen and I couldn't be happier. It's a client. A chap called Higgins. Thinks his wife is having an affair with Reverend Hucks, Vicar of St Claire's in Kentish Town.

'And is she?'

'Yes. But she denies it vehemently, as does the vicar. I actually know the vicar quite well. Fine man. Utterly respectable, but quite besotted by Mrs Higgins. Poor chap. Never known anything like it before. First love at his advanced age.'

'How old is he?'

'Seventy-six.'

'And the woman?'

'Mrs Higgins is, I think, a little older. Seventy-seven or eight.'

Skelton looked to make sure they weren't overheard. 'And this affair has a … physical dimension?'

'My secretary was going into Maples on the Tottenham Court Road and saw them, together, canoodling, coming out of the Grafton Hotel in mid-afternoon.'

'Was he wearing clerical garb?'

'Mufti.'

'And how old is the husband?'

'Eighty-two. He's devastated, of course, and determined to get a divorce. He says there's no future in the marriage.'

'But …' It didn't need spelling out. 'So, he wants to divorce on the grounds of adultery, but the wife would oppose, and the husband has no actual proof that relations have taken place? Would a private detective …?'

'Well, obviously, but if proof were to be obtained the reputation of the poor Reverend Hucks would be dragged through the mud. He'd most likely be defrocked. The shame would kill him. He is a very nice chap.'

'I see.'

'There is another difficulty. You see Mrs Higgins has something of a reputation for raciness. She first made a cuckold of Mr Higgins when they were on honeymoon in Eastbourne in 1881 and has maintained a prodigious record for infidelities ever since. And I could probably find former lovers who'd happily confess to their indiscretions and appear as co-respondent, but then Mr Higgins would have to know about the others.'

'And he doesn't?'

'Not a glimmer. Probably the only person from Kentish Town to Kilburn who doesn't. Fifty years and the business with the vicar is the first time he's harboured any suspicion at all.'

'So, there's a danger that, if he did find out about the others, the shock would …'

'Kill him, yes.'

The meat came and, for a while, both were transported to a corner of culinary heaven where the only utterance possible is 'Mmmmm'.

The joint was wheeled around on a trolley and from time to time the waiter would arrive and offer seconds. Skelton and Cotterell both went for thirds, then had jam sponge and custard.

'I came into the law,' Cotterell said, over coffee, 'because I thought everything would be cut and dried. I thought the law was a book of rules. Like the rules of snakes and ladders. But it isn't at all, is it? It's no more cut and dried than ordinary life. Less so in many ways because other people's problems are so much more complicated than one's own. And the other thing is, justice, in practice, is so often horribly unfair, isn't it?'

'Oh, yes,' Skelton said. 'Anybody who comes into the law thinking it has anything at all to do with fairness or right and wrong is in for a terrible disappointment. It's got to the point where I've started wondering why we bother having trials at all when the toss of a coin would serve the cause of justice just as well, if not better.' The coffee came with tiny biscuits. 'What are these called?'

'I don't know. They're sort of almondy, aren't they? Should we ask for some more?'

'We'd be mad not to. Here's an idea. Tell the old man, Mr Higgins, that you have hired a private detective and that he has listened at doors and looked through keyholes and has ascertained that the Vicar of St Claire's is offering Mrs Higgins nothing more salacious than spiritual guidance and the discussion of Bible passages.'

'That would be a terrible lie.'

'Do you have any particular objection to lying?'

'To clients? No.'

'It would put the old man's mind wonderfully at ease and allow him to live out his few remaining days in peace. You'd probably have to get Mrs Higgins to collude with the lie. Would she do that?'

'I think she'd do anything to protect Hucksy.'

'The vicar? Is that what she calls him?'

'Just speculating.'

'Mr Higgins is eighty-two. Average life expectancy for a man is sixty, so he's effectively been living on borrowed time for twenty-two years. Is he a well man?'

'Not particularly. He's had a lot of trouble with gallstones.'

'There you are, then. You'd probably only have to sustain the lie for a couple of years at the outside. And even if he lives until he's eighty-five or ninety, he'll most likely be gaga and won't know the difference.'

The almondy biscuits arrived and they talked of other matters.

* * *

Edgar was out when Skelton got back to 8 Foxton Row, and since the afternoon's business – reading some nonsense and writing some other nonsense – could be delayed interminably, he decided to devote an hour or so to dozing, first in one of the low chairs, then, when that proved unsatisfactory, on the rug with his head beneath his desk, with a chair and a table carefully placed to aid his standing when his doze was done.

There was a knock at the door. Skelton tried to ignore it, hoping the knocker would assume he was out and go away, but it came again more insistently. A voice, that of Eric, one of the errand boys whose stupidity was on its way to becoming a Foxton Row legend, said, 'Mr Skelton, Mr Rosthwaite is downstairs waiting to see you.'

Quietly cursing and making full use of the chair and the table, Skelton pulled himself to his feet and found the appointments book, meticulously kept by Edgar. There was no mention of a Mr Rosthwaite.

He opened the door. Eric was standing on one foot, like a flamingo.

'I'm not expecting a Mr Rosthwaite,' Skelton said.

'He asked if you was in, sir,' Eric said, 'and I told him you was in 'cos I seen you come in.'

'As I'm sure Mr Hobbes has told you a thousand times,' Skelton said, 'if someone asks whether I'm in, you should say, "I'll check", then you come up here and you ask whether I'm in, and I'm never in unless I specifically say I'm in. Now, is that understood?'

It wasn't, but Eric nodded just as if it was.

'Did Mr Rosthwaite give a first name?' Edgar asked.

'Yes, sir.'

'What was it?'

'Lord.'

Lord Rosthwaite, the sixth richest man in England, was a meat importer who was rumoured to have traded with the enemy during the war. He had bought his peerage from Lloyd-George for £70,000 and when Alfred Harmsworth threatened to expose the sale in the *Daily Mirror*, Lloyd-George promptly ennobled Harmsworth, too, making him Lord Northcliffe, and the story went away.

'Did he mention what he wanted to see me about?'

'Said it was very private.'

'Better show him up, I suppose,' Skelton said. 'And ask Mr Hobbes to come up if he's back yet. And, when you're sure Lord Rosthwaite has gone, bring tea and biscuits. Not before. Remember, *unexpected* visitors, be they peers of the realm or His Majesty the King himself, do not get tea and biscuits.'

Skelton filled and lit his pipe.

Another knock. Eric ushered in the visitor, left the room and fell downstairs. When he reached the bottom, there was a short pause before he called, plaintively, just in case anyone was interested, 'I'm all right.'

Rosthwaite was a hairless man with oversized ears and eyes so small they might not have been there at all. He carefully closed the door that Eric had left open and took Skelton's hand into both of his as if claiming ownership. It was not a tight grip, but it was persistent.

'Mr Skelton,' he said, 'it is a pleasure and a privilege to meet you.'

The accent suggested a la-di-da lower-middle-class home near Liverpool and a very minor public school that had failed to knock the rough edges off.

Skelton tried to rid himself of the double handshake while simultaneously coaxing Rosthwaite into a chair.

Rosthwaite would not be moved. 'The matter about which I'd like to speak with you is of an intensely personal nature.'

Skelton nodded, understandingly. Rosthwaite sat, took out his cigar case, extracted one of Hermann Upmann's finest, cut the end with a blade attached to his match case lit it, and sucked at the thing like a baby at the bottle. Then he leant forward and, in a half-whisper, said, 'It's about this Denison Beck business. You probably already know I've been taking his treatments for the past year or so. And you've probably realised that if word of my condition were to come out in court and reach the press, the effect on the stock market, not to mention Britain's relations with the Empire, could be devastating.'

From the way that Rosthwaite was practically squirming with embarrassment, it was not difficult to deduce that his 'condition' was, more than likely, spermatorrhoea-related, or perhaps something even more embarrassing that Skelton preferred not to think about. While he found it ludicrous to believe that even something he preferred not to think about could have any bearing on 'Britain's relations with the

Empire', he accepted it was exactly the sort of thing that a self-important captain of industry like Rosthwaite would take for granted.

The smoke from Skelton's pipe had a cleaner, bluer quality than that from Rosthwaite's cigar, which was grey and dense.

'I should point out,' Skelton said, 'that, as yet, I have not had sight of a list of Mr Beck's patients nor the conditions for which they were being treated.'

Rosthwaite's sigh of relief came out as a cumulonimbus of cigar smoke.

'But I expect to in the next day or so.'

Some of the cloud was sucked back in again.

'But I can rely on your discretion?' Rosthwaite said.

'My discretion or lack of it is really neither here nor there,' Skelton said as gently as possible. 'A man's on trial for manslaughter. He could go to prison for the rest of his life. I'm briefed to defend him. It is my job to conduct that defence as effectively as I possibly can, and while I can assure you that, in the normal course of events, I would never expose any information which might cause dismay or embarrassment, I might not have much choice in the matter. If it came to it and I was sure that mentioning your name and condition would make a substantial contribution to Mr Beck's defence, I'd be duty-bound to do it.'

'But surely—'

Before Rosthwaite could start banging on about the stock market and the Empire again, Skelton said, 'The thing is, you see, the statue on top of the Old Bailey, the statue of justice with the scales in one hand and the sword in the other is blindfold to indicate that justice – regardless of the effect that it may or may not have on reputation, on share prices, on country or empire – can show no fear or favour.'

Rosthwaite carefully touched the ash of his cigar against the edge of the ashtray and, when it didn't fall off, let it be.

'Needless to say, I am in complete agreement with you, Mr Skelton,' he said. 'Right is right and wrong is wrong and never the twain shall meet, and I know as well as you do that British justice is revered throughout the world, and rightly so. Although, to be pedantic on a small matter, I don't think the statue on top of the Old Bailey is actually blindfold.'

'Isn't she? I thought she was.'

'No, sometimes similar statues are, but I don't think the one up there is.'

'I must remember to look next time I'm up that way.'

Rosthwaite smiled. 'Dickie Matthieu told me the legal fees involved in that patent brawl he had a couple of years ago had practically ruined him.'

Skelton had had nothing to do with the Matthieu case but knew it all the same. Matthieu had manufactured some new sort of drill or lathe some aspect of which had already been patented by Bruce and Laidlaw of Warrington. The case had dragged on for the best part of a year.

'He told me that a top man working on a case like that could expect to end up with two or three thousand pounds.'

Skelton had a horrified inkling where this might be leading.

Rosthwaite had lost his embarrassment. He was never embarrassed when he was talking about business. 'Now, despite what the papers say, you're not really in the top league, are you, Mr Skelton? Not yet. So, what do you make? In a year?'

'I don't see how that could possibly have any relevance to—'

'Presumably your chambers takes a cut of your fees, and your clerk and then there'd be no end of expenses. So, what do you end up with? Five thousand? Ten thousand? It's a hell of a good screw but all the same, it's not first class on the *Île de France* is it? Or your own suite at the Grand Hôtel des Bains? Every little helps and an extra thousand pounds can help a lot.'

'Lord Rosthwaite—'

'It's not as if I'm asking for the world, is it? Just keep my name out of things and—'

'Lord Rosthwaite, I think we should end this conversation now.'

'Whatever you say.'

'Obviously what you propose is absolutely out of the question and I should by rights report you to the police.'

Rosthwaite smoked his cigar, waiting, perhaps, for Skelton to make a counter-offer.

'Under the circumstances,' Skelton continued, 'I think it would be better if both of us pretended that this conversation never took place.'

'Of course,' Rosthwaite said. He stood. 'Don't worry, I

can find my own way out. And, as you say, this conversation never took place.'

As Rosthwaite left, he turned and winked.

Skelton relit his pipe, wondering what was meant by the wink. Then it dawned on him.

Edgar came in with the tea, a tin of biscuits and the afternoon post. 'Sorry, I was delayed. What did Lord Rosthwaite want?'

'He was one of Beck's patients. Some problem he doesn't want people to know about.'

'Ah,' Edgar said. 'I would imagine at least half of Beck's clientele were there to do with downstairs business.'

'He tried to bribe me not to mention his name during the trial.'

'That's very naughty,' Edgar said.

'Which is exactly what I said, except – I think there may have been a terrible misunderstanding.'

'In what way?'

'I said, "I think it would be better if we both pretended this conversation never took place," and I think he thought …'

'Oh, dear. Well, as long as you don't actually act on his suggestion, or take his money, there's no harm done. Although I suppose we could report the matter to the police, except that he'll deny it and it'll be his word against yours and he'll bring the matter up in the House of Lords and then all hell will break loose.'

'Did Aubrey manage to get hold of Beck's client list?'

'I'm not sure. I'll give him a call and get him to send it over if it's arrived.'

'By the way,' Skelton said, 'I told Rosthwaite the statue on top of the Old Bailey is blindfold. It is, isn't it?'

'I haven't looked for ages. I know she's wearing a crown and looks as if she's about to topple over backwards, but I can't remember a blindfold.'

Edgar opened the biscuit tin and found that somebody had snaffled all the ginger nuts so, to compensate, took two petit beurres.

'You never told me what you think, by the way,' he said.

'What about?'

'The cocktail cabinet. Now that you've seen it in the flesh.'

'Well, it's not really my field, is it?'

'All the same, I'd value your opinion.'

'I don't know anything about furniture, and I've got no taste.'

'Exactly, I'd like to gauge its effect on the untrained eye.'

'It's … a … lovely bit of wood. Beautiful grain.'

'It's rosewood,' Edgar said. 'The dark parts are, anyway. The lighter parts are bird's-eye maple. And, of course,' he had the catalogue to hand, turned to the picture of the cabinet and pointed out some of the ornamental features, 'these parts are Bakelite.'

Skelton looked. 'The crevices between the pointy bits,' he said.

'What about them?'

'They're very deep.'

'Y-yes.'

'Be a bugger to dust.'

Edgar reclaimed the catalogue, perhaps a little more roughly than was necessary. 'I have telephone calls to make,' he said, and swept majestically out of the room.

The post contained the usual Wednesday letter from cousin Alan.

c/o The Chaundler Fund, Princess Street, Manchester
Monday, 17th November 1930

My dear cousin Arthur,

I really did not know how busy busy could be before the last few days. I realise that you spend a lot of your time rushing about the country. Whenever I read about you in the newspaper you are one minute at the Warwick Assizes and the next minute in Winchester and then you are doing something or other in Durham or Norwich, as well as all the travelling from Lambourn to London and back and forth and to and fro, so you will know all about what it has been like for us.

We had a very successful four nights in Colne Workingmen's Institute. Since then we have been having one-night bookings in some of the smaller towns. Our band changes its personnel practically every night depending on who is available and whom we meet along the way. One night we had four trombones, accordion, banjo and clarinet. The only fixed entity is Ron, the clarinet player, whom I think I might have mentioned in a previous letter.

Ron (his surname is Liptrot) is a milkman but until quite recently he was in the army, playing his clarinet with one of the Lancashire regimental bands. They train them well in the army. His sight-reading is near miraculous. I asked how he had become so proficient and he told me that you had to be a good sight reader in the army because they put you on a charge for playing a wrong note, send you to prison for two wrong notes and if you make a real blunder, like coming in a bar late or making a squeak with your reed, they put you up against a wall and shoot you. This, I know from my own experience, is probably not that much of an exaggeration.

I was taught to drive in the army by a dreadful martinet by the name of Sergeant Howells. Whether you got it right or wrong, his method of instruction was to shout obscenities into your ear. I cannot imagine the firing squad was ever far from his mind. He pushed poor Gethin Hughes out of the driving seat of a Vauxhall staff car while it was bowling down a hill at about thirty miles an hour just because Gethin made a noise changing gear. Luckily Gethin only suffered a slight injury to his wrist from where he had bent his hand backwards breaking his fall, but he could easily have hurt himself badly or even been run over.

Well, to get back to Ronald Liptrot. As well as being able to sight-read anything you put in front of him, he can also play authentic-sounding jazz and improvise 'hot' solos. This makes him very popular with the younger crowd.

The only problem is that, because of the milkman's hours, he falls asleep a lot. He has to get up at three o'clock in the morning, you see, to cycle to the depot by four. Then he has to load his cart and feed his horse and whatever else it is they have to do. Even though he has usually finished his round by eleven or twelve o'clock, he still has two hours of work to do back at the depot before he can go home. Then, by the time he has had something to eat, had a wash and changed his clothes, it is time to get on his bicycle to get to wherever it is we are playing. He lives in Nelson, which is only half an hour or so by bike from Colne, but since then we have played in Accrington, Oswaldtwistle, Bacup and Todmorden, all of which are more than an hour's ride for him up and down terrible hills. I cannot imagine what his journey home in the pitch-black and the cold must be like.

So, it is hardly surprising that he falls asleep a good deal. It makes not a jot of difference to his playing. He is so proficient that he can play perfectly well when he is half-asleep or indeed half-awake, but sometimes you do have to listen out for the times when the clarinet drifts away to be replaced by snores. A good jab to the shoulder with the end of my banjo usually does the trick. Point at where you are in the music as soon as his eyes are properly open and he is off, bright as ever, until the next time.

The nearest we came to disaster was when, during a particularly loud passage performed by trumpet and trombone (played for that night in rather staid fashion by a plumber and his mate) we missed the snores until it was too late. I turned just in time to see his clarinet fall to the floor. Luckily, the army also taught him how to make running repairs to the instrument with bits of string and rubber bands, so he had it playing again before the end of 'O'Brien is Tryin' to Learn to Talk Hawaiian'.

In light of your comments in your last letter about your dreadful experience at the Lord Mayor's Show, by the way, I asked if, during his time in the army, he had ever had the experience of playing his clarinet while riding a horse. He said he had not but was willing to give it a go on Clarence his milkman's horse and report back. I told him not to go to any trouble because it was not really very important. I hope that was all right.

Well, to get to the bigger picture. The grand plan of the whole venture, as outlined by the Chaundler Fund for the Promotion of Moral Hygiene, is to educate young women in the ways of the world in order to keep them from a descent into sin. And this has become the theme of the preaching element, which, along with the dancing and singing, is incorporated into every one of our meetings.

In the past, as I am sure you are aware, I have always taken care of the preaching, announcements and general chivvying of the audience. Norah takes care of the music, writing out the arrangements and so forth but is generally content to stay 'out of the limelight'.

Speaking in public comes to me naturally and has done ever since the angels first came to me when I was a lad and I began to spread the message of Jesus' joy.

Although I have never had the privilege of seeing you in court, I have read accounts of your oratory in the newspapers and wonder if it is not a gift that runs in the family – although from the praise you garner I can only assume that if I am blessed at all then you must be thrice blessed.

When we embarked on our new mission as 'Moral Hygienists' for the Chaundler Fund, however, it felt wrong for me to be preaching to women and girls about women's temptation and women's sin. I am not even sure that I could address the subject at all. Not with any authority. Apart from the matter of my gender, I am a stranger to romantic love, having never really had time for it. I am not saying that serving God precludes matrimonial thoughts – only a Roman Catholic would believe such a thing – and neither would I disparage courtship and marriage. But it is like making ships in bottles. I can see the attraction – the sense of achievement must be wonderful – but I have never been tempted to have a go myself.

So, we decided that Norah should do the preaching, not only because she is a woman but also because she was once engaged to that awful man Owen Pritchard from the enamelware factory who cruelly abandoned her not three months before the wedding day because Gwen Richards was having his baby. Norah knows what it is to have loved and to have lost. With Owen Pritchard, I believe that she even strayed momentarily towards the stinking gutters of iniquity, although I hasten to add that she never came anywhere near close enough to risk tumbling in.

The trouble is that she has always had a terror of public speaking. She flusters easily, you see, and lives on her nerves. I have always believed that this would be on account of her artistic temperament. You only have to hear her play the piano accordion or sing to know she is artistic, so it stands to reason that she would have the temperament to go with it.

It is not merely a matter of her preferring to stay 'out of the limelight', it could be said that she has been actively afraid of the limelight.

One thing you have to say about my twin sister is that, for all her nerves and artistic temperament, she has never been short of gumption. She agreed with me that it would not be right for me to stand up and speak to young women about love and prostitution and so forth, and since there was no other woman available, and since she has never been known to shirk her duty, she announced that she would do her best to overcome her fears and give it a go.

She prepared hard, wrote out her sermon and committed it to memory. She practised it in the Eccles and though I did not say anything about it, because the last thing she needed was any species of discouragement, it was a dull and lifeless thing that she was doing to which I feared the young women would pay no heed.

Worse still, I feared that they would jeer.

When it came to it, I could see that she was white with fear. Throughout the opening number she was shaking so much that every note she played was a quavering trill.

Well, the time came and it could not be put off. With halting step, she made her way to the lectern and spread out the words she had prepared. She stumbled and mumbled her way through the first sentence. Then she made the mistake of looking out at the sea of glowing faces (we like to do something vigorous, like a one-step, before the sermon, so they are ready for a rest). Poor Norah attempted the next sentence but stammered so much she could not utter so much as a single word.

Cautiously I approached, ready to take over,

but she heard my footfall and gave me such a look – determination mixed with outrage that I should think of intervening. As I say, she does not lack gumption.

I stood still and waited. The audience grew restive. Norah looked up at the ceiling, perhaps in prayer, then she looked down again at the words she had written, pushed them aside and, in a voice rich and strong, spoke, without notes, for ten or fifteen minutes.

I tell you, I almost wept with pride and joy at my sister's glory.

She had those young women in the palm of her hand, speaking their language, never being preachy or pious, but peppering her discourse with jokes and pertinent observations. And when it came to the end, those young women clapped and cheered more enthusiastically than any congregation has ever done for one of my sermons. She, too modest to take a bow or even make a nod of acknowledgement, quietly strapped herself into her accordion and counted us into 'There's A Rainbow 'Round My Shoulder' which we played with such brio that everybody in that room had to dance. They could not help themselves.

The spirit had taken her.

It is a feeling I know well. When I get up to preach, I never have a thought in my head. Deliberately so. If I think about what I am going to say it never comes out right. So, I make my mind a blank and let the spirit take me. Then the words come and the sentences and the thoughts and the ideas and the jokes one after another. At the time it seems effortless. Only afterwards do I realise how much it has taken out of me. Sometimes I have to have a lie down.

I have read accounts of the remarkable speeches you make in court and wondered if it is the same for you. Do you prepare or do you just let the spirit take you? You might not believe in the spirit, of course. I know you have doubts about religious matters, and I respect that, so perhaps you have a different name for what I call 'the spirit'.

After the dance in Todmorden last night, we began to say our goodbyes to Ron the clarinet-playing milkman because we were off to Rochdale, which, by bicycle, must be a good two or three hours from Nelson.

Ron said there was no need for goodbyes because he was coming with us.

I told him not to be so daft. By the time he got home in the morning he'd have to be off starting his milk round. He'd never have time to sleep or eat.

He said he was giving up his milkman's job. Again, I told him not to be so daft. Though the Chaundler Fund pays for our petrol and food, I cannot imagine they would happily stump up the extra for a clarinet player. And besides, the Eccles is crowded enough with just Norah and myself always bumping into each other. There certainly is not room for a third person.

Ron told us not to worry. As an old soldier (he must be all of twenty-five) he knew how to fend for himself.

I could not deny him, and he is certainly a useful addition to our little orchestra, but it is a worry what he means by 'fending for himself' and I hope that it does not mean stealing chickens and eggs from coops and vegetables from allotments and fields as I believe that soldiers are sometimes wont to do.

As I say, we are off to Rochdale tomorrow. I have been told that the Co-Operative movement was started there by the Rochdale Pioneers. I would imagine there will be quite an impressive shop, so that is something to look forward to.

Since we are moving around so much, it will be best to use the above address when you write. The Chaundler Fund will know where we are from day to day and be able to forward your letters.

I am ever yours faithfully in the joy of Jesus,
Alan.

Edgar came back.

'I got on to Aubrey,' he said. 'He's spoken to the police. They say they seized all the paperwork they could find at

Denison Beck's. They've found no client list, although they admit they've only had time for a cursory look.'

'Ask Aubrey to send Rose down there. See what she can dig out.'

Thursday, 20th November 1930

Rose Critchlow, 21, eager, white face, red nose, ginger hair in tight curls, ex-Ranger Girl Guide, beautiful copperplate handwriting, was an articled clerk who, though she'd been working with Aubrey for less than a year, had become his most useful employee.

Edgar had 'discovered' her in Birmingham, where she'd been with her father's firm, and taken her under his wing when the father had died. He suggested she come and work in London, arranged for her to continue her articles at Aubrey's and even arranged accommodation with his former landlady, Mrs Westing in Swiss Cottage. Even though Rose had now reached the age of majority, Edgar, who'd never had children of his own, saw himself *in loco parentis*. He took pride in her achievements and fretted over the setbacks.

At the moment there was a lot of fretting to be done. Earlier in the year, Rose had met a young man, Vernon Goodyear, a PhD student exploring the relatively new science of forensic entomology, mostly based at Bart's hospital. Vernon could speak for hours about the fauna that can be found slowly devouring a human corpse and had, in his laboratory and at his digs, a fine collection of blowflies, house flies and flesh flies in various stages of their life cycles and liked to demonstrate how quickly the flesh fly will respond to a release of the various gases and other substances from a newly dead cadaver.

Rose was clearly entranced by the man and they had seen each other on several occasions socially as well as professionally – picnics and bicycle rides had been mentioned – but whether the word 'love' could be applied was a matter of some conjecture. Though expert in many fields – her map-reading and orientation skills were near superhuman – Rose's knowledge of the heart ran only to ventricles and atria.

And Edgar, whose own understanding of such matters was less than comprehensive, fretted. Was she in love? If she was, did she know? Was the feeling reciprocated? And, most worrying, in her naivety and ignorance was she blundering blindly around the rocky roads of romance about to be banjaxed by the belching bus of heartbreak?

Further complications came when, in July, Vernon had taken the opportunity to further his studies at the university of Heidelberg in Germany. The effect that his absence had on Rose was far from clear, but, perhaps significantly, soon after he had left she had begun a regime of rigorous exercise with Indian clubs with the result that, from the look of her arms and shoulders, you could easily believe her capable of carrying an ox up five or six flights of stairs without breaking sweat. Also, she never seemed to stop working. Twice, Aubrey had called in at his office after some evening engagement to find a light burning and Rose at her desk, studying a book, or old case notes. He was concerned that the nervous strain would eventually tell.

On the previous day, as soon as Aubrey had given her the assignment, she had phoned Marylebone Police Station, where the documents removed from Denison Beck's premises were being held, arranged to see them and gone straight there, working through the afternoon, into the evening, and not getting back home until after ten. The following morning, she was back there at eight, and, in the afternoon ready to present her findings to Skelton and Edgar at 8 Foxton Row.

'They were right,' she said. 'There isn't a client list, as such. But there is an appointments book.'

'Well, that would presumably have the names of the clients,' Edgar said.

'It records appointments with a Mr Smith, a Mr Jones, a Mr Brown, a Mr Wilson. Pseudonyms, I'd imagine.'

'No mention of Lord Rosthwaite?' Skelton said.

'Not unless he sometimes goes by the name of Mr Thompson or Mr Green. Preserving people's anonymity is one thing, but it must have got ever so difficult remembering that Mr Green is so-and-so and Mr White is Lord such-and-such.'

'Perhaps they had some sort of code book,' Edgar said.

'There wasn't a code book among the papers and the police say they took every scrap they could find.'

'Hidden, perhaps?' Edgar said. 'A loose floorboard?'

'Seems an awful lot of trouble,' Skelton said, 'having to rip up floorboards every time you want to know who Mr Jones with the two o'clock appointment really is.'

'Does Mr Beck have a prodigious memory?' Rose asked.

'Hard to say. Would you have thought he has a prodigious memory, Edgar?'

'He wasn't very good at remembering my name,' Edgar said.

'Does he have a secretary?'

'There was a sort of receptionist, a Miss Alison.'

'Perhaps she has a prodigious memory.'

'You're sure the police let you see everything?'

'I don't see any reason why they wouldn't have. I had the impression that they'd barely glanced at the stuff, so they wouldn't have known what to censor anyway. And the chap, PC Root, was ever so helpful. Oh, Mr Duncan said I should have a word with you about that.'

'Yes?'

'Well, as soon as I got to the station, I thought I recognised PC Root, and I just assumed I must have seen him on the beat or doing traffic duty or something, but then it dawned on me, he's the man from the posters.'

'Which posters?'

'Dr Wellburn's Foot Powder.'

'I don't think I know ...'

'Yes, you do,' Edgar said. 'They're all over the underground. With the picture of the fat policeman with huge feet doing traffic duty on a hot day, with sweat practically spurting from his face. "Even on the hottest day, Dr Wellburn's Foot Powder Stops the Stink of Squelchy Feet." And that's the man you saw at the police station?' Rose nodded. 'I'm surprised the police would allow him to do something like that.'

'They didn't. He's very unhappy about it all. Apparently, last August, the *Daily Express* took the photo and used it along with the usual kids swimming in the Serpentine for a "Hottest Day of the Year" story. Then, without asking anybody's permission, these advertising people started using it for the squelchy feet.'

'Without permission?'

'He says he thinks they got the *Daily Express*'s permission. But nobody asked him. And it's embarrassing. He gets recognised in the street. People pass remarks. And his sergeant won't risk sending him out because he says it demeans the authority of the police.'

'Couldn't the police sue?' Edgar said.

'They can't be bothered. Easier just to hide him away in the station all day.'

'Well, he should sue.'

'Gander and Page – the people who do the posters – are one of the biggest advertising agencies in the country.

They'd have hundreds and thousands of pounds to spend on a court case. All he's got is his policeman's wages. So, I said I'd have a word with Mr Duncan, and Mr Duncan said he'd get in touch with Gander and Page, but would you mind if he mentioned your name, Mr Skelton? He doesn't want you actually to do anything.'

'Yes, of course.' Skelton said.

'I'll let Mr Duncan know. I'm sure PC Root will be very grateful. So, do you want me to go through Mr Beck's papers again?'

'I'm sure if you didn't find it,' Skelton said, 'it's not there.'

'Perhaps I should pop over to Mr Beck's consulting room,' Rose said. 'See if I can have a word with Mr Beck or Miss Alison.'

Edgar tutted and said, 'You're not a private detective, Rose.'

'Yes, I know, but by the time Mr Duncan has appointed and properly briefed a private detective, I could have been over there six or seven times. And there's the expense.'

'The bill would go to Mr Beck.'

'Well, I'm sure he'd rather save the money by having me do it, wouldn't he?'

'Mr Beck is not a particularly pleasant man.'

Rose gave Edgar an exaggerated frown with a smile at the bottom to indicate that she was a grown-up woman now who could take a bit of unpleasantness in her stride.

'I'm not sure there'll be anybody there, anyway,' Skelton said. 'Didn't Beck say they were shutting up shop?'

'Even better,' Rose said. 'I can break in and rip up the floorboards to find the code book.'

Edgar half-stood flapping his hands. 'Rose, you mustn't—'

'I'm joking.'

Edgar sat down again but kept flapping. Rose was not known for her jokes, but, especially with her new strength, he could easily imagine her ripping up floorboards.

Skelton felt the teapot. There was still warmth in it.

'Does anybody want a refill? It'll be a bit stewed but I'm quite fond of stewed tea.'

Rose handed him her cup and he did the honours.

'Have you heard at all from Vernon?' Skelton asked.

Edgar breathed in and held it, watching Rose's face, fretting that the question might trigger a bedewing of the eyes or a complete nervous collapse.

There was a pause, and perhaps a blush, but thankfully no tears.

'Oh, he's in his element,' Rose said. 'They are doing up-to-the-minute research in forensic science at Heidelberg. Ehler and Schwann are both there, of course, following up Landsteiner's work on blood groups, and Forsch is extending the Bertillon anthropometrical system to encompass some of Kollman and Buchly's work on facial reconstruction and Schmidt's doing marvellous things in advanced microscopy.'

Edgar and Skelton nodded as if they understood, meanwhile studying Rose's face for telltale hints of emotion.

'Vernon's mostly working with Professor Mayenburg on the effect of heat on the development of blowfly larvae. The difficulty is, you see, that heat in a human corpse can be generated in so many different ways – time of year, weather, depth of burial and so on – and more problematic still, the quantity and variety of other flora and fauna inhabiting the corpse can make an immense difference to ambient temperature.'

'It sounds fascinating,' Skelton said.

'Oh, it is. Quite a long-term study, too, which is why …' she swallowed hard and finished the sentence as quickly as possible, 'they want him to stay for another six months, which, of course, he's accepted because it's such a marvellous opportunity.'

She pretended that something out of the window had caught her attention. Skelton and Edgar exchanged a glance.

'Will he be able to come home for Christmas?' Skelton asked.

'It's difficult, isn't it? With several tanks of blowflies to take care of. They won't look after themselves, will they? And he can hardly expect the assistants to come in on Christmas Day.'

'No, I don't suppose he can.'

'His … parents will miss him … horribly,' Rose said. And Skelton recognised this as an example of what Mila, who knew a little about psychology, would call, 'transference'.

Afterwards, when she'd gone, Edgar wondered whether it might help if she took up smoking.

'It's very good for the nerves.'

* * *

Chester Monroe, now working for the *Daily Graphic*, was doing a fine job keeping the burning car story, as he put it, 'fresh and lively with a new angle every day'.

On the Wednesday it had been the revelation that Musgrave had come into possession of the £1,250 by selling both of his wives' houses – without telling the wives – in order to pay off his mounting debts, the result of gambling and of various paternity suits that had been accumulating. There was also an account of the argument between the two wives over who should take responsibility for the disposal of the poor man's charred remains. The authorities had assumed that the first wife – the mother of his legitimate children – would want to take care of the burial arrangements, but she had refused unless the second wife, who, she was sure, had been the beneficiary of a non-existent fortune that Musgrave had lied about, agreed to bear the cost of the coffin and funeral. The second wife, in turn, had refused to take the body unless the first wife bore the cost. It now looked likely that, unless one of them, or perhaps one of his other women (and there was increasing talk of there being twenty or thirty dotted around the country) would agree to make the arrangements, the body would be buried in a pauper's grave at the public expense. Then came the question, should the expense even of burial in a common grave fall to the City of London, where the body was currently located, or Northampton, where the body had been stored, or Bedford, where it should have been stored, or Coventry, where Musgrave lived. Until agreement could be reached, the body was kept in the morgue at Bart's hospital in London where it had been taken for a full forensic examination.

Thursday's edition bore the headline 'MUSGRAVE'S HAREM'. Monroe had tracked down six women all of whom were, or claimed to be, lovers of the late Harold Musgrave. It was the most entertaining read so far. Musgrave was an inveterate liar – or deranged fantasist, sometimes the difference is hard to spot – with an illusionist's knack for convincing others that his most implausible flights of fantasy and imagination were gospel truth.

The bare facts of his existence, the name on his Auto-Vac-It visitor's cards and the fact of his job, could not be altered, but he invariably suggested that the job was a cover for some other, deeper assignment.

He told one of the women that he was engaged in secret work for the air ministry, while posing as a vacuum cleaner salesman, seeking out likely locations for future aerodromes. She was recruited for the same work and given the mission of persuading – without ever giving the game away – a local farmer to sell a particularly flat meadow and convincing neighbours of the benefits of having an airport on your doorstep. 'In ten years' time,' she was instructed to tell them, 'you'll be taking an aeroplane to see relatives in Manchester or Canada just like you take a bus now. But imagine the inconvenience of having to get on a smelly old bus just to get to the aerodrome. How much better to have the aeroplane ready to go a short walk from home?'

Musgrave had also assured her that there would be no noise problem because scientists had devised a baffle made of radium with which to enclose the engines.

A second lover, Ethel, was told that he was an agent, posing as a vacuum cleaner salesman working secretly for Tom Mix, the American star of cowboy films. Tom was planning a touring show, like Buffalo Bill's Wild West Show from thirty years earlier, with stunt riding, trick shooting, real buffalo and a Sioux encampment where visitors would be able to try their hands at playing drums and smoking the pipe of peace. Musgrave said he was employed as a scout seeking out likely locations where the shows could take place. The buffalo alone, he told Ethel, would need a good twenty acres of prime grassland on which to graze. And obviously, his work needed to be conducted in secret, because finding the location was only the start of a long process of convincing nearby inhabitants that the six-gun-toting outlaws would in fact be sheriffs and marshals *pretending* to be desperadoes and any of the Sioux warriors who still held serious grudges against the white man would be weeded out in the initial selection process.

He told a third, Dora, that he was an agent, posing as a vacuum cleaner salesman for a Romanian philanthropist, a Mr Iamandi, who was looking for worthy causes to which he would donate sums of up to £100,000. Until now, Mr Iamandi had been concentrating on his homeland, but 'as you've probably read', disease and want have been pretty much eradicated in Romania and the orphanages were so well-appointed that the danger that parents might kill themselves so that their children could be given the opportunities they provided was increasingly real. Accordingly, he had spread his net and had chosen England as his next beneficiary. 'Perhaps you could help me, Dora, compile a list of all the orphanages, workhouses, hospitals and schools in the area as well as the names of individuals who might benefit from Mr Iamandi's assistance.'

A fourth, Millie, was told pretty much the same story except that, in this case, he, Musgrave, was the Romanian philanthropist, working on his own behalf incognito. He didn't have an accent and attributed his perfect English, albeit tinged with a slight Midlands twang, to his having attended, in his childhood, an ordinary school in Coventry. 'To be honest, Millie,' he said, 'I've been incognito nearly all my life, but I can only be myself with you.'

Two others were told he was engaged in secret work of great national importance tracking down gangs of Russian spies and saboteurs, whose influence was incalculably strong. He dropped dark hints that local policemen could have been recruited to their Bolshevist cause, along with the local librarian ('does the library contain any books that you might describe as having a politically unsuitable message, such as the works of Mr H. G. Wells or a Frenchman called Zola?'), and even the Member of Parliament ('Yes, of course he claims to be a Conservative. That's exactly what they want you to believe.')

The *Graphic* had photographs of Millie and Ethel, both smiling bravely for the camera with their heads on one side.

'Every word utterly implausible,' Skelton said to Mila, over the shepherd's pie they always had on a Thursday, 'and yet these women never seemed to have had an iota of doubt that he was telling the truth.'

'Perhaps they are all particularly stupid women,' Mila said.

'Nobody's that stupid.'

'Has it occurred to you,' Mila said, 'that hell hath no fury like a woman scorned?'

'The thought had crossed my mind.'

'Any one of these women, not to mention the two wives, could be the murderer.'

Skelton put down his knife and fork and opened the *Graphic*. They examined the photographs.

'Do they look like killers, to you?' Skelton asked.

They didn't. If anything, they looked the sort of people who might give useful advice about digestive difficulties in a branch of Boots the chemist.

'Or one of the husbands,' Skelton said, 'or boyfriends.'

'Or fathers, even; enraged to the point of homicide that this Don Juan, this Casanova, this vile seducer had so heedlessly plucked his daughter's virtue.'

At the top of the page, there was a photograph of the vile seducer himself. It was a half-profile and showed a chubby face with a neatly trimmed moustache and patent-leather hair. The smile revealed uneven teeth. The eyes protruded. Nobody could possibly have looked more like a vacuum cleaner salesman.

'All those women,' Skelton said, 'What d'you think they saw in him?'

'He looks like William Powell,' Mila said, turning the paper round so that she could get a proper look and, on the way, smearing it with gravy from the pie.

'Who?'

'William Powell. The film star. He was in that film we saw.'

'Which one?'

'The one we saw in Slough. Where everybody was blackmailing everybody else and then Louise Brooks was strangled.'

'Which one was William Powell?'

'He was the detective.'

Skelton turned the paper back again. 'Nothing like him.' He looked again at the pictures of the women. 'It's probably just that he's a good salesman.'

'In what way?'

'Well, we know he was a very good vacuum cleaner salesman. The art of good salesmanship, I'd have thought, is to spellbind your customer. And that's similar to the art of the seducer, isn't it?'

Mila was smiling. 'Is that what you think?'

'Well, it's right, isn't it? Men …' less sure of his ground, Skelton spoke slowly, 'some men seduce women by, sort of, spellbinding them with … words and so on.'

Mila was still smiling. 'You've got it completely the wrong way round, haven't you?'

'What do you mean?'

'Women seduce men,' she said, 'by pretending to be spellbound.'

'Do they? I didn't think women ever seduced men.'

Mila gave him a fond but pitying look and went back to her dinner.

Skelton looked at the curtains.

'Did you seduce me?' he asked.

'No. I never wanted to seduce you.'

This was disappointing.

'Didn't you?'

'I wanted to marry you.'

He wasn't sure whether this was better or worse. 'I don't suppose I ever seduced you, did I?' he asked.

'Good lord, no.'

'I didn't think I had. I thought I'd check, though. To be honest, I don't think I've ever seduced anybody. The way it worked in Leeds was – you went out for a walk with somebody, and if you got chips on the way back, there was an understanding.'

Friday, 21st November 1930

Friday's headline was, 'ARTHUR SKELTON: THE MAN WHO
REFUSES TO LOSE.'

The piece started with a brief account of the Hannah
Dryden libel during which Mrs Dryden had hailed him,
to his great embarrassment, as her 'Latter Day Galahad'.
Then there were erroneous summaries of the Ibrahim Aziz
and Mary Dutton cases, falsely and ridiculously claiming
that both had seemed so hopeless that 'no other lawyer in
the country would take them on'. 'But Skelton, as ever the
man of the hour, made sure the truth was shouted from the
rooftops so that the innocent could walk free.' A couple of
paragraphs were devoted to his being a family man living
in rural Berkshire with his wife, two children and beloved

garden. This was a lie. He had nothing against his garden and was grateful to Mr Nailham who came two afternoons a week to keep it looking trim, but it was not and never had been 'beloved'.

The piece finished by telling the tale of the burning car, stressing the vital part played by local reporter Chester Monroe in 'uncovering the FACTS' and wondering whether Skelton would work the same magic with Tommy Prosser as he had with Dutton and Aziz. 'When asked, the great lawyer, never a man to yield his secrets easily, merely smiled playfully and replied, "I'm afraid it would be most unethical of me to make any comment on the case at all".'

'It's not nearly as ghastly as it could be,' Edgar said, when he came in with the tea and morning post. 'As I've said a thousand times before, an article like that, as long as none of the lies suggest that you're ineffective or corrupt – and the execrable Mr Monroe, to give him his due, has done his best to paint you as a hero on a par with Nelson – can do nothing but good.'

'It personalises and belittles what should be an impersonal, anonymous profession.'

'I expect that would be the sort of thing a pompous person might say, so we must all be grateful that you're so unassuming. But you see. The work will come pouring in and every brief will be marked at a thousand guineas. Or would you rather be like poor forgotten Snelgrove?'

Snelgrove was a mutual acquaintance who secured no more than three or four briefs a year, none of them, it was rumoured, marked at more than twenty guineas. Thankfully he had a small allowance from his father, a bishop, but often found himself trying to hide the darns in his socks from the disapproving eyes of the bench.

At eleven, Aubrey arrived for a chat about the Anglo-American Abrasives case.

'Oh, and I just had a quick word with Hedley Page at Gander and Page.'

'Who are they?' Skelton asked.

'The sweaty feet advertising agents. I thought Rose mentioned it.'

'Yes, of course, PC Root.'

'I said we were considering legal action and Mr Page was really being quite disagreeable about it all until I mentioned that we had "The Man Who Refuses to Lose" on our side.'

'You didn't really say that.'

'I did, and he must have seen the *Graphic* this morning because he straight away became a lot more affable. You would be surprised how much weight a thing like that can carry.'

'You see,' Edgar said. 'What did I say?'

'Anyway, we settled.'

'There and then? On the telephone?'

'Agreement to remove all the posters and pay PC Root compensation of £850. I went for a thousand, thinking I'd get seven hundred and fifty, so, not a bad outcome.'

'Excellent,' Skelton said. 'I'm sure PC Root will be delighted. Although, in future ...'

'Yes?' Aubrey said.

'It doesn't matter. It's ... "The Man Who Refuses to Lose".'

Aubrey was laughing, 'I promise never to use the words again. Nor shall I refer to you as the Latter Day Galahad, nor any other soubriquet the press come up with.'

'Conjuror of the Courtroom,' Edgar said, almost under his breath.

'I didn't see that one,' Aubrey said.

'I don't think it's been used yet. I'm giving you advanced notice.'

Skelton gave them a joke disapproving look and pointedly opened the beefy Anglo-American Abrasives file. 'There were a couple of points I wanted to discuss about the supposed relevance of *Carlill versus the Carbolic Smoke Ball Company*. I was wondering whether, if it came to it, Lindhurst's judgement on *Allen versus Gold Reefs of West Africa Ltd* might be more useful.'

Aubrey wasn't listening. His attention was distracted by Edgar, who had stood and was trying to coax life back into the fire. The precision of his trouser creases was shown to full advantage by the slight bend at the waist.

No solicitor in London was better dressed than Aubrey. Though a few years older than Edgar, he still had the figure of an athlete and wore clothes well. He used an excellent tailor, and his suits were cut from cloth that looked, felt, smelt and was ruinously expensive. The stitching in his shirts made you fear for the eyes of the seamstresses.

Skelton noticed the direction of Aubrey's gaze and said, 'His housekeeper pins them to the ironing board.'

Edgar made aware that he was the focus of attention, looked down at his creases and made a show of being modest.

'Oh, I know all about the pin trick,' Aubrey said. 'My batman used it in the war. He'd been a tailor before he joined up, so he knew all the tricks, but he never got results as good as that. Surely there's some sort of starch or glue involved.'

'Well, that's what I thought,' Edgar said, 'but I can't detect any additional stiffness in the fabric.'

'Have you asked the housekeeper?' Aubrey asked.

'Mrs Stewart? I did. But she just gave me a secret sort of look that made me wonder whether there was some sort of guild of housekeepers who guarded their secrets on pain of death.'

Aubrey moved in for a closer look. 'Starch perhaps?'

Skelton shook his head, 'No, we've already been through this. Starch'd leave a white residue and glue'd smell.'

'It doesn't smell at all,' Edgar said, putting a foot on the arm of a chair and sniffing.

'Wax, then?' Aubrey said. 'A little candle wax, rubbed on the inside of the fabric.'

Edgar examined the crease. 'Wouldn't it gum up the iron? And leave residue here and there? And surely there'd be a sheen?'

Reluctantly, Aubrey addressed himself to *Carlill versus the*

Carbolic Smoke Ball Company and *Allen versus Gold Reefs of West Africa Ltd.*

Half an hour of learned discussion ensued, until Edgar got up to move the tea tray.

'What about shellac?' Aubrey said.

'What exactly is shellac?' Edgar asked.

But none of them knew.

Skelton left work an hour earlier than usual so that he could be at Lambourn Primary in time for Elizabeth's school play.

In previous years, the Christmas nativity play had always been an occasion for parental complaints and crushing heartache. Every mother whose daughter is not chosen to be Mary feels cruelly cheated, and far too many children have to resign themselves to being angels and sheep. As well as widespread disappointment, this also resulted in interminable longueurs while lambs and angels filed on and off which inevitably destroyed the dramatic tension set up by the 'will there be room at the inn?' and 'could this baby really be the son of God?' quandaries.

Accordingly, this year, as well as the nativity play, the school had decided to stage a production earlier in the term in which the children who would otherwise have been condemned to baa-ing in white jumpers or floundering in wire wings could shine. The play, called *Incy-Wincy Saves the Day*, concerned the adventures of Incy-Wincy spider and Little Miss Muffet in their bid to save Old King Cole from Red Riding Hood's grandma (who is actually a wolf in disguise).

Mila, a devout atheist, was pleased that her daughter would not be obliged to have anything to do with mangers or stables.

'What part is she playing?' Skelton had asked when Mila had first told him about the venture.

'She's a townsperson.'

'Is it a big part?'

'Not very. The villages and townspeople come on towards the end and help capture the wolf.'

'Is it a speaking part?'

'She has one line.'

The line was: 'Yes, he is a *very* merry old soul.'

Mila had been helping Elizabeth smooth out some of the more objectionable royalist sentiments in the piece with a slight change of emphasis so that instead of, 'Yes, he is a *very* merry old soul,' the line came out as, 'Yes, *he* is a *very* merry old soul,' thereby drawing a distinction between the privileges enjoyed by the king and the privations suffered by the villages and townspeople.

Skelton had wondered whether Mila might be taking the whole thing a bit too seriously and did at one point actually say, 'You don't think …?', but under the weight of Mila's, 'What?' he retreated into, 'Nothing.'

As well as the line, Elizabeth had to join in a final rousing chorus of 'Old King Cole was a Merry Old Soul'. The teacher had instructed them all to sing out and carefully enunciate the consonants. Elizabeth did this around the house at odd hours every day in the run up to the show. It didn't half get on everybody's nerves.

It took Skelton a long time to fold his long spidery frame into the tiny chair provided as seating in the school hall, and it would take him, he knew, even longer to get up again. Neither the girl playing Little Miss Muffet nor the boy playing Incy-Wincy Spider had got the hang of acting. The girl was inaudible and, desperate for approval, delivered every line to her teacher, who stood just offstage. The boy kept waving at his mum in the audience. The mum waved back.

The boy playing Old King Cole was a little better and had mastered a sort of gruff authority, which earned him a couple of laughs, but his cloak was too long. Every time he took a step back, he trod on it, so that when he stepped forward again the ties around his neck strangled him. The wolf, played by a girl, was good too, although the problems inherent in dressing a little girl as a wolf dressed as a grandma had proved insuperable. Finally, the villagers and townspeople came on and Elizabeth, wearing the *bonnet rouge* favoured by the *sans-culottes* of revolutionary France, said her line – 'Oh, yes. *He's* a *very* merry old soul' – with a vehemence that echoed around the school hall like a curse. And though the 'Old King Cole' at the end was sung by the entire cast, only Elizabeth's voice was heard, rising above the rest, with each vowel and consonant carefully enunciated so that, again, it sounded angry – not so much a nursery rhyme as a revolutionary anthem.

Skelton was pleased to note that Mila had tears in her eyes. Elizabeth had done what he had feared during her soppy doll and pink-ribbon years she would never do. She had made her mother proud.

Afterwards, there was tea and bits of cake to be had, and chats with other parents. The cake was of variable quality, but a bread pudding with raisins and spices, overlooked by most, was excellent, if heavy going. Since talking while chewing was out of the question, Mila went off for a chat with Elizabeth's teacher while Skelton found a quiet corner where the hint of cinnamon could be properly appreciated.

Later, Mila returned to find her husband experimenting with a lopsided French fancy that Mrs Warburton, the school secretary, had foisted on him.

'Did you know that Elizabeth has been falling behind in maths?' Mila said.

Skelton had no idea.

'It does rather explain why she brings her spelling books and her composition books home so regularly to show off the gold stars, but never the maths book. Are you listening?'

He wasn't. A slight nod of the head told her he was tuned in to a conversation taking place behind him. Mila tuned in, too.

Three mothers were gossiping about somebody called Mrs Clayton, possibly one of the other mothers, who, significantly, worked part-time at a shop in Maidenhead that sold vacuum cleaners.

One of the women was saying, 'Why else would she have put rouge on and that afternoon frock she got from Madame Ivor just to go to work?'

'I thought she was seeing the man from the jam factory,' one of the others said.

'I'd say she could run two at a time easy,' said a third. And the other two, with hands over their mouths, went 'ooh' and secretly giggled.

Saturday, 22nd November 1930

Skelton liked Saturdays. There was a routine to them that hadn't changed much in two or three years; a comforting spell of ordinariness that stood in contrast to the mayhem and murder he dealt with all week and brought reassurance that, at least as far as his family was concerned, all was for the best in the best of all possible worlds.

He got up first, saw to the fires and made tea. Mrs Bartram arrived just after seven and started putting out the breakfast things.

Then Mila got up. For three or four years, she'd been teaching a Saturday morning archery class at the Lambourn Academy, a posh local girls' school. In the early days she had nurtured a hope that from the spoilt brats in her charge she could forge a race of Bolshevist Amazons equipped to do battle. These days, though, her primary goal was to stop the girls giggling when they missed the target and dispel the notion that hopelessness in any physical endeavour was proof of their femininity.

'It's still quite foggy out,' Skelton said. 'Will they hold the class if it's too foggy to see the targets?'

'I wouldn't have thought seeing the targets would make much difference one way or the other to their ability to hit them.'

Elizabeth came down dressed for her ballet class and executed a few *pliés*, using the back of a dining chair as her barre, while twittering about the previous afternoon's triumph like a diva after a Covent Garden first night.

Lawrence had his piano lesson on Saturday morning but here there had been a change to the routine. Emrys, who had taught him since he was six, reckoned that he showed promise and had recommended a teacher who could take him to a more advanced level. This was Mr Pilsudski, an affable Pole, who came to the house in an ancient Humber. Emrys had also advised them to acquire a better piano, so they'd ditched the barely tuneable upright and replaced it, at ruinous expense, with a Broadwood baby grand, which now lurked, a threatening presence, in the big bay window.

By nine, breakfast was done, Mila and Elizabeth had left the house and Lawrence was in the front room learning a new piece with Mr Pilsudski. Mrs Bartram was in the kitchen making pies.

Skelton started putting his coat on for his Saturday morning walk, then realised that Mr Pilsudski might be gone by the time he got back and needed paying. He went up to his study, wrote out a cheque and sealed it in an envelope.

'Sorry for interrupting,' he said, sneaking into the front room. 'Just wanted to make sure you got this.'

He put the envelope on top of the piano.

'Your son has beautiful hands,' Mr Pilsudski said. 'And I can see where he gets them from.'

Skelton looked at his hands. He'd never taken much notice of them. Like the rest of him they were thin and spidery.

'Hold out your fingers. Like this. Stretch. Now put them here. You see ... all the way from C to E, with no effort. The right hand in the piece we are studying is in octaves. Lawrence is having a little trouble maintaining the stretch and despairs that he will ever be able to stretch a tenth. But a little more growing and he will have your hands. Stretch a little further ... no, keep your thumb where it is on the C. Look, Lawrence, all the way to F and then, a little further, G. Have you ever played the piano, Mr Skelton?'

'Not really, no.' Skelton said. 'We never had one when I was a kid. But I have got a cousin who plays the banjo and another cousin who's apparently attained some renown on the piano accordion.'

'You should learn. You have musician's hands. You should learn the piano and the cello. See, my hands. Oh, I can stretch a tenth and beyond and beyond, but they are like hammers, like shovels. I have the power, but I work so hard to achieve any sort of delicacy, any sort of lyricism. Your hands, and your fingers, so long, so thin, so elegant … they are precision instruments. The power comes from the wrist, you see, but the delicacy, that must come from the fingers.'

Skelton tried a few delicate notes on the keyboard. Mr Pilsudski smiled and nodded encouragingly. Everybody likes the idea that they have a great gift that has never been properly nurtured. Perhaps, Skelton wondered, he had missed his vocation and, if only his mum and dad had given him the opportunity, he could now be the toast of the concert halls playing for the crowned heads of six continents.

He tried a few more notes. Mr Pilsudski smiled again. Lawrence wrinkled his nose. 'Are you going for your walk, Dad?'

All week, Skelton had been having difficulty opening and closing the front door. It was easy to see where it was sticking. There was a mark on the sill where it had scraped. He reckoned that if he could slip a sheet of very coarse sandpaper underneath and work the door backwards and forwards, he'd have the problem solved in no time.

There was no sandpaper in the conservatory nor in the shed at the bottom of the garden, so he started his usual Saturday morning walk with a trip to Brigland's, the hardware shop in the village.

'Wouldn't the door just push the sandpaper away?' Mr Brigland asked.

Skelton thought about it. 'You could be right. I'd have to stick it down somehow. I wonder, is there a sort of glue that can stick sandpaper to a door sill for an hour or so, then stop sticking so it can come up without leaving a mark?'

'No,' Mr Brigland said.

'What about tacks? I could nail it down, then, when I was done, take the nails out and fill the holes in the sill with … is there something you could recommend that would fill nail holes in a door sill without it showing?'

'Sawdust mixed with glue, I suppose, might do the trick.'

'Where would I get the sawdust from?'

'You usually get it by sawing up some wood.'

'I've got some wood.'

'Well, that's a start … is that lady trying to get your attention?'

Skelton turned. Outside the shop a woman in a green suit and matching hat with a feather was examining some buckets. As soon as he turned, though, the woman left.

'I thought she was looking at you.'

'I don't see why.'

Skelton quickly agreed that the sandpaper was a bad idea and that Mr Brigland should pop round himself with his tool bag and do the job properly.

He walked his usual route, down Brickett's Path to the woods and then back home along the lanes. There had been a mist earlier, but it had mostly cleared leaving an attractive haze that blurred the greens, reds and browns like an Impressionist painting.

The names of trees, plants and birds were a mystery to him. Particularly birds. They'd had birds in Leeds when he was a kid, but there had never been a perceived need to tell one from the other. Since moving to the countryside, he had noticed that some of the birds you saw were bigger and/or more colourful than the ones you got in Leeds, and now and then it occurred to him to look them up in a book, but only in the same way as it sometimes occurred to him to buy an overcoat that fitted properly or find out how electricity works.

Just before the woods, he paused by a gate and filled his pipe. Behind him, about fifty yards distant, he caught a flash of green and saw the hat with the feather. Was the woman following him?

He wondered whether he should be afraid. People who feel that they or their loved ones have been wrongfully convicted have been known to blame their solicitors or barristers. According to Holland in Bedford, Tommy Prosser had physically attacked three solicitors and put one of them in hospital. Could the woman in green be an avenging wife or mother concealing a weapon in her handbag?

The woman was small. He was tall. Just in case, he picked up a muddy fence post, then threw it away because he was being silly and called out, 'Hello, can I help you?'

The woman popped her head around a tree just for a second.

Skelton walked back towards her hiding place.

'Hello.'

The woman appeared again.

'You're Mr Skelton,' she said.

'That's right.'

There was a long pause. Twice the woman looked back the way she'd come wondering whether she should retreat, then, with great decisiveness she advanced.

'I'm Mrs Clayton,' she said.

Skelton remembered the name – the woman about whom the other mothers had been gossiping on the night before after Elizabeth's play. For decency's sake, he pretended not to.

'Have we met?' Skelton asked.

The woman reached into her handbag – easily big enough to contain a knife or gun – took out a handkerchief and dabbed at her nose.

'I just wanted you to know it wasn't what they all think it was,' she said.

'I'm sorry, you have me at a loss,' Skelton said, keeping up the pretence if only for the sake of form.

'I work at Bowman's in Maidenhead.'

'I don't think I know it.'

'We sell vacuum cleaners.'

'Is this about the late Mr Musgrave?'

'It wasn't like they say it was. I was seeing him, but there was never any funny business going on. It was all a matter of the heart and the head ... never anything—' She broke off and dabbed at her nose a little.

'If we walk on to the main road,' Skelton said, 'there's a bench there by the bus stop. We could sit and have a chat, if that's what you want.'

'I'd like that very much,' Mrs Clayton said. She was close to tears.

The bus only ran once every two hours on a Saturday, so there was nobody waiting. Cars and motorcycles buzzed by from time to time but otherwise it was a good spot for a chat.

Skelton lit the pipe he'd filled at the gate.

'I admired him,' Mrs Clayton said. 'I admired the man. I've been reading all these silly stories in the papers about the lies he told all those other women and to be honest I don't think any of them knew him at all. They've just made it all up to get their names in the paper. Or if they did know him, it was only a bit of flirting. He was a terrible flirt. Anybody could see that. But I always saw that as a professional skill. Part of his salesmanship. And he probably made up the silly stories to amuse. Part of the flirting. But none of them can have been that close to him. You see, I knew the real Harold Musgrave.'

'I'm sure,' Skelton said, trying to sound sincere.

'He was a very brave, very decent man. He was a war hero. But I'm sure you know all about that.'

'Er … not really …'

'He was a lieutenant in the Hussars.'

'I knew he'd served but—'

'He was in France. Saw terrible things. Then he was wounded. In the head. At the side here. Shrapnel. Nearly killed him. He had a lump at the side of his head. Quite obtrusive, really. It was the first thing I noticed about him, to be honest. The first time I saw him coming towards the shop, it was pouring with rain, but he wasn't wearing a hat. And I thought he must have lost it. And I asked him, and he said he could never wear a hat because of the lump on the side of his head, and I said, where did you come by that then, and that's what got us talking. And I told him about losing my husband and he was very concerned, very sympathetic about that. I mean it was a long time ago now – fourteen years – and you do get over these things. But that's what I mean. We talked. That's what we did all the time. We talked. He'd take me out to this place down by the river where we could sit out and chat, and then when the colder weather came, he'd book a room there so we could talk there, because you can't really talk properly in a public place where people might hear, can you? But there was never any funny business.'

Skelton wondered whether her definition of 'funny business' would exclude sexual congress or include straightforward congress but exclude any variation. But he didn't ask.

'He wrote poetry, did you know that?' Mrs Clayton said.

'No, I didn't.'

'He used to read me his poetry.' She stared into the middle distance and recited in a deep, sing-song voice.

'O come, dearest Emma! the rose is full blown, And the riches of flora are lavishly strown; The air is all softness, and crystal the streams, And the west is resplendently clothed in beams.'

'That's lovely,' Skelton said.

Mrs Clayton didn't seem to hear but continued:

'We will hasten, my fair, to the opening glades, The quaintly carved seats, and the freshening shades; Where the fairies are chanting their evening hymns, And in the last sunbeam the sylph lightly swims.'

She paused. Skelton waited until he was sure she had finished.

'That's lovely,' he said again. He wondered whether it was a good poem or a bad poem but had no criteria by which to judge. His own knowledge of poetry was limited to the ones he'd learnt at school. Perhaps Musgrave hadn't written the thing at all but learnt it out of a book. Again, no idea.

'I miss him such a lot,' Mrs Clayton said and dabbed again with the handkerchief.

The chill, which had seemed so attractive for walking, wasn't so good for sitting. The bench was in deep shade and there was a not entirely pleasant smell of bushes. It was a difficult conversation to end.

'I just didn't want you to get the wrong impression about him or about me,' she continued.

'Of course.'

'And although I have no reason to be ashamed of anything I've done, I am a very private person. I know there's gossip, but I really don't know what I'd do if it got any further or got in the newspapers or got mentioned in court.'

Was she, like Lord Rosthwaite, about to offer him a bribe?

'Of course. I promise I'll not breathe a word of this conversation to anybody.'

'Thank you,' she said.

She clearly found the conversation as difficult to end as he did, so they sat in awkward silence for a while.

A bird began to sing nearby, loud and beautiful and clear. Skelton caught a glimpse of it on a fence post – brown with spots on its chest. He made a mental note to look it up in a book when he got home.

Sunday, 23rd November 1930

Gillian McPhail, who ran the discussion group Mila was attending at Birkbeck, lived with her husband Bob, a two-year-old daughter, Ellie, and a wire-haired fox terrier called Pompey in a decent-sized house in Maida Vale. Like Skelton and Mila, they had no live-in servants, just a housekeeper/cook and a nanny both of whom only did weekdays, so Sunday lunch was a feat Gillian achieved single-handed.

Skelton didn't usually like coming into town at the weekend, but the roads were empty, the children were safe visiting friends, the sun shone now and then, and Mila, beside him in the Bentley, kept him entertained with gossip about other members of the discussion group, some of whom, she suspected, were having affairs.

'The first week she came in a ratty old cardigan and a tweed skirt,' she said, about a woman called Nora. 'Three weeks later she's in a low-waisted bouclé tweed thing with silk stockings and enough rouge to cause medical alarm. Meanwhile he's had his hair cut, polished his shoes and always has a clean collar. And every week they do this pantomime at going home time, "Oh, are you catching the 63, too? I'll walk down with you," as if the whole thing wasn't prearranged. Honestly, it's some of the worst acting I've seen since the Lambourn Amateur Players did *Dear Brutus*. I'd imagine she's single. She doesn't wear a ring, anyway. But I'm fairly certain he's married.'

'The soup's gone wrong, so I've thrown that down the sink,' Gillian McPhail said, as she took their coats. 'The beef looks all right, but I've made the mistake of doing Yorkshire pudding with it forgetting you're from Yorkshire, so you'll pass harsh judgement.'

'Oh, I'm sure—' Skelton said.

Gillian ignored him. 'Bob …' she called upstairs, 'they're here.'

Pompey, the dog, who had been barking steadily from somewhere, appeared like a rat out of a trap and bit Skelton's trousers.

'I'd suggest kicking him,' Gillian said, 'but experience has proved he'll just think you're playing and bite more.'

Skelton bent down and pulled the dog's ears. It stopped biting, looked up and wagged its tail hard enough to put its arse in danger of flying off.

Bob appeared carrying Ellie, who had a curly moustache. Introductions were made and hands awkwardly shaken.

'She's been painting herself,' Bob explained. He licked a finger, rubbed at the paint and tasted it experimentally. 'I don't think it's poisonous. Is it poisonous, Gill?'

'We'll know soon enough if she falls over or something,' Gillian said. 'Are we going to have sherry?'

'Oh, I'd have thought so. Come through.'

Bob put Ellie down, told the dog not to do whatever it was thinking of doing and took them through to an artsy-craftsy living room where everything was in need of minor repairs. He sat them down and provided them with sherry.

'Gillian said you work in the Civil Service,' Mila said.

'Yes, I do.' Bob pulled a face. 'Agriculture and Fisheries, but please don't assume I know anything about either. It's probably a wonderful job if you like cereal crops. Do you have a particular fondness for cereal crops?'

'Not in their raw state, no.'

'Oh, everybody likes them once they've been turned into bread and cakes and what have you, but in the field they're green for a bit and then they turn yellow and that's about it. It's not enthralling, is it? And then they do the same thing a year later.'

'I expect farmers like it.'

'I don't think they do, really, but they've no choice but to put up with it. And as for fish ...'

The dog jumped on the sofa next to Skelton and looked at him lovingly.

'That is odd,' Bob said. 'I've never seen him like a human being before. He's indifferent to Gillian, he holds me in contempt, and I don't think he's that keen on Ellie. Where is Ellie?'

'I think you put her down in the hall.'

'Did I? Excuse me.'

Bob went out to the hall and spent a difficult minute or two trying to stop his daughter blinding herself with the spokes of an umbrella.

Lunch was ramshackle, but enjoyable.

'Are they supposed to look like that?' Gillian said as she introduced roast potatoes to the table. Skelton assured Gillian that the Yorkshire pudding, flat like a pancake and blackened at the edges, was 'Exactly like my mother made it', which was substantially true. Skelton's mother was a terrible cook. And later they all agreed that lumpy gravy was preferable to the smooth stuff because it provided sudden moments of concentrated flavour.

They spoke, or rather Gillian and Mila spoke, about some article they'd both read in a learned journal about the limitations of Freudian psychoanalysis on patients with anything but the mildest forms of mental disturbance.

Bob asked Skelton about the Musgrave case, and Skelton, trying hard to protect his beef from Pompey, who had never been taught not to jump up at table, did his best to give coherent answers.

'Is it true about all the women Musgrave was supposed to have seduced?' Gillian asked.

And they talked about that, for a while, then got on to Musgrave's stories about Tom Mix and aerodromes.

'Did I read somewhere he claimed to be working for MI5?'

'That was one his many fantasies.'

'Actually, there could be a grain of truth in that one, somewhere,' Bob said. 'They did have some strange and shady characters working for them just after the war. I caught a blighty at Thiepval,' Bob indicated his chest. 'Doesn't bother me now, but it got me a desk job at the War Office. I used to have regular dealings with the hush-hush people. Man called Kell, have you heard of him? Colonel Vernon Kell, I think he ran MI5, although there was another man called Thomson who ran something called SIS that was the same sort of thing. Anyway, after the war, Kell had his budget cut back to the bone and had to lay off his men, so he – I might have this completely wrong, of course, not my department so I've only got rumour to go on – but what I heard is that he started recruiting freelancers and paying on result. It didn't last long because they had all sorts of ne'er-do-wells and charlatans fabricating evidence about anarchist bombers for a fiver in the back pocket. This Musgrave chap could easily have been one of them.'

'He wouldn't still be working for them, would he?'

'I wouldn't have thought so,' Bob said. 'Not if he's telling people about it. Not telling is the first rule of spying, I would have thought.'

'Unless it's a double bluff.'

'What, he tells people because they'll never believe it's true, so he escapes suspicion? Couldn't the same be said about Tom Mix?'

'Or for that matter, could Tom Mix be working for MI5?'

Cigarettes and pipes were smoked, coffee was drunk.

'Would a postprandial stroll be of any interest?' Bob asked. Mila and Gillian seemed keen, so Skelton's vote remained silent. 'We've got Regent's Park to the east, or Hyde Park to the south, but neither are really walking distance. We usually go up to Paddington Recreation Ground.'

'What's there?' Mila asked.

'Nothing of any interest. A running track, some tennis courts, a few square yards of muddy grass and some very scruffy trees.'

Gillian and Bob made a fine-looking couple as they walked along with Ellie in her pushchair and Pompey on his lead. Mila, who walked with them, chatting and making faces at Ellie, could have been Gillian's sister. Skelton, limping slightly behind, towering over them with his horse face and pebble-glasses, dressed inappropriately in his Homburg hat and black overcoat, felt like a dull uncle to whom they owed some duty of care.

Near the park gates, they encountered a dumpy man in tennis clothes, carrying a net of balls and a racquet in a press.

'My goodness, here's a how-de-do', he said, and broke into something halfway between a smile and a sneer that made his big shiny face look even bigger and shinier.

Mia and Gillian made some surly introductions and

he shook hands, 'Digby St Clements,' he said. 'I'm one of the less bright sparks at Lady Gillian's Birkbeck discussion group.' He laughed to indicate he was being absurdly modest and actually he had the brains of twelve or thirteen other men and twice as many women.

With care, as if he'd practised the move many times in front of a mirror, he spun his tennis racquet into the air and caught it neatly. 'Been having my usual Sunday afternoon knockabout,' he said. 'I was actually up against Henry Frobisher. Do you know him?'

'No,' Mila said, her surliness attracting 'What d'you think has got her goat?' glances from passers-by.

'Used to be a fairly big wheel at the Queen's,' St Clements said. 'Must be a bit rusty these days, of course, because even a worn-out has-been like me could take a few points off him.'

Mila took a step back, and with surprising warmth said, 'Oh, well, I was going to suggest I give you a game some time. But if you're used to playing with ex-champions ...'

O, lor, Skelton thought. *She's up to something. And it's sly.*

'No, no, not at all,' St Clements said.

Mila looked around to Bob and Gillian, doing things with her eyebrows to tell them to play along with her. 'Perhaps we could get up a four for doubles.'

St Clements looked at Skelton, who clearly was not included in this arrangement.

'I'm *hors de combat*, I'm afraid,' he said. 'Dicky hip.'

'That sounds a delightful idea, then,' St Clements said.

'I'll book the court. They're just over there. Say, one o'clock next Sunday?'

When they were out of earshot, Gillian whispered, 'What was all that about?'

Mila smiled enigmatically and Skelton said, 'I'd guess that, for some reason, Mila dislikes that man and wants to humiliate him on the tennis court.'

'Spot on,' Mila said. 'Congratulations. He is a vile little man.'

'Loathsome,' Gillian said.

'He once said he doesn't believe women should have the vote, because they're too emotional and can't understand a logical argument,' Mila said. 'And this is proved by the fact that every time you try to explain this to women, they're unable to follow your reasoning and often get angry.'

'He said this out loud?' Bob said.

'He did.'

'And he's still alive?'

'Gillian discourages weaponry in class.'

'I'd have no objection to a bit of cheesewire, though,' Gillian said. 'Or one of those tubes Renaissance assassins used to use to drop poison in your ear.'

'But how do you intend to humiliate him on the tennis court?' Bob asked. 'I haven't played for years and Gillian … you were good at school, weren't you, Gill?'

'I wasn't bad.'

'The only person who has ever beaten Mila on the tennis court, as far as I know,' Skelton said, 'was Cissy

Pemberton, a schoolfriend who subsequently went on to give Suzanne Lenglen a run for her money at Wimbledon. In any sport you care to mention, my wife is shamefully competitive and has, over the years, acquired an arsenal of psychological tricks designed to undermine an opponent's self-confidence, their will to win, and sometimes their will to live before and during the game. She is unhinged. And a cheat.'

'I don't cheat.'

'You do. You cheat playing Ludo with the children.'

'I don't.'

'There's no such rule as no jumps after a three.'

'People shouldn't make up games where it's so easy to cheat. It's almost impossible to cheat at tennis.'

'Almost. Exactly. There's always that little loophole you like to turn into a gaping maw.'

'But I win, don't I?'

'Of course you do.'

'So, what else could possibly matter?'

Skelton turned to Bob and Gillian, 'You take my point.'

Mila ignored him. 'Mixed doubles. Bob and I against Gillian and St Clements. Play your best game, Bob, and leave any tricky shots to me. Same for you, Gillian. Best game and I'll make sure you get plenty of easy returns. As far as possible, we need to make sure that St Clements can be blamed for every point you and he lose. Halfway through the first set, I promise he will be tripping over his laces and thinking there's something wrong with his racquet. By the end of the match he will doubt his right to call himself a man, or indeed a human being.'

'Cheesewire,' Skelton said. 'Would actually be kinder.'

Monday, 24th November 1930

He found himself preoccupied by eels. On the train into Paddington, in *The Times*, he read that students had disrupted an anti-vivisection meeting at the Westminster Central Hall, by releasing several containers of live eels that they'd smuggled in and throwing them among the crowd. People fled and the meeting was abandoned in chaos.

A release of eels – like a trampling of elephants – confirms the suspicion that there is only chaos. Our brains are in the habit of making patterns of events creating the illusion that there is some order in the universe, but there isn't. As a species we've just got good at making patterns and the universe takes a long time, billions of years, to reveal its irrationality. Just because day has regularly followed night ever since humans started noticing, it's no guarantee it will tomorrow. You can't trust these things. Elephants could trample the sun or eels cause the earth to stand still in its orbit.

As soon as he got into the office, he telephoned Sir Bernard Spilsbury, the Home Office pathologist at Bart's and got through to an assistant, who told him that Sir Bernard was away on business. Could he help at all?

Skelton asked whether it was correct that the fatal wound to Musgrave's skull was definitely at the back rather than to one side. The assistant spent a couple of minutes looking out the notes, then came back to the phone and confirmed that it was indeed at the back.

'Was another wound, or a lump of some sort visible at one side of the skull?' Skelton asked.

'There is a very distinctive lump at the side of the head visible in the photograph,' the assistant said.

'I wonder, could you arrange to have copies of the post-mortem photographs sent over?'

Skelton put the phone down slightly disappointed. He knew it was extremely unlikely that an autopsy would mistake an old war wound for the results of a much more recent assault, but one lives in hope.

He rang Holland, the solicitor, in Bedford.

'Do we have Musgrave's medical records?'

'Only for the past couple of years.'

'Not his army medical records, then? He was apparently quite badly wounded.'

'It's difficult. The Auto-Vac-It people had him down

as a lieutenant in the Prince of Wales Dragoons, but the Dragoons have no record of him at all.'

'I met one of his lady friends. She seemed to think he was in the Hussars.'

'I'll get on to them.'

'Although, maybe a cavalry regiment was one of his stories. I'd have thought that, since he's from Coventry, it's most likely he'd have been in the Royal Warwicks.'

'I'll give them a try, too.'

'And he may, of course, have lied about his rank.'

'Good point. I'll chase it up.'

'I'd be very grateful.'

Skelton stood and looked out of the window. The wind had caught a flour sack, or perhaps a pillowcase making it dance in midair like the ghost in a story that had terrified him at school. It started him thinking about elephants and eels again.

Justice was victim to the same nonsense, the same disorder. People convinced each other – and themselves – that, because of a certain chain of events, a sequence of cause and effect, this person must be innocent of the crime and this person guilty, but those chains and sequences were no more reliable than the elephants or the eels.

'Are you all right old chap?' Edgar asked, coming in with the morning post and the rest of the day's business.

'Absolutely fine.'

Eric, the idiot errand boy, close behind, managed to put the tea tray down with minimum spillage. Skelton spotted there were butter Osbornes among the biscuits – a good start to the day.

As Edgar had predicted, the *Graphic*'s 'Man Who Refuses to Lose' headline had brought the work pouring in. He was wrong about them all being marked at a thousand guineas, though. One of them – a convoluted matter of companies suing each other involving three countries and principles of law, which, like problems of differential calculus, you could hold in your mind for a moment, but look away and they were gone – was marked at fifteen hundred.

'Could we pass on that one?' Skelton asked.

'But … fifteen hundred guineas.'

'Man that is born of woman hath but a short time to live, and is full of misery. At the moment, the misery is being more than adequately supplied by Anglo-American Abrasives, any more would be surplus to requirements. Isn't there anything fun?'

'Fun?' Edgar said. 'Well, I suppose that'd be toss up, between on the one hand *M R C Oxenbergh versus P. J. Croft* and, on the other hand, *Jefferson, Graham & Co. Ltd. trading as 'Ivory Enamelware' versus Wilson and Bray Hygienic Porcelain of Wolverhampton*. The first is about knickerbockers, the second lavatories.

'What's the lavatory one?'

'Wilson and Bray have, over the past couple of years, been producing a range of products stamped with the words "Ivory White". Jefferson, Graham & Co. Ltd. claim to have registered the word "Ivory" as a trademark in 1921. And are suing Wilson and Bray for infringement.'

'And these are "Ivory White" lavatories, are they?'

'Lavatories, sinks, baths.'

The schoolboy urge to say 'lavatory' loudly and frequently in court ran deep in Skelton.

'That one's good. What's the knickerbocker one?'

'Rather short notice, I'm afraid. Astley's fallen prey to laryngitis.' Astley was another barrister at 8 Foxton Row. 'So, we're doing what we can with his cases.'

'When is it?'

'Tomorrow. It's not the sort of thing that would drag on, very straightforward brief. A Mr Croft ordered a pair of plus fours from Mr Oxenbergh, a tailor. When the plus fours were made, Mr Croft refused to pay for them claiming that they were not plus fours, as worn by outdoor gents and golfers, but knickerbockers, as worn by lady cyclists and schoolboys. So, Mr Oxenbergh is suing.'

'Who's the solicitor?'

'Harding.'

They both knew Harding. Excellent chap.

'And prosecuting?'

'Luckhurst.'

They both knew Luckhurst, too. Dim. Plodding.

Skelton took the brief and turned the pages. There weren't many of them. 'And the case revolves around the exact differences between the plus four and the knickerbocker?'

'Exactly.'

'And what is the difference between the plus four and the knickerbocker?'

'As far as I can make it out it's a matter of the overhang.'

'Do we have an expert witness?'

'Harding's conjured up a chap from Tautz.'

'What's Tautz?'

'A shop. Specialises in hunting and sporting wear. There's an advertisement there somewhere.'

Skelton found a press cutting and read, 'Breeches and jodhpurs, side or astride.'

'That's the one. Prosecution's got a chap who writes for *The Tailor and Cutter*.'

'Who's up?'

'Mr Justice Tomlinson.'

They both knew Tomlinson as well; a man who gave the lie to the phrase 'sober as a judge'.

'Should be all right.'

Skelton handed the brief back to Edgar who, shuffling it with the other papers, spilt a little tea on it. He took out a perfectly ironed handkerchief to dab it up.

On the rare occasions that Mrs Bartram ironed handkerchiefs, the edges always came out corrugated. Edgar's hems were flat. Probably flatter than they'd been when the handkerchief was brand new.

'Does Mrs Stewart pin hankies to the ironing board, too?' Skelton asked.

'I wouldn't be in the least bit surprised,' Edgar said. There was a hint of acid in his voice.

'Oh, dear,' Skelton said. 'Do I detect a note of disenchantment?'

'It's the cocktail cabinet.'

'The Czech cubist cocktail cabinet?'

'In the rosewood and bird's-eye maple, yes. I'm afraid Mrs Stewart has taken against it. She said it would harbour inaccessible dust.'

'In the crevices. I did suspect there might be a problem.'

'If it comes down to "either that cabinet goes or I do" – and, the way she's been talking about it, it may well come to that – I shan't know which way to turn.'

'Surely life without Mrs Stewart would be worse than life without your cocktail cabinet?'

'It is an extraordinarily beautiful cocktail cabinet.'

Skelton gave Edgar another moment to mourn, then drained his tea and said, 'What's next?'

'*Rex versus Michael Mullen*,' Edgar said. 'A safe was taken, intact, from a jeweller's shop and discovered, some days later, still intact and unopened, hidden in bushes beside a canal towpath, by a man walking his dog. The police—'

'Where is this?'

'Hayes.'

'Middlesex?'

Edgar nodded and continued. 'The police, knowing that the thief would return to open his treasure, left the safe where it was, but kept a covert watch on it. Early the following morning they saw Mr Mullen approaching the safe carrying a bag clanking with tools, apprehended him, and, finding the bag was full of drills, crowbars and explosives – just the stuff you might use to break into a safe – made their arrest.'

'And what did Mr Mullen say?'

'He said he was on his way to remove a tree stump in a friend's garden. When, however, the friend was questioned, while acknowledging that he did, indeed, have a tree stump in his garden that he'd like to have removed, denied ever having requested Mr Mullen to do the job.'

'And what did Mr Mullen say to that?'

'He said he wanted to surprise him,' Edgar said.

'And does Mr Mullen have previous convictions?'

'A little shoplifting some years ago, but nothing of any significance.'

'Does he have any history of stump removal?'

'Not specifically. General building.'

'There you are, then. Poor innocent chap walking along the towpath early in the morning off to do his pal a favour, out spring the bobbies and accuse him of all sorts when the only evidence is a bag full of drills and crowbars.'

'And explosives.'

'You might use explosives to blow up a tree trunk, mightn't you?'

'I've never considered the matter,' Edgar said.

'I bet Mr Glazier has, though.'

Producing Mr Glazier, from Lower Dunworth, possible murderer of Harold Musgrave, with his face patch and hook hand as an expert witness would be enough to put the wind up any jury and most judges. It was a racing certainty that he'd blown up trees in his time – in fact, hadn't he mentioned that during the war he'd blown up forests. He might even have photographs to show.

Edgar could see the attraction too. 'I'll write to him, shall I?' He stood to put the selected briefs on Skelton's desk.

'Have you seen the backs of your trousers?' Skelton said.

Edgar turned and lifted a leg to look.

'What about them? Have I sat in something?'

'You've been sat in that chair all morning and there's not a trace of concertinaing. Razor-sharp crease and the rest smooth as sheet steel. She's worth a dozen cocktail cabinets, you know that, don't you?'

Edgar didn't reply immediately but busied himself with the papers for a minute or two before blurting, 'It's the most beautiful thing I've ever owned.'

Tuesday, 25th November 1930

The post-mortem photographs of Musgrave's corpse were less grisly than Skelton had feared partly because the flesh was so badly burnt and the expression so distorted that the thing more closely resembled a gargoyle on a church in some sooty industrial town than anything human. The bump, as the assistant had said, was clearly visible on the side of the head.

Percy Croft, defendant in *M R C Oxenbergh versus P. J. Croft*, had inherited a fortune from his father, but nonetheless lived frugally in a small house in Camberwell without even so much as a 'daily'. He practised vegetarianism and saved empty soup tins in a shed at the bottom of his garden. He preached the benefits of wearing Dr Jaeger's sanitary woollen underwear next to his skin and smelt of Vick's VapoRub.

As told in the brief, earlier in the year he had ordered, from Mr Marcus Oxenbergh, a tailor, a plus-four suit in green Donegal tweed. There were two fittings, which passed without incident. When the suit was ready, however, Mr Croft, having tried it on, said it was unsatisfactory and refused to pay. Mr Oxenbergh was suing him for the £8. 4s. 9d. owing.

The nature of Mr Croft's complaint was that the lower part of the suit, which had appeared to be plus fours in every respect during the earlier fittings, had turned out not like plus fours at all, but more like knickerbockers.

Skelton managed a quick word with him before the trial. Mr Croft wanted to make it clear that it wasn't the money that mattered. It was the principle of the thing. The kind of people who cheat honest customers by describing knickerbockers as plus fours were a menace to society and had to be stopped.

There was, Skelton surmised, more to it than that. Mr Croft was a little man, no more perhaps than five foot one or two in height and he squeaked like a frightened piglet. Knickerbocker suits were what schoolboys wore – or had worn before the war, anyway. Mr Croft had got it into his head that Mr Oxenbergh was deliberately mocking him. Skelton found it hard to fathom why a tailor would fashion a garment in such a way as to make fun of a client, but that, perhaps, was because he was six foot three and had a sonorous, rumbling voice. Remove a foot from his height and half an inch from his vocal cords and he too might begin to see sniggerers everywhere.

In court, photographs of Mr Croft wearing the suit, as well as the suit itself, were produced in evidence.

Mr Oxenbergh droned on for a while about the bands that gather the hem of the trouser into the leg and went into a lot of technical detail about the difference between knickerbocker trouser bands and plus-four trouser bands.

He also maintained that he had suggested, when Mr Croft had declared himself dissatisfied, that he change the bands at no extra charge. But Mr Croft had refused the offer.

Skelton could see that the judge, Tomlinson, had hoped to derive more entertainment from the case, but both Mr Oxenbergh and his counsel, Luckhurst, had spoken in dull monotones without any regard for the comic potential of trouser bands. Oxenbergh looked as if he was trying to contain a gastric event.

The expert witnesses were called. They weren't much fun, either. The judge, Tomlinson, had clearly never heard of Tautz and seemed sceptical that a magazine called *The Tailor and Cutter* could exist.

Skelton tried to keep himself engaged by examining trousers. There they were, the two expert witnesses, arbiters of taste and style, and neither of them had creases anything like as good as Edgar's. Pretending to make a note about some salient point he drew a cocktail cabinet and some nicely pressed trousers.

Finally, Skelton rose for his closing speech and Tomlinson, who knew his reputation as an orator but had never seen him in action, roused himself and leant forward. Skelton gave him a reassuring smile, grasped his lapel, looked around and, as if addressing a full courtroom, with recalcitrant jury and packed, hushed public gallery rather than the sparsely populated acreage of a civil courtroom, thundered, 'My Lord, I put it to this court that the case we are examining here is – despite all the nit-picking about the width of bands, the overhang and number of buttons – the case we are examining here is simple and straightforward *criminal* – and I do not use that term lightly – *criminal* fraud.'

He looked around. Croft and Oxenbergh were both watching him, awestruck and breathless. Tomlinson smiled. It was going to be all right.

With all the melodrama a lesser advocate might employ in defence of, say, a simple country girl who, on the eve of her wedding, had strangled, with her own hair, an evil baron intent on exercising his *droit du seigneur*, Skelton spoke of the funny sorts of trousers people had taken to wearing these days and pointed out that the essential difference between the knickerbocker and the plus four was the width, depth and generosity of the *drop*.

'We were shown pictures of famous men, members even of our own and much-loved Royal Family, may God bless them, wearing plus fours that floated out to such an extent that they looked like – and I intend, My Lord, no disrespect in my use of this word but choose it the more graphically to illustrate my point – *petticoats*.'

He concluded by saying that the principal problem with the offending suit was nothing more and nothing less than the amount of fabric used. Mr Oxenbergh thought that he could boost his profits a little by saving a yard of fabric, with the result that the garment instead of *ballooning* like plus fours should *balloon*, instead *hugged* in an unmistakably characteristic and essentially *knickerbockerish* manner.

Tomlinson snorted a laugh on 'knickerbockerish', then pretended he hadn't.

Skelton went for a second laugh. 'And though, as Mr Oxenbergh pointed out, some of Mr Croft's initial instruction could have been interpreted in a "knickerbockerish" light, it is clear that Mr Croft had no desire that the general impression given by the finished garment should, in any respect, carry with it the smallest trace of "knickerbockerishness".'

Tomlinson pretended to drop his pen and ducked down beneath the bench to retrieve it.

'I therefore would humbly suggest to this court that not only should Mr Croft be found not guilty of failure to pay the £8. 4s. 9d. owing, but that Mr Oxenbergh should be delivered into the hands of the police and taken from this court to the Central Criminal Court and there face charges of fraud and of common theft. My Lord, I rest my case.'

Tomlinson suppressed another snort, gave judgement for Croft, the defendant, adding that, although it was up to other authorities to decide whether to charge Mr Oxenbergh as had been recommended, he would urge leniency and suggest that forfeiting the £8. 4s. 9d. and costs should be punishment enough.

As he left the bench, Tomlinson nodded a thank you to Skelton.

In celebratory mood, after the trial Percy Croft invited Skelton to join him for a high tea at a vegetarian restaurant in Peckham. Wondering whether the man smeared himself with VapoRub before putting on the Jaeger underwear, Skelton politely declined.

Edgar was waiting for him outside the courtroom, with Rose, looking as if she'd been running, in tow.

'Rose has something to show you,' Edgar said. From the school satchel she used as a briefcase, Rose began to take a quarto-sized Manila envelope. Edgar stopped her. 'Not here. Somewhere private.' He turned to Skelton. 'Back to Foxton Row?'

Skelton didn't want to go back to Foxton Row. It was a cold day and he doubted that Eric, the idiot errand boy, had remembered to stoke up the fire in his room. Also, he'd been looking forward to tea and cakes.

'Kemble's?' he said. This was a restaurant he and Edgar favoured at the Aldwych end of Drury Lane.

'Hardly what one would describe as "private",' Edgar said.

It was true. Kemble's was decorated in an uncompromisingly modern style. The walls were covered with mirrors in such a way that, from most of the tables, you could see the back of your own head. Also, Kenneth, the proprietor, was an enthusiastic gossip.

'We'll get a booth and be discreet,' Skelton said.

They ordered tea and a selection of cakes, and sat largely in silence until they'd arrived. Rum baba, some slices of Battenberg, millefeuille, fondant fancies. When Rose was absolutely certain that she could not be seen in any of the mirrors and Kenneth was far away over by the cloakroom, she took out the envelope again.

'Mr Duncan said you should see them as soon as possible,' she said. 'I warn you. They're not very nice.'

They were photographs. The first showed a man, naked apart from some sort of harness which secured him to a frame, being caned by a woman in a leather mask, leather trousers held up by strategically placed braces, and nothing else. Any erotic interest was countered by the man's corpulence and a general aura of goose pimples.

The next one showed the same woman, dressed in the mask and trousers, and a gentleman – a different gentleman – naked and kneeling with his hands tied behind his back. The lady held two paddles, like table-tennis bats, one of which seemed to be covered in fur, the other in needles.

'I'm so sorry you've had to see these terrible things, Rose,' Edgar said.

'Where did you get them?' Skelton asked.

'Denison Beck's consulting rooms,' Rose said.

'I think you'd better start from the beginning.'

Rose checked to make sure Kenneth was still over by the cloakroom, leant forward and whispered, 'I went to Mr Beck's consulting rooms in Wimpole Street, only Enoch told me it was all locked up.'

'Who's Enoch?' Skelton asked.

'The porter chap who answers the front door. He said it was all locked up and Mr Beck was at his flat in Belgravia and Miss Alison had gone back to her parents in Bruges.'

'Bruges in Belgium?'

'She's Belgian.'

'I'd never have guessed.'

'So, I told Enoch I was from the solicitors and asked if he had a pass key because I needed to get into the consulting room to look for a document. And he said he didn't have a pass key. Then he had a funny turn and had to sit down on the stairs. He didn't look at all well.'

'He didn't look well when we were there,' Edgar said.

'And I asked him what the matter was, and he said he'd be all right in a jiffy if he could get his hands on ten or fifteen shillings. Well, I couldn't help him, because I only had four and sevenpence in my purse, but I said I'd fetch him a doctor and he said it wasn't anything a doctor could help him with and gradually – I won't go into all the ins and outs because it took ten or fifteen minutes to get the whole story out of him – but the gist is he's a morphine addict. I knew a bit about it because I'd been reading up on the 1925 Dangerous Drugs Act and the 1928 amendments. Apparently, a lot of old soldiers are morphine addicts. Enoch had shrapnel in his stomach and there was nothing they could do for him in the field hospital, so they just pumped him full of morphine and shipped him home. Then he had lots more morphine in the hospital here and by the time they let him out he was addicted. If he tries to stop, he gets very ill. He's been getting his morphine from the doctor ever since, but the trouble with that is that over time you get used to it and you have to have bigger doses, and the doctors don't want to give you bigger doses so you have to get it illegally. He gets his from a man called Spanish Joe. Only it's expensive. Just to make up the difference between what the doctor gives him and what he needs to stop getting ill costs him more than two pounds a week. Before the place was closed down, he could manage that because Mr Beck's patients would give him tips, a shilling or two and sometimes five or ten shillings. But now he's not getting the tips so he can't afford to buy the extra, which means he's feeling poorly all the time and getting worse. Well, it didn't seem right just to leave him there in the state he was in but, as I say, I only had four and sevenpence in my purse. So, I offered to make him a cup of tea, which felt a bit like offering somebody with TB a drop of Famel Syrup, but he said he'd like one and showed me where he had a gas ring and a kettle in his backroom. And then he asked me what I wanted from Mr Beck's consulting rooms and I said we were looking for a list of all his clients and he thought for a bit and then said if I could get him five pounds, he'd give me something much better. Well, like I said, I wanted to help him because he looked so poorly, so I didn't really care if the "something much better" turned out to be useless. And I've still got a lot of money in the bank from selling my dad's house and everything, and I knew there's a Midland a ten-minute walk away up Baker Street, so I went and got him five pounds and he gave me these. They're taken in the basement in what they call "The Special Treatment Room".'

She turned over the photographs until she found the one she wanted.

'That's Raymond Vane isn't it?'

Edgar looked. Raymond Vane was a film actor who'd recently starred as Red Jake the pirate in *The Curse of Tortuga*. The photo, which showed him bound tightly with several yards of rope while the lady in the leather mask and trousers stood over him holding a selection of mediaeval instruments of torture, was blurred, but Raymond Vane's dimpled smile was unmistakable.

'That is indeed Raymond Vane.'

'And here's Lord Rosthwaite,' Skelton said. Rosthwaite was naked and in chains. The lady was tickling his tummy with a cat o'nine tails.

From other photographs they were able to identify one cabinet minister and one former cabinet minister, three members of parliament, a judge, a noted barrister, two other film actors, a minor member of the Royal Family and a championship jockey (with a saddle on his back and a bit between his teeth being 'ridden' by the lady who was a good foot taller than him and a couple of stone heavier).

'Did Enoch tell you who took the photographs?' Skelton asked.

'There's a secret camera in the Special Treatments Room. I think Mr Beck took the photographs with blackmail in mind.'

'Is this what he meant by having influential friends working on his behalf?'

'Oh, and there is one other thing,' Rose said. 'I asked Enoch whether he knew the name of the lady in the photographs and he said she's called Marcia the Whip. But, look at this …' She selected one of the photographs and from her school satchel took a newspaper clipping, arranging them side by side on the table. 'What do you think?'

The newspaper clipping was a photograph of Mrs Edith Roberts, the alleged victim of Beck's manslaughter. It was hard to tell because Marcia the Whip was wearing a mask, but there was something about the jawline and the hairstyle. Rose showed another of the photographs and next to it put one of Edith Roberts in her Gaiety Girl days. In both photographs she was striking a pose – the identical pose.

'I thought Mrs Roberts had a bad back,' Edgar said. 'How much whipping can you do with a bad back?'

Skelton licked his finger and used it to pick up the leftover fragments of millefeuille on his plate. 'By all accounts, her visits to the consulting rooms did her the world of good so it could be that whipping is the ideal exercise for a bad back.'

Rose started putting the photographs back into the envelope.

'The question is,' Edgar said, 'now that we've got the photographs, what should we do with them?'

'Well …' Skelton said and was lost in thought for a moment. Then, 'It just occurred to me that Lord Rosthwaite may have been right.'

'About what?'

'He said that if all this came out in court and the press got wind – I thought at the time he was talking about embarrassing medical conditions – the effect on the stock market, not to mention Britain's relations with the Empire, could be devastating. It actually could, couldn't it?'

'I expect so,' Edgar said. 'But they said things like that when Woolworth's first opened on Oxford Street, didn't they?

'I suppose the correct procedure,' Skelton said, 'would be to hand everything over to the Director of Public Prosecutions and let him do with them what he will.'

'Unless of course the Director of Public Prosecutions is one of the clients.'

'Good point. Perhaps we should have another chat with Mr Beck first. Find out exactly what was going on.'

There was one slice of Battenberg left. Skelton divided it into its four segments, offered them to Rose and Edgar and, when they refused, popped them into his mouth one by one.

'Could I ask a question?' Rose asked.

'Yes, of course.'

'Do people really pay money to be tied up and thrashed?'

'It's called masochism,' Edgar said. 'Named after Leopold von Sacher-Masoch who wrote—'

'Yes, I know about *Venus in Furs,*' Rose said. 'But I thought it was just something in a story. I didn't know people really did it.'

'Well, it seems, from the ample photographic evidence,' Skelton said, 'that they do.'

'Why?'

'I have absolutely no idea. Do you have any inkling, Edgar?'

'N-no.'

And in that slight hesitation, Edgar opened a world of possibilities that Skelton hoped would never be explored.

Wednesday, 26th November 1930

Denison Beck's flat was in a mews not far from the Cadogan Hotel where Oscar Wilde was arrested. He answered the door himself, in his shirtsleeves, his hair unbrushed.

His greeting was surly.

'Are you sure this isn't something that could be dealt with on the phone?'

By way of answer, Skelton pulled a quarter-inch of photograph out of the envelope.

'Oh, you've found those. You'd better come in.'

The flat was nowhere near as Marie Antoinette as the consulting rooms. Chairs, sofa, rugs and curtains were all in drab greens and yellows. The room admitted little in the way of daylight. Even though it was a bright morning out, the electric light was switched on.

There was a half-empty bottle of brandy and a glass on the table, next to an overflowing ashtray. Beck didn't invite them to sit, so they remained standing.

'Did Enoch give them to you?' he asked.

Skelton nodded.

'I feared he might. Did you pay?'

'Five pounds.'

'You could easily have beaten him down to ten bob. Who's seen them?'

'Enoch, myself, Mr Hobbes here, Aubrey Duncan and Aubrey's assistant, Rose.'

'Nobody else?'

'Enoch mentioned that the plan was to use them for purposes of blackmail.'

Beck ran a hand through his hair. 'I'm afraid that all backfired horribly. It's the reason I'm in the mess I'm in. I suggested to one or two of the clients I might have photographic evidence documenting their ... peccadilloes. Rather than helping me, they said that if I breathed a word they'd have the charge beefed up from manslaughter to murder and then they'd make sure I'd hang. And I have no doubt they could do it. Would you like a brandy? Whisky?'

'It's a little early.'

Beck poured himself a generous measure.

Edgar lit a cigarette, emptied the ashtray into the grate and gave the fire a bit of a stir. It was cold. 'I wonder,' he said.

'is the electrical therapy side of the business a going concern, or is it there just as a cover?'

Beck's pride was wounded. 'I am a fully qualified medical electrician. Many of my clients know nothing at all about the Special Treatments Room.'

'Did Mrs Roberts take the electrical therapy or was she exclusively Marcia the Whip?'

'Oh, you worked that out, did you? That's what's so unfair about the whole matter. I'm accused of killing a woman with equipment she never went near. And there seems to be a battle going on. Half the judiciary, like you, think the evidence against me is negligible, and the other half know that, if that is the case, they can merely get the police to manufacture more evidence, and perhaps they have the power to secure a conviction with no evidence at all. And it gets worse. One of the clients – a judge – told me that this man …' Beck rummaged through the photographs until he found one of a client dressed as a baby with nappy and dummy lying across the lap of Marcia the Whip, who was dressed impeccably as a Norland nanny. 'I knew him only as Mr Green. Do you know who that is?'

Skelton looked closely. The face was obscured by shadow.

'It's Norris Lazell,' Beck said.

Norris Lazell was known, or at least rumoured, to run a south London gang the members of which had a reputation for ruthless and unmerciful violence. Members of his gang had frequently been arrested and some of them sent to the gallows, but Lazell, like the Chicago gangsters whose exploits filled the newspapers, always made sure nothing could be traced back to him.

'If Lazell found out I'd had this photograph taken, he'd kill me, probably in some slow and unimaginably painful way. You heard about Walter Ingram?'

Walter Ingram was a rival gangster. His body had been found welded into an oil drum along with twenty or thirty rats.

'In fact, I'd imagine that if he found out you'd seen the photograph, he'd kill you, too. And Enoch and Aubrey Duncan and … who was the other person you mentioned?'

Skelton and Edgar looked with suspicion at every passer-by on Sloane Street.

'So, what should we do with the photographs?' Skelton asked.

'I'd say we hide them in a drawer and pretend we've never seen them.'

'Pervert the course of justice, you mean?'

'If that's how you choose to describe it.'

'Couldn't I get disbarred for that?'

'Better than being welded into a bin full of rats, wouldn't you say? In Chicago, I believe, they use Tommy guns. They drive past in a car spraying bullets.'

Skelton pulled his hat tighter down on his head. The action, he knew, would not protect him against a Tommy gun attack, but he felt he had to do something and pulling your hat down is something to do.

* * *

218

The usual Wednesday letter from Alan was waiting for him at Foxton Row.

c/o The Chaundler Fund
Princess Street
Manchester

Monday 24th November 1930

My dear cousin Arthur,

Many thanks for the gramophone records. Was it you who did the packing, or the shop where you bought them? Whoever it was did a marvellous job and they arrived intact. My favourite is 'Airman! Airman! Don't Put the Wind Up Me' and 'Sitting on a Five-Barred Gate', both of which we shall most certainly include in our repertoire (in fact, as I'm writing this at one end of the Eccles, Norah is writing out the band parts for 'Airman! Airman!' at the other.)

I have a confession to make. The more we go about our new mission with the Chaundler Fund, the more I become aware that we may be working under false pretences.

Norah, by the way, after her shaky start, has become a compelling and persuasive preacher. She does herself proud, she does the mission proud and she does the Chaundler Fund proud. But more and more we are unsure whether she is speaking to the right people.

As you know, our role as Moral Hygienists is to save the young women who come to our meetings from the snares and temptations of loose living and the slippery slope that leads to prostitution. But here's the thing. Over the past few weeks, we must have chatted with hundreds of young women before and after the meetings, but – and Norah will bear me out on this – we have yet to meet one that I would say is in danger of finding herself on the slippery slope. The fly in the ointment to my way of looking at things is wholesomeness. The places in which we hold our meetings – church halls, working men's institutes – are wholesome, our appearance is wholesome, the way in which we address them is wholesome, the songs we sing are wholesome, and, even though we play tangos, jazz and tunes with titles that some might describe as suggestive, there is something you cannot quite put your finger on about the way we play them that is wholesome. And thus, for the most part the young people we attract are wholesome.

But there is another element to the congregation that we – having been instructed by the Chaundler Fund to concentrate on the youngsters – barely notice. Every night, there is a fair smattering of older women. To be honest, at first we assumed that they were the mothers and aunties of the younger ones, come perhaps in the role of chaperone.

It was Ron, the clarinet player, who taught us otherwise.

As you may remember, when he decided to team up with us, we warned him that we would not be able to pay or even feed him. He assured us that as an old soldier he would be able to fend for himself.

This is how he does it.

Obtaining money for food and drink is easy. All he has to do is go into a pub, take out his clarinet, stand on a table and play 'The Flight of The Bumblebee', at possibly double the tempo that Rimsky-Korsakov intended it to be played. It is a feat that is bound to leave any audience agog. He follows it with a ragtime piece called 'Kitten on the Keys', originally composed for the piano, but adapted for clarinet with the most entertaining swoops and slides. People first of all pay money to hear the tunes again, then they pay to hear requests. Ron, as well as being a near-miraculous sight-reader has an astonishing ear and memory for a tune. At times people even bet him that he doesn't know the tune they are about to request. He always wins.

So that is how he makes money for his food, drink and clothing. He finds accommodation every night simply by announcing, at the end of the meeting, that he has nowhere to stay and if anybody could offer him a bed for the night, he would be very grateful. And always one of the older women, the ones we took to be aunties and mothers, would volunteer to put him up. And we thought that was nice. Kind aunties and mums taking the homeless young chap into the bosoms of their families.

Then, one day, Solomon, a cornet player who works during the day as a clay blunger at Dudson's, heard us saying something to that effect and slyly pointed out that the women were not mothers and aunties and that Ron was a very good-looking and charming young fellow.

It took – such is our naivety – a good few minutes before the implications of what he was saying came home to Norah and me, and then a much longer time for us to work out what, if anything, we should do about it. If it was true what Solomon was implying, then Ron's behaviour was clearly unacceptable, not merely on the broader moral grounds, but also because it flew in the face of our mission as Moral Hygienists leaving us open to accusations of gross hypocrisy.

Solomon told us that since the first night we came to the Stoke-on-Trent area, Ron has been staying with the same woman, a Mrs Shipley in Hanley.

Obviously, if it was true that Ron and Mrs Shipley were engaged in some sort of unfitting liaison, we would have to inform him that his services were no longer required. But neither Norah nor I were willing to do this on the grounds of what really amounted to no more than gossip from Solomon, so we determined to get to the bottom of it all by going to see Mrs Shipley.

We found the house, part of a run-down terrace on a dingy road. We knocked. Mrs Shipley came to the door. She said that Ron had popped out, but insisted we come in and have a cup of tea.

She made us tea and even had a bit of cake, that she told us Ron had bought. Her son would be home from school soon, she said.

It is difficult to tell people's ages when their lives have been hard. A thirty-year-old woman who has given birth to five or six children and struggled to feed them can look about the same age as a fifty-year-old duchess. Mrs Shipley was perhaps thirty or thirty-five but had only one child and had also managed to retain a youthful posture and instead of the pinched wrinkles you see so often, she had an open, intelligent face.

Not wanting to rush to judgement, we thanked her for having Ron to stay and hoped he wasn't being too much trouble. Her reply – she mentioned that the only trouble was his snoring, but he usually stopped if you held his nose – was shameless.

There is nothing more confusing than a contented sinner. Since it was impossible to believe that she did not know the difference between right and wrong, one could only assume that she flaunted her sin so shamelessly and so readily in the hope of eliciting some reaction. If we were going to condemn her to hell fire, she wanted to get it over with so that she could kick us out before cutting the cake.

Jesus, when he encountered the woman who had been accused of adultery by the scribes and Pharisees and sentenced to be stoned to death, said, 'Let he who is without sin cast the first stone.' Then, he told the woman he did not condemn her and instructed her to 'sin no more', and we have every reason to believe that, chastened by and grateful for Our Lord's intervention, she truly renounced her adulterous ways.

Then in Luke 7, He has his feet washed with tears by the woman, often assumed to be a prostitute, whose sins are many. And He says, 'Thy sins are forgiven.' And 'Thy faith hath saved thee.'

You see, saving people from sin who want to be saved from sin is all well and good, but the Gospels are a little more ambiguous about what to do in the case of unrepentant sinners. As I understand it, from Matthew 18, you're supposed to have a word with the sinner. If that does not work you get a lot of people, the congregation of your church, for instance, to have a word. And if that does not work, then 'Let him be to you as the Gentile or tax collector'. By which I suppose Our Lord meant banished from decent society, but it's hard to be sure.

St Paul in his first letter to the Corinthians, advises them, when they encounter a man who is living adulterously with his own stepmother and seems, if anything, quite proud of doing so, 'to deliver such an one unto Satan for the destruction of the flesh, that the spirit may be saved in the day of the Lord Jesus'.

Chatting there with Mrs Shipley, drinking tea and eating cake, to be honest, the very last thing on my mind was delivering her to Satan for the destruction of her flesh.

She met a boy in 1917. They intended to get married. Then he got called up and dragged off to the barracks in Lichfield. They tried to arrange a marriage first time he got leave, but it proved too difficult and not long after that he was sent to France and never came back. The boy, called Leslie, the same as his dad, was born a few months later. Shipley is her maiden name. And she calls herself 'Mrs' rather than 'Miss' because 'some people are funny about a boy having a "Miss" as his mum'.

Because she never married, she was unable to claim a war widow's pension. She got a job at one of the potteries, but as soon as the slump came in '21 she was laid off and had not worked since and probably never will now.

I rarely have time to read the newspapers, but Mrs Shipley keeps abreast. Apparently, it was thought, when the American stock market crashed October before last, that it would have no effect over here. This has proved incorrect. In the past year – I did not know the figures but have seen the evidence clearly enough

– unemployment has doubled and there are those who say it could double again next year.

Dole for one such as Mrs Shipley is a pittance if they'd let her have anything at all. At times it seemed her only choices were starvation or the workhouse. Men were her salvation.

'There was a chap for a while who used to visit every Tuesday and Friday afternoon. A married man. He was good fun. We couldn't go out or anything because we'd be seen, but we'd have a laugh. I used to live for those Tuesdays and Fridays. And yes, he gave me money. I was a "kept woman", I suppose. But I can't think I could have got by any other way. And when he went there was a chap who moved in for a bit and then another one who had a sort of country cottage out towards Cheddleton where he used to take me, and he had a bike there and taught Leslie how to ride it. And if you want to call it prostitution, then that's what it is, but I've kept my boy fed and clothed and I've had a very nice time doing it. I've had companionship. Sometimes that's all I've had. I mean, Ron buys me a bit of cake now and then, but he's hardly a sugar daddy is he?'

And then she said: 'I've been up your dances and heard what you have to say and I'm all for what you're talking about. It's a terrible thing for a young woman to have to do, but what you should know is that some of the time, the reason the young women don't have to go on the streets is 'cos their mums are already there. I mean, I'm all right. I've managed to look after myself a bit and if I do my hair nice and put a bit of rouge on, I can look presentable enough to stay off the streets and be a "kept" woman. I've been able to be choosy about the men I've had to do with. And I hate to think what it must be like for them as can't be choosy. And anyway, Leslie's twelve now and I hope I can keep him at school so's he can get a decent job in an office and keep me because if he doesn't, I'm going to be out there on the streets. I don't see as I've got any alternative.

'And don't tell me there's widows' benefits you can claim. Yes, some people get a war widow's pension, but then there's Mrs Batkin who used to live over the road. Five kids. Her husband came home gassed. It took him three years to die and then they turned round and said she couldn't have a war widow's pension because even though it was the war that killed him, he didn't actually die in the war. I don't know what happened to her in the end. She moved away. Probably in the workhouse.

'Have you seen the forms you have to fill in to get the Widows' and Orphans' Pension?'

I had to confess that I had not, although I have since been to the trouble of acquiring one. The filling in does not seem too difficult – unless of course you cannot read or write – but the form includes a page and a half of information about who is entitled to the

227

benefits and under what circumstances, none of which makes a blind bit of sense.

I quote, 'And whereas by Section 18 of the Pensions Act it is provided that a person whose husband, father or mother, as the case may be, had died before the commencement of the Pensions Act is entitled to a pension in the like circumstances and under the like conditions as if the husband, father or mother is deemed to have been insured at the time of his or her death for the purposes of the Pensions Act if he or she would have been or would have been deemed to have been so insured by virtue of any employment if the Pensions Act had then been in force ...' and so on and so on. Can you, a Cambridge man and a trained lawyer, understand a word of that? I certainly cannot and I would imagine there are armies of curmudgeonly officials who do not understand it, either, but rather than owning up to their ignorance, for fear of making a mistake, deny everything to all-comers.

Leslie, the son, a smart boy who knows a lot about trains and is a wizard at mental arithmetic came home, then Ron. He was a bit taken aback to see us there. Caught red-handed in adultery by his religious colleagues. We complimented him on his choice of cake and said we would see him later for the meeting, thanked Mrs Shipley for her kind hospitality, and left.

I certainly do not think that Mrs Shipley, or Ron for that matter, should be delivered unto Satan for the destruction of the flesh.

I am sure that in your line of work you frequently encounter real sinners who perhaps deserve to be delivered unto Satan and that you have done much good work in saving the innocent from false accusation. Religious instruction, and particularly the letters of St Paul, do rather steer one towards a belief in moral absolutes, but more and more, I am finding it hard to make that clear distinction between the black and white of sin and virtue. Everything, once you start properly to explore the circumstances, is in the grey area between.

Mrs Shipley would be in no doubt that these men with whom she has adulterously consorted have brought joy into her life. What if your vacuum salesman Harold Musgrave bought more joy with his amorous exploits than Norah and I can ever hope to with our missionary work? Are we wasting our time? Do I really believe that there is a genuine distinction to be made between virtuous joy and sinful joy? Are the virtuous more filled with joy than sinners, and, if so, why do they so rarely look it?

Such thoughts are unsettling. If God is, in this way, testing my faith, then I pray most fervently that I shall not be found wanting.

I am ever yours faithfully in the joy of Jesus,
Alan.

P.S. Some of the records you so kindly sent are by 'Jack Payne and his BBC Dance Orchestra'. Am I to assume from this that Mr Payne's music can be heard regularly on the BBC? I have always assumed that a wireless set would not be a practical proposition in the Eccles because of aerials and batteries and so forth, but Ron tells me that with modern equipment this might not be the case. If Ron is correct in this respect, investment in the right sort of equipment would enable us to keep our repertoire bang up to date, which would be a great advantage these days when fashions in music and in dancing seem to change so quickly. It would not do to be seen by the young people as 'old hat'.

Thursday, 27th November 1930

Monroe had another of his 'scoops'. A woman from Rugby, Warwickshire, had been in touch with the *Graphic* to say that she was one of the many who had had a romantic entanglement with Musgrave, but unlike those others she knew the identity of the killer and it was not Tommy Prosser at all.

One day, in early July, she met Musgrave during her dinner hour and he took her for something to eat. When she had to go back to work, she watched him walk back to his car, which he had left parked on Albert Street. As he was crossing the road, he was approached by a man who engaged him in a sharp argument. At one point it looked as if blows were about to be exchanged. Eventually, Mr Musgrave had broken away and got into his car, but the man followed, still haranguing him and continued to do so even as the car drove away.

That man was none other than Lawrence of Arabia.

'Did you see this, Edgar?'

'What? The thing about Lawrence of Arabia killing Harold Musgrave? Yes, I did. If you read down to the bottom paragraph, to avoid the inevitable libel suits it makes it clear that Lawrence was actually nowhere near Rugby on the day in question but that he is serving in the RAF, stationed in Plymouth, and is so busy testing new speedboat designs he wouldn't have a moment spare to assault a vacuum cleaner salesman. So, it must have been somebody who merely bears a resemblance to Lawrence.'

'It's a useful story all the same. Does help establish that the killer could have been any one of a hundred who felt wronged by his philandering.'

'Did you see the bit where she says Musgrave had told her he was tracking down Russian saboteurs for MI5?' Edgar said. 'That and scouting for aerodromes are his two favourite stories by the looks of things.'

'Chap I met told me that the MI5 thing could, at a stretch, be true.'

'Is it actually legal to know that MI5 exists?'

'Not sure.'

'I'm fairly sure, even if you do know, it's treason to mention it.'

'I expect they'll come and hang us in a minute.'

Edgar had been thumbing through a bulky magazine. He passed it over to Skelton. 'Have a look at that.'

Skelton examined a picture of somebody's living room in which everything was white, or off-white, or cream, as if somebody had been ever so clumsy with a bottle of bleach.

'What am I supposed to be looking at?' Skelton asked.

'In the corner. By the screen.'

'What?'

'The cocktail cabinet.'

'That?' Skelton said, pointing.

'It's exactly the same as mine except hers is bleached oak.'

'Oh, yes,'.

'It's the Yellow House at Fetcham. Syrie Maugham.'

Skelton recognised the words 'yellow' and 'house', but the rest was just funny noises.

'Syrie Maugham,' Edgar repeated, to press home his point.

'Is that a person?'

Edgar raised an eyebrow. His chief, for all his brilliance, was lamentably ill-informed about things that actually mattered.

'She's possibly the most influential interior designer of the age,' Edgar said. 'Has a shop on Baker Street, you must have passed it. Used to be married to Somerset Maugham.'

'The writer?'

'*The Moon and Sixpence, Of Human Bondage.*'

'I've heard of him. And his wife …?'

'Ex-wife …'

'… ex-wife, designs rooms like these?'

'Celebrated here and in America.'

'She does it for a living, then?'

'Most certainly.'

He looked back at the picture in the magazine. Though his loyalty usually lay with his clerk, in this case he had a lot of sympathy with Edgar's housekeeper, Mrs Stewart. He tried to imagine living in such a room and the fuss there'd be every time somebody came to visit with muddy shoes, or spilt cocoa on the settee. Your life wouldn't be worth living.

'You see my point,' Edgar said.

'Not really, no.'

'I've got Syrie Maugham on my side, haven't I? Proof that I'm right and Mrs Stewart is wrong.'

'Mrs Stewart's objections aren't to do with aesthetics or taste, though, are they? It's the practicality. Who does Syrie Maugham's dusting?'

Edgar looked crestfallen. 'I don't know.'

'Have you shown Mrs Stewart the picture.'

Edgar nodded.

'And she wasn't impressed?'

'She said who ever thought up a room like that should be locked up in a sewer and left to drown.'

'Strong feelings, then.'

'Very. She said the King of Siam could have a cubist cocktail cabinet for all she cared, it'd still be a bugger to dust. Mirrored surfaces, glass, chrome, she's happy to polish all day. But those crevices …' Edgar stared at the wall.

* * *

A parcel arrived with the lunchtime post from Holland, the solicitor in Bedford, containing Harold Musgrave's army medical records. They'd been right about the rank and regiment being made up. He was Corporal Musgrave of the Royal Warwicks. He'd signed up in 1915 and shipped out to Le Havre in the same year, seen action at Ypres, and taken part in the Battle of Albert and the Battle of Le Transloy before being wounded at the first Battle of the Scarpe in 1917.

The records consisted of pages of doctors' notes in many different hands.

Skelton pieced together the story.

Musgrave had essentially been blown up. He had broken an arm, several ribs and suffered shrapnel wounds to the left side of his skull. The doctors at the field hospital had patched him up as best they could and when, after three days, he regained consciousness and gave indication that he might stay alive for a little longer, he was shipped back to England. At a military hospital in Kent, the doctors had done things to the wounds to prevent further infection, set and splinted the arm, strapped the ribs and, not expecting much in the way of a favourable outcome, removed the shrapnel from the head and put the bits of skull back together as best they could.

Again, days passed before he regained consciousness, after which his recovery was surprisingly fast. His brain had clearly taken a terrible jolt. He had to learn all over again how to speak and did so in much the same way as a child does, albeit in an accelerated way, first making 'da-da' and 'ba-ba' sounds, then acquiring words and forming sentences. Curiously, he had, it seemed, never lost the ability to read, although this did not become apparent until he could speak the words from the page.

When it was felt he had made sufficient recovery, he was transferred to a convalescent hospital in Warwickshire where the doctors reported he was soon walking comfortably and seemed to have regained all of his mental faculties. The only significant anomaly being his taste for spinning elaborate stories, especially when flirting with nurses, although the doctors did not consider these to be 'delusions' serious enough to count as evidence of mental disorder, especially since they had no knowledge of what the man had been like before he had suffered the head wound.

Skelton turned back to the post-mortem photographs and looked at the lump at the side of the head, trying to imagine how a skull could deform into such a shape. It was a ridge just above the right ear that protruded what must have been getting on for an inch.

Then something occurred to him. He went back to the doctor's notes. He looked again at the photograph. There was an anomaly. The notes made it clear that the wound was on the left side of the skull. In the photograph it was on the right side. He remembered that Mrs Clayton, when speaking of the wound, had indicated the right side of her head. But that's what you do, isn't it? When somebody has stray custard at the corner of the mouth, you show them like a mirror image.

He telephoned Spilsbury's office. Again, Spilsbury was out, and he spoke to the same assistant as before.

'When the copies of the photographs that I have were made,' he asked, 'could it be that they were done back to front or some such so that left became right and right became left?'

'I'm afraid I wouldn't know anything about that.'

'Were you actually involved in the examination of Mr Musgrave's body?'

'Not personally, no.'

'I wonder whether I could speak to somebody who was.'

'Dr Reid might have been.'

'Could I have a word with him?'

'I think he's downstairs at the moment. If he's free, I could ask him to telephone you from there, shall I?'

'That would be very kind.'

Skelton put down the telephone and picked up the photographs again, holding them up to his head to make sure he wasn't doing something daft. He was fairly sure that doctors, when they talked of right and left, were definitely speaking from the patient's point of view and not their own.

After ten minutes Dr Reid rang back.

'Do you remember, when you were examining the body, was there any indication that an arm had been broken or ribs?'

'Several bones were broken, but I believe that happened when the body was removed from the car.'

'What about the bony ridge at the side of the head. That was definitely on the right-hand side was it?'

'I'm not sure what you mean.'

'The lump at the side of the head. It shows quite clearly on the photographs.'

Reid was amused. 'Oh, that. No, that's not a bony ridge. That's the remains of a hat, most likely the inner band of a cap, that had sort of been fused to the head by the heat.'

Skelton breathed hard. Musgrave, Mrs Clayton had told him, never wore a hat.

'You've still got the body in cold storage, haven't you?'

'Yes, there was some difficulty about its release.'

'I'm sending over Musgrave's medical records from the army. They've only just turned up. I'd like you to re-examine the remains in light of what they say.'

'Is that really necessary?'

'Oh, yes, I think so. Because that bloke you've got there in storage, I don't think it's Harold Musgrave at all.'

Friday, 28th November 1930

Late on Thursday afternoon, Sir Bernard Spilsbury, the Home Office pathologist, had issued a revised report saying that he had read through the newly emerged medical records and, upon re-examining the body, had discovered no evidence of a previously broken arm or ribs and, most notably, no evidence of a shrapnel wound to the left side of the head. He therefore declared a case of mistaken identity. The corpse was not that of Harold Musgrave.

The press were informed. Chester Monroe was peeved that the scoop wasn't his exclusive but kept his nose to the grindstone up to the *Graphic*'s deadline. As well as the front page – 'BLAZING CORPSE NOT MUSGRAVE' (he'd wanted 'A Corpse of Mistaken Identity' but had been overruled by the editor) – he had two follow-ups on the inside pages: 'WHO IS THE MYSTERY MAN?' AND 'WHERE IS MUSGRAVE?'

It was a fine opportunity for extravagant conjecture.

Musgrave could have been attacked by an aggrieved husband or lover and, in the resulting struggle, delivered a fatal blow to his assailant, then, half-maddened by the horror of what he had done, set fire to the car, run away, and had been in hiding ever since.

Or, in order to escape his debts and commitments, Musgrave had withdrawn his money, found some unwitting victim who vaguely resembled him, killed him in order to fake his own death and had run off with one of the more favoured members of his 'harem' to start a new life, perhaps in South America or the Far East.

Or – the two-corpse theory – a desperate bandit had killed Musgrave, left his body concealed somewhere, stolen the car, then made some elementary error, perhaps with the choke, which had flooded the car with petrol such that a single spark was enough to set it alight.

Or, Musgrave, as he had often intimated, was working on business of national importance. He had captured a foreign agent, killed him, burnt the evidence so that people would assume that the corpse was him, then assumed the foreign agent's identity in order more effectively to foil a gang of similar agents plotting to assassinate the King and key members of the government.

And so on.

Meanwhile, in Bedford, arrangements were made for the release of Tommy Prosser.

There were a couple of reporters waiting for Skelton as he got out of the taxi at the Old Bailey, one of whom, Brougham, who worked for the *Daily Herald*, he knew slightly.

'Do you think Musgrave could have killed the man in the car, Mr Skelton?' Brougham asked

'It's not my concern now, is it? I was instructed to defend Tommy Prosser. All charges against Mr Prosser have now been dropped. He's being released from prison, I think today, so that's the end of my involvement with the matter.'

'Who do you think the corpse might be?'

'I don't have the faintest idea. I'm sure the proper authorities are doing their best to find out.'

'Where do you think Harold Musgrave is now?'

'Ooh, is that him over there?'

Brougham looked and, while his back was turned, Skelton skipped into the courthouse.

Jefferson, Graham & Co. Ltd. trading as 'Ivory Enamelware' versus Wilson and Bray Hygienic Porcelain of Wolverhampton turned out to be a damp squib. Before the trial even properly began, the judge and prosecution counsel became entangled in a discussion about whether 'Ivory White' had been registered using the terms of registration specified in the 1905 act and whether that registration was encompassed by Part A or Part B of the 1919 act, and whether the dispute was about the actual words 'Ivory White' or the words together with the script with which they were written. This went on for most of the day at the end of which the judge adjourned the case until such time as the various matters at stake could be more exactly defined with the result that Skelton only got to say 'lavatory' twice.

Skelton and Edgar went for tea at Kemble's, and Rose, who'd been waiting at court with paperwork that needed Skelton's signature, was invited to join them.

'Just for a minute, though.'

They ordered sandwiches, savouries and cakes. Skelton got on with signing what needed to be signed and checking over what needed to be checked over while Rose toyed listlessly with a devilled egg.

After a while, she excused herself and went to the Ladies' Room.

'Is she ill, d'you think?' Edgar asked.

'She does seem to have lost her bubble.'

'Heartache, I believe, can be as debilitating as typhoid.'

'Did a doctor say that?'

'No.'

Rose came back and Kenneth, the proprietor, brought over the cakes.

'I wonder if I might ask a question of a somewhat personal nature, Mr Hobbes?' he asked.

'As long as it's not too personal,' Edgar said.

'I was just having a word with Tony at the cloakroom and

he says, when he took your coat, he couldn't help noticing your trousers. He takes a lot of pride in his appearance, of course, because he's French. And he was wondering where you get them pressed.'

'My housekeeper does it.' Edgar explained about the pinning and – no, as far as he knew, no starch, glue or wax was involved in the process. 'She invariably presses them while I'm out and tends to keep her professional secrets closely guarded. But if I do ever find out, I promise you and Tony will be the first to know.'

'That's very kind of you, Mr Hobbes. Can I just mention that the apricot baskets might be a bit cloying after the egg and anchovy? I'll bring over some coffee meringues just in case. No extra charge.'

'That's very kind of you, Kenneth,' Skelton said.

Edgar looked around. Kemble's, being so close to Drury Lane, Aldwych and the Strand, attracted a theatrical clientele and Edgar, a keen theatregoer, enjoyed star-spotting.

'Is that Ivy Close? Don't look.'

They didn't need to. The mirrors did the looking for them.

'Who's Ivy Close?' Skelton asked.

'In the green crêpe with Chinese embroidery. Before the war the *Daily Mirror* hailed her as the world's most beautiful woman. She must be forty if she's a day, but you'd never know it would you? Oh, Lord.'

'What?'

'Coming through the door.'

Skelton switched his attention to a mirror that covered the door and saw Chester Monroe approaching. His overcoat seemed to be yellow, his hat a lurid shade of green and his shoes shone with many colours, like shot silk.

'Who is he?' Rose asked.

'The reporter who does all the awful stories in the *Daily Graphic*.'

'Mr Skelton, Mr Hobbes,' Monroe said, grinning. 'One of the lads at Foxton Row said I might find you here.'

'Which one?' Edgar asked.

'Ooh, dear. Wasn't he supposed to say?' Monroe swung off his overcoat in a practised gesture, pulled a chair from an adjacent table and turned it back to front before sitting down to give the impression that though he was at their table he wasn't actually *joining* them.

Rose had not encountered Monroe before and her expression, as she examined his check suit in a strange bronze fabric, his striped shirt with pointed collar, his garish tie, and his disconcerting shoes tightened into a horrified pout.

'In his defence,' Monroe continued, 'I can vouch for the fact that he didn't yield the information easily. Cost me a tosheroon and two tickets for Will Hay at the Holborn Empire.'

'Mr Skelton, after a difficult day in court, is entitled to a little privacy,' Edgar said.

'Of course he is. Stands to reason. And that's why I'm going to come straight to the point. And the point is, in one word, Musgrave.'

Skelton stirred his tea and didn't bother looking up. 'What about him?'

'Where is he? And who is the mystery corpse?'

'As I explained to the *Daily Herald* this morning,' Skelton said, 'I was instructed to defend Tommy Prosser. Now that charges against Mr Prosser have been dropped, I no longer have any interest in the matter.'

'My readers do, though. The mistaken identity is the best twist the story could possibly have had. If it hadn't really happened, I might have been tempted to make it up. And the "Where is Musgrave?", "Who is the Mystery Corpse?", is solid gold. As attention-grabbers go, it really does take the biscuit.'

'As I say …'

'In *Writing for Newspapers,* John Spencer Meyer of the University of South Dakota, makes two crucial points. When you've got a good story, first – what we've been doing very successfully – you have to keep it running. Second, you haven't got a story at all – doesn't matter whether it's politics, crime, human interest – you haven't got a story until you've got a hero and a villain. Well, we had our villain, didn't we? Or rather we had several possible villains. Was it Tommy Prosser, one of Musgrave's harem, or one of their husbands, boyfriends or fathers or was it … and I can't tell you how proud I was of this one – Lawrence of Arabia? We had our villain. And we also had our hero, "The Man Who Refuses to Lose".'

'Oh, for God's sake,' Skelton said.

'I want you to stay with the case, Mr Skelton. My readers

want you to stay with the case. My editor wants you to stay with the case.'

'I don't know what you're talking about. I'm a barrister and – how many times do I have to say this? – I no longer have any involvement with the case. I'm sure the police are doing all they can to find Mr Musgrave and to establish the identity of the deceased. Go and talk to them.'

'My editor's prepared to pay £2,000 plus any expenses incurred.'

'That's a preposterous sum,' Skelton said. 'To whom, for what?'

'To you, if you'll stay on the case.'

'I don't know what you're talking about and I suspect that you and your editor have even less idea. Barristers don't go round looking for missing persons. As I say, get on to the police – or hire a private detective. Aubrey Duncan, I'm sure, would be more than happy to recommend a competent private detective who'd be willing to move heaven and earth for £2,000. The whole notion is utterly out of the question. There's nothing more to say.'

'Well, I'm sorry you feel that way, Mr Skelton,' Monroe said.

'It has nothing to do with feelings. It's just facts.'

'Well … if you change your mind …' Monroe said, and like a conjuror, produced a visiting card from thin air and left it on the table, '…you know where to find me.'

'Ridiculous man,' Skelton said, when he'd left.

Edgar was looking at the card wistfully.

Skelton sighed. 'What?'

'I know how you hate all this sort of thing but …'

'No. Edgar. Please. Do not for another second entertain the thoughts I fear you are entertaining.'

'The Hannah Dryden case pretty much doubled your fees overnight. The "Man Who Refuses to Lose" had you so inundated you could cherry-pick whatever case took your fancy. And if you feel there are ethical questions to be considered, I'm sure you know of several charities that could do some marvellous work with £2,000.'

'Edgar … I'm close to my wits' end here. I shouldn't have to say this … I neither have the time, the resources nor the know-how to track down Harold Musgrave, and as for finding out the identity of the dead man – I don't think anybody knows how you'd go about that.'

'I do,' Rose said. Skelton and Edgar had almost forgotten she was there. 'Mr Goodyear might know, anyway.'

It took them a moment to remember that Mr Goodyear was Rose's covert and possibly illusory *inamorato*, Vernon.

'He's doing a research project at the University of Heidelberg in Germany,' Rose continued.

'Yes, we know all about that, but—'

'Do you remember, I told you about Professor Forsch, one of Vernon's colleagues at Heidelberg?'

'Remind me.'

'And how he's extending the Bertillon anthropometrical system to encompass some of Kollman and Buchly's work on facial measurement.'

'How does this …?'

'The technique essentially is to take a human skull and, using these tables of measurements and comparisons that Kollman and Buchly have compiled, reconstruct a likeness of the skull's owner when they were alive and had flesh on the bones. Professor Forsch's main interest is forensic, but he's also collaborated with the archaeology department working on skulls found at the Heuneburg excavation and produced drawings of what ancient Celts might actually have looked like.'

'And who can say they're accurate?'

'From bones long buried in the trenches, he also reconstructed the faces of soldiers killed in the war, and his drawings matched army records and could be recognised by relatives so that names could be put on headstones.'

'It is, as you say, very impressive work, Rose, and I'm sure the police will be very interested, but, as I've said, it really is none of our business any more.'

Though every fibre of his being rebelled against it, Skelton was eventually persuaded to accept Monroe's offer by Edgar's sentimentality.

'Rose could go,' the clerk said, as they walked back to Foxton Row. 'We could send her over there, to Germany. The *Daily Graphic* would cover her expenses. She and Vernon could spend some time, thrown together as it were, and … at least something might get settled.'

Skelton knew he was beaten but pretended to ignore his

clerk and watched a man painting some railings.

'It always takes a lot more work than you'd imagine, doesn't it?' he said. 'You'd think they'd have invented a brush that can do the front, back and sides of a railing all in one go, up and down once and move on to the next.'

Sunday, 30th November 1930

Bob and Gillian were perfectly dressed. Mila had suggested they go for something that looked a bit like tennis whites, but which were either showing signs of great age or last-minute improvisation. Gillian was wearing a white pleated skirt of a length that hadn't been fashionable since before the war, a rather dainty cream blouse with a lace collar, a greyish pullover three sizes too big and presumably borrowed from Bob and a dark green cloche hat. Bob had dug out the cricket whites he hadn't worn since Oxford. They'd yellowed and still showed signs of ancient grass stains. Both carried plimsolls to change into. Bob's were black. Their rackets looked like survivors from the age of the underhand serve.

Mila was wearing a yellow linen suit over a white blouse.

Her shoes and racket were modern and Wimbledon standard, but soiled and scuffed for disguise. Like Gillian, she wore a cloche hat.

Skelton, as a non-combatant, was dressed in his usual Homburg and ill-fitting black overcoat.

Ellie the daughter and Putney the dog had been left at home with the nanny.

Their effect on Digby St Clements, who wore an outfit that looked as if it had been bought that morning from Lillywhite's, was very satisfying. He looked around cautiously. What if someone saw him playing with this crew of ragamuffins? He'd never be able to hold his head up in the saloon bar again.

By the time they'd arrived at the court he'd consoled himself with the idea that the game would probably be over in no time at all. The possibility that any of them might take a point off him seemed remote. In fact, there was a good chance he'd never have a serve returned.

He smirked. They shook hands and he suggested a knock-up to 'get the juices flowing'. Mila galumphed gracelessly around, nurturing a false sense of security in her opponent by striking the ball whenever possible with the wood of the racquet. Bob shouted encouragement when either she or Gillian actually returned a ball but never managed to return one himself.

It was too cold to be standing around. Skelton had seen Mila pull these stunts before and, besides, had spent far too much of his youth standing on the side lines, watching girls and boys play tennis knowing it was a courtship ritual in which he could never hope to participate.

'I'm going for a walk,' he said. Mila saluted him with her racquet.

Towards Paddington, he knew there was a junction of two canals that somebody had once said looked a bit like Venice. It was something to aim for.

It took about fifteen minutes of brisk walking to get to the canals, and when he'd done so he decided that if this was, indeed, what Venice looked like then Venice was overrated. There was a towpath that might have made a pleasant summer stroll, unless it vanished into an endless tunnel somewhere, but it was cold and forbidding down by the water.

Skelton noticed that the street of stucco houses overlooking the canal was called Blomfield Road.

This was, he remembered, the address of Denison Beck's alleged victim, Mrs Edith Roberts, also known as Marcia the Whip. He couldn't remember the exact number but suspected it was somewhere in the twenties, so he walked up that way.

One of the houses had a mourning wreath on the front door. Skelton thought it was probably not the house of Mrs Roberts. She had died sometime in October and though a year's mourning had been considered proper etiquette before the war, these days a couple of weeks seemed generous. On the other hand, the wreath was looking fairly dog-eared.

A maid came out of the house holding her apron like a hammock.

'Excuse me,' Skelton said, 'is this the house where Mrs Roberts used to live?'

'Oh, you're him, aren't you? Mr Skeleton.'

'Skelton.'

'That's right, Skeleton. You're doing the—'

'Yes, I'll be defending Mr Beck in court.'

'Can I just say, it is terrible the things they've been saying about him. Sorry, can I just get rid of these?'

The apron was filled with scraps, crusts of bread and bits of cake. Skelton followed the maid down to the canal where ducks were already assembling. She tried to be fair, throwing scraps to the shy ones at the back, while the more aggressive ones fought over the big bits that had fallen on the towpath.

'It looks as if they know you.'

'So they should. Every day, on the dot. I'm Evie, by the way. Look out for that big 'un. He'll have your leg off if you give him half a chance. Do you want a go?'

Skelton accepted the crust of bread she offered, broke it into smaller pieces and aimed for a small black bird with red on its beak that was hovering on the edges of the pack. Annoyingly, a bigger brown duck stole that piece. Red beak started to swim disconsolately away, but Skelton managed a couple of long lobs that hit a mark almost directly under his beak.

'You're a good thrower,' Evie said.

'I used to play a bit of cricket.'

'I bet you were ever so good.'

He wasn't. But it was nice of Evie to think so.

'Have you seen, Mr Beck? Is he all right?'

'He seems in very good health.'

'He's not in prison, is he? They haven't put him in prison?'

'No. He's at home.'

'He's ever such a nice man, always had beautiful manners.'

'Did you go often with Mrs Roberts, when she went to Wimpole Street?'

'No. She went on her own. Got a cab and went on her own. No, I only met Mr Beck when he came here, and I gave him his tea and so on.'

'He came here to Blomfield Road?'

'All the time. Is it all right to say?'

'What do you mean?'

'Mr Beck said it would be best not to say anything about him coming here, not after they started accusing him of goodness knows what, but it's all right to say to you, isn't it? You're on his side, aren't you?'

'Yes. I'm on his side.'

'He brought such a lot of happiness here. And, with her bad back and what happened to her husband, I thought Mrs Roberts deserved every scrap of happiness she could lay her hands on, and Mr Beck made her ever so happy. Brought the colour back to her cheeks and everything.'

As well as Marcia the Whip, then, Mrs Edith Roberts was Beck's lover. No case had ever proved more baffling.

'Was marriage ever mentioned?' Skelton asked, wanting to make absolutely certain that he hadn't got the wrong end of the stick and Evie was indeed talking about a romance.

255

'Not as such, but you could see by the way they were together it wasn't far off. Mr Beck told me I wasn't to tell anybody.'

'So, you didn't mention any of this to the police or anybody?'

'He told me specifically not to mention it to the police.'

There was sound reasoning in this. If the prosecution found out that Mrs Roberts, as well as being Beck's patient, which she never was, was also his lover, it would be much easier to bump the charge up from manslaughter to murder. A lover's tiff, an argument, a heavy hand on the voltage dial. He'd hang for that.

Which would be better? To let him hang, or to try to save him from the noose by revealing the existence of the photographs thereby invoking the wrath of Norris Lazell who would kill Beck anyway, along with Rose, Edgar, Aubrey, himself and possibly the Director of Public Prosecutions.

Skelton wished he was a duck.

When the bread was finished, they began to walk back to the house, with Evie rattling on about the good that Mr Beck had done for Mrs Roberts' back.

'Her relief when the pain started to get better – I've never seen anything like it.'

He was right then. Cracking a bullwhip was indeed the ideal exercise for a bad back. He made a mental note to recommend it to anyone he came across who suffered from lumbago.

'She practically stopped taking the pills altogether.'

'What pills were these?' Skelton asked.

'The ones the doctor gave her for the pain.'

He knew from Mrs Roberts' medical records that she had down the years been given various medications to ease her pain, none of which had been particularly effective.

'And of course she'd tried no end of massages and osteopaths and … what are the other ones …?'

Skelton knew, because at one time he'd tried most of them himself, to see if they could help with his hip. 'Chiropractors.'

'That's the one. And the tea. She loved the tea.'

'What's that?'

'Comfrey.'

'I tried that myself, for a bit,' Skelton said. 'I've got a dicky hip.'

'I noticed you were walking a bit funny – sorry, no offence.'

Comfrey, otherwise known as 'knitbone', had been recommended by some well-meaning client.

'Chap I used to know said I should give it a go,' Skelton said. 'So, I got hold of some and brewed it up, but I couldn't get on with the smell or the taste, so I only had it once or twice.'

'You have to drink it every day for months before it does any good. Mrs Roberts used to have it cold with lots of sugar. It grows wild, further down the canal and up the waste ground in Kilburn. She used to send a lad picking it for her. Gave him twopence a bunch. Here, you should try it again.'

They were back at the house now. A couple of bunches of comfrey were hung out to dry in the porch. Evie took one down and gave it to Skelton. He smelt it and turned up his nose but stuffed it into his overcoat pocket out of politeness.

'Try it cold with lots of sugar.'

He walked back to Paddington Recreation Ground slowly, stopping now and then to fill and light his pipe. He'd have liked to have been invited into the house to see whether there were any whips in the umbrella stand or leather trousers hung on the line to dry, but the invitation never came.

The game had finished by the time he got back to the tennis courts and Digby St Clements was doing his best to overcome the humiliation he'd suffered at Mila's hands with a brave show of superciliousness.

'And you certainly found your form in those last couple of sets,' he was saying. 'Managed to steal quite a lot of sneaky points off me. Serves me right, I suppose, for being too much of a gent and giving you an easy time. But I did think it important to make sure you *enjoyed* the game, because that's the point, isn't it? I tell you, though, if you work a little harder at that backhand and your serve, you could really make some progress.'

Mila gave him a playful smack on the head with her racquet and hurt him quite badly.

'Must be off,' St Clements said, 'got to see the master of my old Oxford College. I think the cheeky blighter wants me to deliver some lectures.'

And he went.

Slowly, Mila, Bob and Gillian collected their ragtag assembly of discarded overcoats, pullovers and scarves, and left the court.

Gillian had burnt a ginger cake for tea. Luckily, Pompey had a good appetite and afterwards had the decency to be sick somewhere discreet.

Monday, 1st December 1930

The purser took Rose's landing card. She trailed across the quay, dragging her suitcase, her school satchel and a stout leather hatbox that contained a charred severed head, wrapped in muslin and encased in sand.

An initial exchange of wires on the Friday morning had revealed a time problem. Professor Forsch was committed to a series of lectures in America and would be sailing the following Friday. Accordingly, if the thing was to be done at all, he would need the mystery skull by Tuesday at the latest.

The other difficulty was the simple problem of conveying a charred human head through customs.

Aubrey, who enjoyed any challenge that allowed him to show off his ability to pull strings and influence people, had sprung into action. Between Friday evening and the Sunday evening, when Rose was put on a train, he had obtained letters of authority from J. R. Clynes, the Home Secretary, Arthur Henderson, the Foreign Secretary, Konstantin von Neurath, the German ambassador, and Sir Bernard Spilsbury, the Home Office pathologist. He would have liked one from the King, too, but the poor chap was indisposed and not to be disturbed.

The biggest challenge was getting hold of the head itself. Spilsbury was weekending in Suffolk, and though he agreed to send a wire to one of his underlings at Bart's with permission to remove the head from the corpse, the underling had been unwilling to act without a properly signed order. Accordingly, on Saturday afternoon, a motorcyclist had been despatched to Saxmundham with a document for Sir Bernard to sign.

Frank Chettle, editor of the *Daily Graphic* was at first doubtful that Rose was the right person to send when he had experienced reporters to hand who knew Germany and how to deal with recalcitrant officialdom. Edgar had spent most of Saturday on the telephone, arguing that only Rose had the 'influential contacts' required to oil the wheels to persuade the powers that be at the University of Heidelberg to co-operate. Even the most experienced of their reporters would find himself bogged down in a mire of incomprehensible academic bureaucracy.

Once persuaded, Chettle had put the *Graphic's* various departments to work. In a matter of hours, they had provided Rose with a passport, sorted out her travel itinerary and presented her with cash, a portfolio of tickets, timetables and hotel reservations together with a little book of useful German phrases.

Rose had been on boats before, but only rowing and sailing on lakes and rivers, never anything seagoing. The thought of seasickness had not occurred to her until she saw the ship itself, docked at Dover, the size of a terrace of houses, ever so slightly bouncing up and down in the almost calm waters.

When the ship encountered the slow swell of the English Channel, instinct made her want to stay on deck, where the air was fresh and the freezing wind slightly more than bracing, but a Sea Scout had once told her that, to avoid seasickness, you should go to the lowest accessible part of the ship for there the movement will be the least. So that's what she did, making her way to a bar half-filled with people trying to get drunk.

She found a seat out of the way behind a thing that looked navigationally important and reproached herself for not bringing a book about boats. It would have been instructive to pass the time looking up what all the bits were called. She knew some words – like 'companionway', 'bulwark' and 'stanchion' – but was shamefully ignorant about their meaning. She thought of asking a passing steward, but they were all rushing about with tin basins and towels for the people who were being sick.

Determined not to think about sick or anything related, she huddled in her corner, undisturbed, clutching her suitcase and the hatbox with the head in it.

She actually didn't feel one bit sick, now she thought about it, but she was very hungry. Mrs Westing, her landlady had provided her with a bag of captain's dry biscuits, but they were deep in the suitcase. To find them she would have to unstrap and unlock the case. This would mean letting go of her hold on the hatbox. A sudden lurch of the ship could easily have sent it scurrying away. A trip to the ship's lost property to reclaim a severed head could not be countenanced.

When the hunger itself started to make her feel sick, she picked up the suitcase and hatbox and stumbled over to the bar where, with one foot on the hatbox to make sure it didn't escape, she bought and ate a roll with a slice of sausage in it and some chocolate. They made her feel more hungry.

Her itinerary told her that she had an hour and three-quarters between getting off the boat and catching her train, during which time she would have to deal with customs and passports, find the station, then find the right train.

Wanting to be first off, she was standing at the rail long before the ship reached land and chose a spot near the stern where she could see there was a sort of fence for the gangplank. The cold was intense. Then she noticed, as the ship approached the harbour, that the more experienced passengers were gathering midships.

Her mistake cost her almost half an hour. She was the last passenger down the gangway.

'The customs shed is that way, Miss,' the purser said. 'Can you manage that,' he indicated the suitcase and hatbox, 'or should I call a porter?'

'I can manage, thank you,' said Rose.

Ten minutes went by while an American family in front of her, mum, dad and daughter, a girl of about Rose's age, explained, shouting so that the officer, who spoke fluent English, would be able to understand, that they were on their way to Amsterdam. The mother wanted to see *The Night Watch* and the Rijksmuseum. The daughter wanted to know where she could buy clogs.

Eventually the officer was able to get rid of them, waved Rose forward and asked what she had in her luggage. She told him. It's always best to tell the truth. He motioned a colleague forward. After a short conversation in Flemish, the colleague opened a flap in the counter and herded Rose into an inner office.

She took from her satchel her letters from the Home Secretary, the Foreign Secretary, the German ambassador and Sir Bernard Spilsbury, and showed them. The officer, despite the very official crests and expensive paper, was not impressed.

Carefully he examined the hatbox. For a moment his hand toyed with the buckles, but a second thought dissuaded him from opening it. What if it contained a bomb? What, come to that, if it actually did contain a head?

'I will have to look at the list,' he said, and began slowly to turn the pages of a much-thumbed document he took from a desk drawer. Rose got the idea that it itemised what was and was not allowed to be brought into the country. It made no mention of charred heads.

The officer shook his head, knocked on the door of a back office and summoned his superior, a much fatter man with mustard on his uniform.

He seemed to know the correct procedure, found a form in a filing cabinet and began to fill it out, demanding to know Rose's address, and date and place of birth, details of the hotel where she was to stay in Heidelberg, Vernon's name and address, Aubrey's name and address, the name and address of the *Daily Graphic* and the limited information she had about Professor Forsch.

When the form was filled, he read it through with an air of hopelessness. Nothing in it could help him reach a decision.

He made a telephone call. When that proved inconclusive, he made another, then another. It was clear that each call was to somebody of increasing importance. From the expression on the official's face and the tone of his voice, Rose guessed that the final call was possibly to the King of Belgium, or maybe the Pope.

Finally, reluctantly, he stamped several documents, made chalk marks on the suitcase, hatbox and satchel and allowed Rose to pass.

She ran to the station. She knew that Cologne in German was *Köln*, but she had no idea what it might be in Flemish. None of the signboards were much help but saying 'Cologne' and '*Köln*' repeatedly to a porter eventually led to his pointing at a train. Whether it was the right one or not no longer mattered, whistles were being blown. She jumped on, clutching hatbox, suitcase and satchel just as it pulled out of the station.

If you get on the wrong train in England, chances are the next station would be no more than twenty or thirty miles. Here, the next stop might be Moscow, or Istanbul or Shanghai. What would become of her if she was found by Chinese officials to be in possession of a severed head?

She was grateful to find an empty compartment, hoisted the suitcase and hatbox on to the luggage rack and sat down. Her ticket was for first class. The compartment was second class, but she didn't imagine anybody would object, and the idea of struggling with her luggage up the length of the train in search of a slightly more comfortable seat did not appeal.

There was a hubbub in the corridor. The compartment door crashed open and seven men, German by the sound of them, came in, laughing and jostling and pushing each other. They slung their haversacks onto the luggage racks nearly dislodging Rose's precious hatbox.

It was only then that they seemed to notice that the carriage was already occupied. A dark-haired chap addressed her. '*Es tut mir leid, Madam, ich habe Sie dort nicht gesehen.*'

'*Ich spreche kein Deutsch,*' Rose said. It was one of the sentences she had mastered from the *Daily Graphic* phrasebook.

One of the other men, a little younger, perhaps younger than Rose, bowed slightly and said, in barely accented English, 'My friend was apologising for he failed to notice you sitting there when first he entered the compartment.'

The younger man made some announcement to the others in German. They were chastened. They took off their hats. Some of them took off their coats, too. Huge and muscular, they jostled like a herd of Aberdeen Angus corralled into a telephone box, breathing heavily through their mouths.

'Please forgive our uncouth behaviour, miss,' the younger man said. 'We have had a most extraordinary sojourn in your country.'

The others nodded enthusiastically. Rose managed a weak smile.

'May we introduce ourselves? I am Erich, and this is Johann, Karl, Gunter *Eins*, Gunter *Zwei*, Fritz and that's Gerd.'

'I am very pleased to meet you all. My name is Rose Critchlow. Are you all travelling to Cologne?'

Erich laughed. 'Why, yes, miss,' He puffed himself up, 'We are the *wasserball* team of the Cologne swimming club,' and added, because Rose looked confused. 'Water polo.'

'I'm terribly sorry not to have recognised you, but I don't really follow water polo. Won't you sit down?'

Obediently the men found seats. The compartment was big enough for eight ordinary people, or maybe six German water polo players. They huddled and nudged, trying conscientiously not to crowd or touch Rose.

'Have you been competing in England?' she asked.

'Yes, miss, we have. In London. Do you know it?' Erich said.

'That's where I come from.'

'Are you visiting Cologne? The cathedral is, of course, very beautiful, but please also be sure to pay a visit to admire the natural beauties of the Stadtwald Forest. The walks are quite lovely in the snow. Do you skate, miss? Because we would be honoured if …'

'No, I am here on business,' Rose said, and added, because she liked the sound of it, 'Home Office business.'

Erich didn't look entirely convinced, 'Are you a spy?'

'No, I'm an articled clerk for a solicitor. I'm going to Heidelberg.'

'Heidelberg?'

Gunter *Zwei* echoed, 'Heidelberg?'

Erich and Gunter had a conversation in German.

'Gunter says that he has an aunt in Heidelberg who sometimes takes in boarders. He is sure that she would make you very welcome should you wish to stay with her.'

Rose told him she was staying in a hotel that had been booked for her. 'My work takes me to the university there.'

Erich nodded, impressed.

There was a long pause during which Erich smiled at her relentlessly.

'Your English is very good,' Rose said.

'My grandmother, my father's mother, is English.'

Rose wanted to say, 'That must have made things difficult in the War,' but, worried it might be deemed impolite, instead asked, 'Did you win your match in England?'

'Not so much win.'

'It was a draw?'

'You know in Heidelberg,' Erich said, changing the subject, 'the students are very good scholars but not such good swimmers. Do you swim, miss? If you do not and if you wish to visit Cologne, I would be delighted to offer my services as your swimming teacher.'

Rose thought now would be an appropriate time to mention Vernon.

'My friend, Vernon, an Englishman, will be waiting for me in Heidelberg.'

'Ah,' Erich said. And nodded again.

Not long after that, he fell asleep.

She had almost called Vernon her 'boyfriend'. She wanted to. She wanted to say it aloud. Silly, of course. Vernon was her friend.

She read. On the train in England, she'd started reading a book recommended by Mrs Westing; *The Unpleasantness at the Bellona Club,* by Dorothy L. Sayers. It passed the time, although she found the hero, Lord Peter Wimsey, most irritating even though he shared many traits with Aubrey Duncan, and she quite liked Mr Duncan.

There was a bottle of lemonade – if it hadn't broken – in the suitcase along with the captain's biscuits, but, even though she was still very hungry, the idea of opening her suitcase and exposing her blouses and underwear to a German water polo team made her blush, so she pressed on with *Unpleasantness at the Bellona Club,* until her gurgling stomach caught Gerd's attention and he looked up. He had not known many ladies and was surprised that they made such noises.

Since, on balance, the embarrassment of gurgling was worse than that of having your underwear examined, she stood and reached up to the luggage rack. Immediately Erich and Fritz leapt up to help her and Erich said, 'Allow me.' He pulled down the suitcase, dislodging the hatbox, which teetered. The embarrassment of a severed head falling on to the floor would, of course, easily trump both gurgling and underwear, so she leapt to control it, but Fritz was ahead of her, and, with the precision of a champion *wasserball* player, batted it back to position.

Trying as hard as possible to conceal its contents, Rose opened the suitcase and found the captain's biscuits and the mercifully intact lemonade. Fritz lifted the case back to the luggage rack.

They all looked at her, pityingly, as she took tiny joyless bites out of one of the biscuits. Erich opened his knapsack.

'Perhaps I could offer you something a little more toothsome,' he said. 'Our English hosts insisted on providing us with food for the journey. We ate our fill on the boat, but there is a great deal left over. English food.'

He opened a snap tin and showed it was half-full of pork pie and cheese sandwiches. The others opened their knapsacks too. Gunter *Zwei* had four bars of Dairy Milk chocolate. Gerd had sausage rolls.

'Please,' Erich said.

Rose took a sausage roll, just to be polite. Then a quarter of a pork pie, three cheese sandwiches and half a bar of Dairy Milk. She should, Rose thought, have been ashamed for making such a pig of herself but the *wasserball* players, far from minding her greed, seemed as fascinated by the sight of an Englishwoman eating English food as they would be by, say, a python consuming an entire goat.

Every second bite, she said, 'Thank you,' and 'You're very kind,' and they nodded and urged her to take more.

When she opened her lemonade, they opened bottles of beer and proposed toasts in German to which she responded with 'Cheerio' and 'Good health'.

Rose went back to *Unpleasantness at the Bellona Club.* The *wasserball* players held subdued conversations in German or dozed.

At Bruges, newsboys sold papers and magazines – English, French, Dutch, German – to passengers who leant out of the windows.

It grew light outside. They passed allotments and houses like Rose had never seen in England, different shapes, some clad with brightly coloured tiles. After Liège there were flames from factory chimneys and the train paused for a moment on a bridge over a road where she could see men standing outside a cafe, laughing.

At the German border, officials got on the train. They

inspected passports but seemed uninterested in luggage. So that was all right.

At Cologne, the *wasserball* team helped her down with her bags, then, on the platform, shook her hand one by one and repeated their offers of accommodation and swimming lessons.

They left her alone.

The Heidelberg train didn't leave for forty-five minutes so she made for the steam of the station cafe. Through the window, she could see men and women eating and drinking. Twelve years ago, some of them would have been in the trenches, shooting and being shot by British soldiers. They would have had husbands, fathers, brothers killed, perhaps by people she knew. She wondered whether Germans had Armistice Day, and the two minutes' silence. And how would they treat an English woman?

She imagined them standing around and taunting her, possibly opening her luggage.

'What's in the hatbox?' they would say. And she would reply, 'The severed head of an Englishman.'

Perhaps that would make it all right.

She entered. Nobody gave her a second glance.

The smell was different. Coffee and a tobacco smell much sharper than you get in England – more like pipe tobacco even though she couldn't see anybody smoking a pipe. The harbour had smelt of the sea and oil the same as an English harbour. The train had the usual train smells of coal and musty upholstery. This was her first proper smell of abroad.

Again, keeping the hatbox tight between her feet, she ordered two ham sandwiches, a piece of something halfway between bread and cake that the label said was *Butterkuchen* and some coffee. She took German money from her satchel to pay. The sandwiches came with pickles.

Warm and fed she sat back in her chair and looked around. A German station cafe wasn't the Hindu Kush or Kanchenjunga, but it was still an adventure. And she was doing all right, wasn't she? She had been on a train, spoken with a *wasserball* team, ordered food and paid with foreign money without coming a cropper. She hadn't let the side down – whoever the side was, these days. For years it had been the Girl Guides. Now, she supposed, it was Mr Duncan, and perhaps Mr Skelton and Mr Hobbes. To get grandiose about it, she might even say it was the British legal system, or Britain. Oh, and for the time being, the *Daily Graphic*.

She shared her compartment in the train to Heidelberg with a sad man with a huge moustache who looked a bit like Chester Conklin, and an elderly couple who did not seem to like each other very much. Nobody spoke. She read some more.

Outside snow began to fall. A schoolfriend had had a picture on her pencil case with the title, 'Germany in the snow'. It showed pine trees, mountains and a house that looked like a Swiss chalet. There was nothing like that to be seen from the train window, but she knew the mountains were much further south.

Vernon was waiting for her on the platform at Heidelberg.

They shook, rather formally, with their left hands – the Boy Scouts' handshake.

'Can I carry madam's severed head for her?' he asked with a smile.

Rose had forgotten about his smile.

The hotel, on Sofienstrasse was on the *Daily Graphic*'s list of reporters' favourites primarily because it was next door to a lively bar that stocked, in addition to the usual German beers and spirits, a good selection of Scotch and Irish whiskey and bottled Bass.

Outside the station, Vernon had headed for the tram stop. Then Rose took out the paper wallet filled with German money that she'd been carrying in her school satchel.

'Where did you get that?' Vernon asked.

'The *Daily Graphic* is paying for everything. We can take a taxi.'

'I've never done that here,' Vernon said. 'In fact, I don't remember taking a taxi anywhere.'

'I got one once or twice in Birmingham,' Rose said. 'On business for my dad. You'll have to tell the driver where to go, though, because I don't think my German accent is right.'

A taxi was waiting at the rank. Vernon spoke to the driver and they got in.

Rose checked in to the hotel and a porter took the suitcase up to her room. She carried the hatbox and satchel herself.

'Are you hungry?' Vernon asked, when she came back down to the lobby.

'Starving.'

'I think you could probably leave that in your room.'

'D'you think it'll be safe?'

'I would have thought so.'

Rose took the hatbox back to her room.

'There's a place where a lot of the students go, not far,' Vernon said when she came back. 'We could go there, and you could sample some of the local delicacies,' he laughed. 'Except they don't really have delicacies in Germany. Not for dinner, anyway. Some of the puddings and cakes are good but dinner is mostly pork in one form or another in bulk.'

'Sounds perfect.'

The snow had turned to sleet and was coming down more heavily.

'Come on,' he said. They ran up the street and down another street on to a cobbled lane with fairy-tale buildings on either side. Vernon pushed open an arched door and they stepped into a party. They battled down the stairs, past young men braced against the bannisters, into the large hall, with archways on either side that gave glimpses of other small alcoves and rooms. The smell of beer, tobacco and – another smell, maybe sweat, maybe sausages – was overpowering. Most of the people were young, but others looked as old as the furniture, with bodies as bulky and stout as beer casks, their buttocks spread over the oak benches. There were women there too, scarlet-faced from the heat.

'Welcome to Heidelberg,' Vernon said.

'What?'

He shouted, 'Welcome to Heidelberg.'

She saw hands reach out to shovel fork-loads of frankfurters, krenwurst, sauerkraut and spuds into open mouths. It was washed down with tankards of beer, bigger than pint glasses in an English pub. Big lumps of bread soaked up the juices. Waitresses threaded their way round the tables with more beer, more sausage, more bread. There seemed to be a lot of spillage.

Vernon led Rose by the hand to a long table at the back of the hall. Their neighbours looked like farmhands. They smoked long-stemmed pipes that they didn't bother to lay down when they drank, just moving them to the corners of their mouths. When they saw Rose and Vernon, they smiled a welcome and moved their bulk further down the bench to accommodate them.

A group of young men lurched past. One of them shouted something and they all laughed.

'A lot of these people are students,' Vernon said.

'A lot of these people are drunk,' Rose said. 'Are those Brownshirts?' She pointed at a group of men in khaki uniforms at a table across the way.

Vernon nodded.

Rose had read about the Brownshirts in the *Daily Herald*. They were fascists, like Mussolini's Blackshirts, followers of a man called Hitler and his Nazi party. Recently the Nazis had done very well in the Heidelberg local elections and become the strongest group in the town council.

Her father had been a long-time member of the Labour party. As a solicitor he had specialised in cases involving industrial injuries, strikes, lockouts and unfair dismissals. The Nazi party, the National Socialists, even though they had that word 'socialist' in their name, had nothing at all to do with the socialism her father had believed in. They mostly seemed to be anti things – anti-Semitic, anti-communist, anti-anybody who opposed what they called 'the war spirit'. The only thing they seemed keen on was brawling. There had been riots here and there. Shops owned by Jewish people had been ransacked and looted.

Rose, a Girl Guide through and through, considered herself, like Kim in the Rudyard Kipling novel, a 'little friend of all the world'. She subscribed to what the Girl Guides handbook described as 'The Knights' Code'. 'Defend the poor and help them that cannot defend themselves. Do nothing to hurt or offend anyone else.' 'Help others by thinking the best of them, speaking only well of them and doing well by them.'

This, she supposed, made it impossible for her to be a Nazi.

'Where do they get their uniforms?' she asked.

'What?' Vernon said.

'Where do they get their uniforms? Is there a Nazi shop somewhere? Like the Scout Shop in Birmingham. Or do they have to send off for it?'

'I don't know,' Vernon said. 'I've never seen a Nazi shop.'

'Do they have to pay for it themselves? It looks good quality. I can't imagine it'd be cheap.'

'Perhaps they get a discount,' Vernon said. 'A lot of the big firms support the Nazis.'

'Why?'

'Because they're against the communists and what the big firms are most worried about are the communists.'

A waitress came to take their order. The menu was on a board over the other side of the room and Rose wouldn't have understood it anyway, so she asked Vernon to order for her.

'Do you want beer or schnapps?'

Rose frowned and looked at what other people were drinking.

'They don't do tea,' Vernon said. 'And I think even a glass of water would give rise to sidelong glances.'

'Beer, then.'

Vernon spoke German to the waitress. She asked a couple of subsidiary questions, which Vernon understood and to which he gave what seemed like satisfactory answers.

'Your German is very good,' Rose said when the waitress had gone.

'Just about good enough to order a meal, but not for much else. I've had to learn a lot of technical stuff for the university, but I'm still a novice with some of the basic grammar and, oh, the endless pronouns! I like the way they run words together, though, – like *der Windschutzscheibenwischer* and *der Handschuh*.'

'What's a *handschuh*?'

'It's a glove – a hand shoe. Good, isn't it?'

'And the other one?'

'Literally, as far as I can make out, "wind protection slices wiper".'

'What?'

'Windscreen wipers on a car.'

The Brownshirts laughed raucously.

Somebody from a group at another table, clearly students, but dressed as workers in flat caps and open-neck shirts, shouted something at them, and the Brownshirts shouted something back.

'Are they communists?' Rose said, pointing at the ragged-looking students.

'How did you know?'

'They look the same as the communists in Birmingham,' she said. 'Sometimes they used to come round to the house. They either wore red ties or no ties at all and they'd always rather stand than sit in bourgeois-looking chairs.'

'What's a bourgeois-looking chair?'

'Anything comfortable.'

Vernon laughed. 'Is there anything special you'd like to do while you're here? You're stuck until Professor Forsch finishes with your head. We might as well make the most of it.'

'I don't know. Perhaps see the castle and go on a boat on the Rhine. Or is that too dull for you? Have you done all those sorts of things already?'

'No, not at all. Professor Mayenburg keeps me hard at it. And I've been working with Lessing as well on frog muscles. I know what you're thinking, "What's that got to do with entomology? Complete red herring!" – but there are crossovers to do with lactic acid fermentation and its relationship with oxygen availability.'

Rose let Vernon talk. Even if she could have heard what he was saying she probably wouldn't have been able to understand it, but that didn't matter. His enthusiasm was calming.

The waitress put a tin plate piled high with pork and dumplings in front of her and followed it with an oversized glass of beer.

'I'm never going to be able to eat all this.'

'I thought you said you were starving.'

'I know. But I have my limits.'

'You see. The beer helps wash it down. What have you been up to, anyway?'

Rose told him about some of the cases she'd worked on with Aubrey Duncan, about Edgar's new flat in Belsize Park and about Joan, the woman who had taken over Edgar's old room at Mrs Westing's. She seemed very nice and worked in the hosiery department at Gamages.

'Does that mean you get a discount on stockings?'

Rose coloured, unsure whether it was right for them to be talking about ladies' stockings.

'What are these things called?' she asked.

'Oh, those are *knödel*. Dumplings. Don't you like them?'

Without warning, a short stout man lurched from behind Rose and pushed his face towards hers.

'*Deutschland und England gegen die französischen Tyrannen! Wir haben zähne Ausdauer*! Together, yes?'

He lurched off again.

Vernon was on his feet and shouted '*Du Grossmaul*!' at his back. Rose pulled on his arm to get him back into his seat

'What was that all about? Was he angry about the war? Is it because we're English?'

'No, he seems to think Germany and England should gang up against the French.'

'Why?'

'No idea. Aren't you going to finish that?'

Rose pushed her plate towards him, but before Vernon could dig in, he stood and said, 'Oops. Time for us to get out of here quickly.'

Rose, alarmed, looked around. The Brownshirts seemed to be placid and so were the communists. 'Is there going to be trouble?'

'No, but there's a chap over there who's just produced a piano accordion and I think he intends to play it.'

Vernon took her back to her hotel. In the lobby they shook left hands. He went off to his digs. Rose went up to her room. She was in bed by half past ten, but overtiredness and noise from the bar next door kept her awake until after one in the morning.

She remembered, when she was much smaller, reading a story in a magazine about Alma Dent, Girl Reporter. Alma was only supposed to be some sort of secretary on the newspaper, but her insatiable curiosity, courage and persistence led to her unmasking a gang of criminals or some such. The details were hazy.

Here she was, Rose Critchlow, in a hotel in Germany paid for by the *Daily Graphic*, having carried a charred human head o'er land and sea. She had sat in a *bierkeller* with real Nazis and communists. What stories she would have to tell her grandchildren.

She imagined the grandchildren, then looked to one side and saw who their granddad was.

Tuesday, 2nd December 1930

She woke with a start, saw how light it was outside and found her wristwatch on the nightstand. She had arranged to meet Vernon by the hotel reception desk at nine and it was twenty to. Thankfully the bathroom was free, and she'd only brought one change of clothes so there was no choosing to be done.

Vernon was sitting in a chair, reading a German newspaper.

'Sorry I'm late,' she said.

'You're not.' He eyed the hatbox. 'I see you've brought Mr Nobody. Would you like …?'

'No. I'll hang on to him, if that's all right. Then if he gets lost it'll be my fault.'

'Have you got a scarf?' Vernon asked. 'It's very cold out.'

'I forgot it.'

'Here.' Vernon took off his own scarf, long, blue and knitted by his mum, and wrapped it around her neck twice. 'My coat buttons all the way up to the top,' he said.

They went to a cafe near Universitätsplatz, and ate bread, jam and coffee – much nicer coffee than the stuff she'd drunk at Cologne station. Conversation was stilted, the result, no doubt, of sharing a breakfast table with a charred head.

Professor Forsch was a round-faced man with tiny black eyes and a calm slowness about him. He spoke good English but hesitated over every other word, carefully weighing it before allowing it to be voiced.

He removed the head from the sand in the bag and tutted over the muslin it had been wrapped in. Rose exchanged a glance with Vernon. Would that spoil everything?

Forsch took his time, turning the head over. He took out a magnifying glass to look more closely. 'He was dead before being burnt,' he said. It was a statement, not a question. 'The high temperature inside the skull causes dura mater retraction. It exfoliates from the bone and leads to blood exuding from the sinuses. The blood then coagulates and forms heat haematoma.'

Forsch looked up and Vernon nodded as if he understood. Perhaps he did understand. Rose thought it proper to ask a question.

'And what exactly is "dura mater"?'

Forsch smiled. 'It means "tough mother". It's the protective lining around the brain. It is important to distinguish the

286

heat haematoma from an epidural haematoma caused by blunt trauma – as we see here.' He indicated a spot at the back of the skull.

'And how long will the reconstruction take?'

'I have to take many, many measurements and …' he picked a fragment of charcoal from the cheek, '…perhaps try to estimate …' Lost in thought, now, he took a surgical probe from a pot on his desk and gently pressed it into the burnt flesh. He seemed pleased by what he found.

'The *Daily Graphic* is paying me handsomely for this work, so I have accordingly made arrangements so that I can devote myself exclusively to its completion. But I'm afraid that …' He looked up at the door as if waiting for a knock. 'I may be distracted by one or two … administrative problems.'

'I had heard there were difficulties,' Vernon said.

'Some of the students have made the running of my department problematic. They find one of the technical staff, Frau Rosenberg, to be an "unfit" German and have made it their business to bring about her dismissal.'

Rose wondered whether Professor Forsch's English had failed him. 'Unfit' suggested that she couldn't run up a hill without having to stop, panting for breath halfway, a failing that surely wouldn't disqualify her for an academic post, much less being a German.

'"Unfit"?' she asked. 'In what way?'

Professor Forsch looked nervously up at the door and shook his head. 'Personally, I find Frau Rosenberg very capable but …' he whispered, 'there are political difficulties. Not so long ago the great Emil Gumbel – you know the name, perhaps? – one of the professors of mathematics, was forced to resign.'

Forsch tidied away his magnifying glass and emptied the muslin and sand into a bin. 'Perhaps in two days, Fraulein, I will have something to show you.'

Outside, it had just started to snow again.

Vernon looked at the sky wondering how heavy a fall it would be. 'Do you want to go to a cafe or something?' he asked.

'I'd rather just walk around for a while, look in shops, get my bearings.'

'As long as you're not too cold.'

Rose wondered if he would take her hand, pretending to test how cold it was, but he didn't.

Skelton was on his feet at the Old Bailey for *Rex versus Michael Mullen*.

Mullen, 32, of Tottenham Hale, London, an employee of the Enfield Tin Canister Co was charged with theft from a jeweller's shop in Hertford Road, Enfield from which a safe had been removed, intact and unopened, containing jewellery and cash with an estimated value in excess of £1,000.

The following day, a man walking his dog had discovered the safe, still unopened, hidden in bushes near a canal towpath.

On the assumption that the felon would eventually return to collect it, the local police arranged for officers to keep a 24-hour covert watch on the safe.

The next morning, before dawn, Mr Mullen was seen approaching the safe, lighting his way with an electric torch. He carried a heavy, clanking tool bag. Before he could make clear his intentions, however, the officer, hiding beneath a bridge nearby, happened to sneeze. Mullen, alarmed, dropped his tool bag and made as if to run away but the officer, Constable Akerman, managed to apprehend him and take him into custody.

The bag was found to contain a selection of drills, crowbars and explosives. Mr Mullen had two previous convictions, one for shoplifting and one for taking away a bicycle without the owner's permission. He was also considerably in debt – the result of indiscriminate gambling – and he had previously worked for a locksmith, so knew something about locks and safes.

In his statement, Mr Mullen said he knew nothing about the safe on the towpath and was walking to the house of a friend in order to remove a tree stump in his back garden.

The friend, George Birchwood, was contacted. He knew Mr Mullen quite well – they both worked for the same employer – and he did, indeed, have a tree stump in his back garden that he wanted to be rid of, but he had made no arrangements with Mr Mullen to do so.

Mr Mullen said that he wanted to surprise Mr Birchwood by waking him in the early hours of the morning with a huge explosion and then placating his subsequent anger by showing him the shattered tree stump. He said that he and Mr Birchwood often played tricks on each other.

This was confirmed when Birchwood, appearing as a prosecution witness, under cross-examination from Skelton, admitted that he had once hung a sign on Mr Mullen's front door saying 'You May Telephone From Here', and, another time, he had glued a sixpence to the pavement outside Mr Mullen's house – although that was several months ago and, as far as he knew, Mr Mullen hadn't noticed it yet.

When asked whether removing a tree stump could ever be seen as a 'practical joke', however, Mr Birchwood replied, 'No, not really.'

Skelton managed to score a couple of points when questioning the police witness. The tools in the bag that Mullen was carrying were essentially woodworking and gardening tools – exactly the sort of things you'd use to remove a tree stump, but entirely inappropriate for opening a safe. If Mullen's locksmith experience was as extensive as the police evidence tried to present it, surely he'd have come equipped with locksmithing tools – picks, skeleton keys and so forth?

But on the whole, it was turning out to be what Skelton called a 'blah-blah trial' in which one person says this and another person says that, but no piece of evidence or argument is ever compelling enough to impress a jury one way or another or even interesting enough to keep them engaged. There is, he knew, nothing more dangerous than a bored jury. A bored jury will retire, the foreman will say, 'So what do we think? Guilty?' and the others will agree just to get the whole tedious business done with.

But Skelton did not despair, for he knew what was coming, and when Mr Glazier – ex-major (Royal Engineers), explosives expert, chairman of the Great Dunworth Parish Council – brought his black metal face patch, hook hand and air of reckless glee to the stand he knew that everything was going to be all right. Two members of the jury let out an audible gasp. Glazier bared his teeth at them in the lopsided grimace that served as a smile.

Skelton led him through a brief account of his war record and experience with explosives and then asked about different kinds of explosive, their properties and uses.

Glazier laid great stress on the fact that though gunpowder – black powder of the sort that Mullen had in his possession – would, if packed correctly into a tree stump, make a delightful bang and possibly send earth and roots flying all over the place, it would have no effect whatsoever on a reinforced steel safe other than, again, to make a big bang loud enough to alert every policeman for five miles around that something was amiss down by the canal.

Glazier went on to say that he had planned to bring examples of various kinds of explosive to court and to demonstrate their properties with some very small, controlled explosions, but the court officials had forbidden this.

'They did, however, allow me to bring my mascot here, little Benjamin Bunny.' From his pocket, Glazier took a tiny toy rabbit. 'Who I made to demonstrate how easily gelignite can be moulded.'

Mr Justice Bentham, on the bench, said, 'You mean to say …?'

Glazier bared his teeth. 'Yes, indeed, My Lord. This is a jelly bunny. And now …' Glazier did something with the ears, 'he's a jelly mouse.'

With a commendable show of *sang froid*, Bentham asked, 'Would it perhaps be advisable to clear the court?'

'Gelignite is perfectly safe, My Lord. Indeed, people have even been known to eat it in small quantities without exploding. Danger arises only when it begins to sweat out its nitro-glycerine – and at the moment this little mouse seems perspiration-free – or when it meets some sort of detonator.' Glazier took out a small metal cylinder and said, 'Like this one.'

The Clerk of the Court, who knew something of explosives, braced himself.

'Now, this,' Glazier continued, 'is, of course, a dummy. It would be foolhardy in the extreme to bring a detonator into a public place. It was, indeed, a detonator just like this one that took away half my face in 1916, but I produce it just to give some indication—' He stopped suddenly and examined the cylinder closely. 'It is the dummy, isn't it?' he whispered to himself. 'Blow me, if I didn't pick up the wrong one. No, no … as you were, it definitely is the dummy.' He flashed the smile again. 'The point being that this, jelly and detonator, is the stuff you'd need to blow a safe.' Skelton then, to keep

292

the jury entertained, asked him a series of questions which invited him to furnish the court with exact details of how one might blow a safe; details that, years later, every member of the jury would remember and, perhaps, pass on to children and grandchildren who might, equipped with this useful knowledge, turn to a life of crime.

Cross-examination by Smethurst, the prosecution counsel, if anything bolstered the defence case, especially when Glazier pointed out that, since Mullen clearly had no idea how to break into the safe, it was unfair to charge him with the theft of the jewellery and cash it contained on the grounds that he would never be able to take possession – a comment that earned him a mild reprimand from the bench.

The jury was gone for less than an hour. Not guilty.

Glazier joined Skelton and Edgar for a celebratory drink in the King of Denmark.

'I take it you'll no longer be requiring my services for the Tommy Prosser trial?'

'No, that's all over. Tommy's been released.'

'Pity. I had a good time today,' Glazier said. 'I might do more of this sort of thing.'

'In what way?' Edgar said.

'I might become one of those bastards who sues everybody in sight on the slightest provocation. It is such fun, isn't it?'

Skelton looked doubtful.

'Well, I don't imagine it's so much fun if you do it for a living,' Glazier said, 'but now and then.'

'Oh, it's not that I don't think it's fun,' Skelton said. 'It's just … I'm not sure it's supposed to be.'

Edgar supped his ale reflectively. His chief was getting in some funny moods these days.

Wednesday, 3rd December 1930

Rose, who had, in the past, slept soundly in a leaky tent during a storm-tossed night in Cwm Pennant valley, could do no more than doze for a few moments at a time in her German hotel room. She had excitement bubbling in her stomach.

After delivering the head to Professor Forsch, she and Vernon had spent the rest of the previous day together. They had lunch, explored the castle, took a boat trip on the Rhine and had dinner, all the while chatting endlessly about their parents, about scout and guide camps they'd been on, about his research and her work with Mr Duncan. She had never felt so easy talking to anyone, girl or boy.

At six in the morning, she gave up trying to sleep, took

her sponge bag and towel down to the bathroom and turned the taps wondering if hot water would be available. They made a noise like a pneumatic drill that must have woken up every guest in the hotel, but the water and steam came out at such a rush that she knew the noise could last no more than a couple of minutes.

As she soaked, she spotted a sign on the wall, written in German. It looked insistent. The only part of it that Rose recognised were the various words meaning 'the'. She feared it said something like, 'No baths before 8.00' or 'Do not turn on the taps to their fullest extent'.

She rubbed soap on her sponge and thought about Vernon.

The ache she had felt when she was in London and Vernon in Germany, the joy she had felt when she saw him at the station and the bubbling excitement she'd felt all night, had left her pretty convinced that she wanted Vernon to be her boyfriend. But she wondered, in practical terms, how the transition from 'friend who is a boy' to 'boyfriend' was usually made.

It was silly. She'd known lots of girls who had boyfriends, and some who'd had fiancés, husbands even, but never thought to ask them how you go about organising the transition.

First, presumably, one would have to establish whether the boy wanted you to be their girlfriend. That alone was quite a mountain to climb. Could she ask? Would that seem gauche, just to come right out with it. *Would you like me to be your girlfriend?* Or did one just *know*. She hoped it wasn't a case of just *knowing* because she didn't know at all what Vernon thought of her. The fact that he always seemed happy in her company meant nothing because she had never seen him when he wasn't in her company so had no control sample with which to compare the experience. Perhaps he was like that with everybody.

Kissing and holding hands probably had a lot to do with it. They'd walked around streets and so on for a whole day without holding hands, so it would seem quite silly somehow if, for no apparent reason, she suddenly grabbed his hand. What if he pulled his own hand away? And it was the same with kissing. If he pulled away from a kiss, and possibly even wiped his mouth, that would be much, much, worse than him pulling his hand away.

It wasn't done, of course, for a lady to kiss a gentleman. She had to wait for the gentleman to kiss her.

The kissing, she supposed, would formalise the transition from friend to boyfriend and set one on a path to engagement and marriage.

In frank and open discussions, whispered late at night under canvas and often steered by Beth Tyrell, her shockingly outspoken patrol leader, the subject of 'going all the way' had cropped up. Most girls thought that if you went all the way before marriage no boy would ever respect you. Girls who did that sort of thing inevitably ended up as unmarried mothers and likely as not prostitutes with venereal diseases. Other girls thought, more simply, that, never mind the boy's respect, if you fornicated you would lose the respect of God and burn for all eternity in the fires of hell.

Rose wasn't sure. She didn't particularly believe in God or hell.

Although she'd never been, or wanted to be 'fashionable', she did like to think of herself as a 'modern thinker'. She knew that writers, artists and intellectuals like Bertrand Russell, D. H. Lawrence and the Bloomsbury people thought that having sexual intercourse before you got married was generally a good idea and that men who lost respect for girls who 'went all the way' were just silly.

The water had gone cold and the ends of her fingers were wrinkled. She towelled herself off and, shivering in her dressing gown, crept back along the freezing corridor to her room.

By seven-thirty she was dressed and ready for the day to begin. Vernon had arranged to come to the hotel at noon. Before that, she had chores to attend to.

The *Daily Graphic* had stressed the importance of getting the results of Professor Forsch's investigations back to them as quickly as possible. She had sent them a telegram (the people on the desk at the hotel, she discovered, could do this for you, even if it was in English) to say that the Prof. expected to be finished by Thursday. They had replied that if this meant early on Thursday morning then it might be possible to send the results by airmail and they would arrive just about in time for the Friday morning edition. She double-checked to make sure it was true and learnt it was. The last posting for the Heidelberg airmail service on a Thursday was 9.30 a.m. There was no Friday service.

The only alternative to the airmail service would be to send the report by telegram. The pictures could go by wire, too, using a piece of apparatus called a belinograph or a telediagraph – Rose had no idea that such things existed. The *Graphic* had been in touch with a Heidelberg newspaper, the *Heidelberger Tageblatt*, which apparently had, or had access to, the appropriate machinery. Rose was advised to pay a visit to their offices, on Brunnengasse, to make sure that everything was in working order and they would be able to send Professor Forsch's report – text and pictures – as soon as it became available.

Brunnengasse was a short walk away from the hotel, towards the university. She had passed it the previous day.

It wasn't the most prepossessing of buildings, but then she remembered the *Birmingham Daily Mail* office wasn't much to look at, either. The entrance hall could have done with a mop and a dust. At the desk, she asked a young chap whether he spoke English. He said he didn't, but spotted another, older chap in a lurid green suit and brown felt hat, walking past, called him over and said something in German. The older chap introduced himself as Willy and, in fairly good English, asked if he could help.

Rose told him that she represented the *Daily Graphic* in England and explained her business.

Willy's manner suggested he might be making fun of her. Or flirting. Sometimes the two can be indistinguishable.

She wasn't used to people flirting with her. And yet, on the train Erich had definitely flirted and now here was Willy. She wondered whether the Germans were by nature a flirtatious people or whether they found slightly gawky girls with red noses, woolly hats and big ginger coats particularly attractive.

He told her that he was just a humble reporter on the newspaper and knew nothing about the important business of sending and receiving telegraphs, but he had a vague idea where the telegraph room was.

'Come,' he said, 'we will go exploring together and see what we can find.'

Willy took her downstairs into a dingy basement and made a great pantomime of opening this door and that in the manner of Howard Carter opening Tutankhamun's tomb. Eventually they found a room filled with complicated-looking typewriters and ticker tape machines.

A couple of chaps were bent over the machines, working furiously. When Willy asked if they could interrupt him, they shouted something that may have been rude. Willy smiled apologetically at Rose and withdrew.

'They seem to be very busy at the moment. There is, I think, some very big story happening, although usually the very big stories turn out to be very small stories once all the fuss has died down.' He laughed and offered her a cigarette.

She shook her head. 'I need to check, you see, whether they'll be able to send the report tomorrow as soon as it's ready.'

They went back up the stairs to the entrance hall.

'I am sure that everything will be fine. But right now, the big story must have … precedence?'

'Precedence, that's right. But what if there's a big story tomorrow as well?'

'Then you must get in touch with me … here is my card … and I will speak to the editor and the editor will insist that your report should take precedence over everything else.

The card said he was Willy Brechenmacher Auslandredakteur. Rose wasn't sure whether the 'Auslandredakteur' was part of the name or his role on the newspaper. She had the impression, both from the general quality of the card (embossed on thick board) and from his confidence, that he had the ear of the newspaper's editor, that he was something rather more than a junior reporter.

'And maybe later I could show you around. There is a beautiful restaurant in the old town.'

He was asking her out. Rose looked at him. He was forty if he was a day and probably married.

'I'm afraid I'm meeting my boyfriend in a few minutes for lunch and then later we will be having dinner, too.' There. She'd said it. She'd called Vernon her 'boyfriend'.

Willy fell against the wall as if an arrow had pierced his heart.

'A boyfriend!' he said. 'A German man?'

'English. He's working at the university.'

'An English intellectual. I did not think that English intellectuals like girls.'

Rose wasn't sure how to react, so she smiled as nicely as she could and said, 'Well, I'll perhaps see you tomorrow, then.'

She skipped backwards out of the door and onto the street.

Vernon was waiting for her at the hotel. She wondered whether she should tell him that a German man had asked her out for dinner to see if it would make him upset or angry but didn't in case he wasn't.

At 8 Foxton Row, the morning post brought a letter from Alan.

c/o The Chaundler Fund, Princess Street, Manchester

Monday, 1st December 1930

My dear cousin Arthur,

Something has happened and I need to get it off my chest, and you are the only person I can think of who will be able to consider the matter from an objective and impartial standpoint.

Norah and I have grown accustomed – if that is the right word – to seeing the results of poverty. We have seen malnutrition and starvation and the cold and filth in which people are expected to live, and I suppose that in Fetterick in Scotland, when the ghost people – particularly those who seemed to have lost their senses through want – when they first came out of their houses to find what warmth and food we had to offer, we thought we had seen the worst it could get.

In Derby, the morning after the dance, as we were packing up the Eccles to leave, two gentlemen, one a Baptist Minister, another from the Public Assistance Committee, asked us to come with them on a visit of mercy and bring the Morris.

They directed us to a yard next to the windowless back wall of a factory where there was a cluster of derelict buildings. At one time they might have been engine sheds or some such, but they clearly had not been used for a long time. The bricks were sooty black and eroded, the mortar falling out, and the wood so rotted you could put a finger straight through it as if it had been wet paper.

We left the car and they took us into one of the buildings, lighting the darkness with a lantern the man from the Public Assistance Committee had brought. There was mud underfoot, or at least we hoped it was mud, but the smell suggested otherwise. They came to a rickety staircase and warned us to ascend carefully, one at a time, because the treads were as rotten as everything else. The stairs led up to what may once have been a set of rooms where people might have lived or had offices.

The man from the PAC opened a door and held up his lantern to reveal a woman, wrapped in sacks, looking up in terror, as if we had come to butcher her. She was holding a baby beneath the sacks and two other children, tiny infants almost indistinguishable from the sacks, clung to her. They buried their faces in the woman and one of them began to whimper. A fourth child lay to one side, motionless and blue.

Norah hurried to examine the fourth child and, having done so, turned with an awful face that told us she had found no pulse or breath.

There was no furniture, heat or light in the room, although there were a few scraps of food, an empty milk bottle and more sacking. It was very, very cold. The stench was almost unendurable.

The minister tried to calm the woman, to tell her that we had come to help and meant her no harm. He said that we would take her to the Public Assistance Institution – which is apparently what they call the workhouse these days – where she and the children would be fed and clothed and bathed and given medical attention. This made the woman more afraid still and she shrank back.

The PAC man explained quietly, although it did not need to be explained, that the woman could be compelled to go with us but seemed so frail and so fierce that he feared a struggle might cause a fit or some such. He had seen it before.

Norah approached, sat down next to the woman and began to sing a song so quiet you could only just hear it. It did not seem to have words, or rather the words could have been in some ancient foreign language with lots of lul-lul-lul sounds at the back of the throat. I have heard her sing to babies like that before. When I sing to babies, I usually try to match my loudness to that of their crying. Sometimes it can shock the infant into a stunned silence, which can turn to smiles when you start making faces at them. Norah's method works better, though.

The woman seemed confused by the singing and tried to pull away, but the two bigger children showed their faces, and their interest seemed to calm the woman, too.

Norah looked up at us, smiling, and said we should leave for a while, but please could we leave the light with her. The calm authority with which she spoke left us in no doubt that she knew what she was doing.

Outside we sat very still in pitch-darkness apart from the little crack of light that came under the door from the lantern.

I asked, in a whisper, who the woman was, and the man from the Public Assistance Committee said he did not know. Her existence had been discovered by a soldier, on leave, drunk and lost, who had blundered in. The soldier had told his mother, the mother had told the minister and the minister had told him. And he and the minister had been there earlier in the day but had only succeeded in terrifying the woman and the children to the extent that they feared she would do herself or the children harm. Possibly she was deaf and dumb.

'So why did you think we would be able to help?' I asked. And the minister told us that his daughter had been at the dance the previous night and there was a girl outside with some sort of disfiguring skin disease, too terrified to come in but saying she was happy to sit there and listen to the music. Norah somehow got to know she was there – I knew nothing of this but did remember seeing the girl later in the evening – so she went outside and sat on the step with her and after a long time, persuaded her to come in. And the minister thought that Norah would be able to help here, too.

And besides that, neither of them had a car and we did.

Norah had stopped singing and was speaking now. You could not hear the words but there was the same lilt to the voice. There is always something about a Welsh accent that is close to singing, a lot closer than the harshness of the Lancashire voice, anyway.

After a long while, Norah came out grimly carrying the baby that the woman had been cradling. One look was enough to see that this child, too, was dead. The woman, leading the two older children came close behind.

The minister went back inside and picked up the

corpse of the other dead child and we carefully trod back down the rotten stairs.

We did not know what to do with the dead. Norah spoke quietly to the woman again and then took the baby to a sort of outhouse near where we had left the car, where there was more sacking and some rotten straw. She said we should lay the dead in there and the minister should stay with them, then we should stop at the police house – the PAC man knew where it was – and ask him to arrange for the collection of the bodies.

We left the lantern with the minister and put the woman and the children in the back of the car, them and Norah in the back, the PAC man and me in the front. As we drove away, I noticed that the scene – the minister, sitting among the straw with the two dead children, lit by the lantern – bore a grim resemblance to a nativity. Nobody spoke as we got them in the car. Mostly, because we were trying not to breathe the smell was that bad, and I did not want to open the window of the Morris for fear that the icy blast would cause harm. Afterwards, worried about nits, we spent several hours working on our hair with a comb dipped in petrol. It is usually effective, only you have to be careful not to do it by candlelight.

The workhouse was a little way out on the Uttoxeter Road. I drove slowly, uncertain whether the woman or the children had ever been in a motor before and afraid that a jarring pothole might make them afraid. Nobody made a sound until we had delivered them into the hands of the workhouse people. They seemed kind. The Public Assistance man told us he would stay behind to complete the necessary arrangements and would make his own way back, so Norah and I drove away.

Again, neither of us spoke for a long time. Then Norah started crying and shaking and I pulled over to the side of the road to do a bit of crying – I am not ashamed of this – of my own.

A few days later we received a letter from the Public Assistance man saying they had learnt that the woman had been living in a comparatively decent couple of rooms nearby with a husband in work at the factory, but the husband had been laid off and had hanged himself.

The woman could not pay the rent so was evicted and found shelter in the engine sheds.

Fred and Louisa Gosling, the two Chaundler Fund volunteers we got to know in Derby, have a lot to do with making sure people know how to claim their unemployment allowance and so on, so we asked them, how, in a civilised country, children can be allowed to die in such circumstances. They told us that it can happen in any number of ways. Most people have a natural disinclination to accept charity, and even when the 'charity' is actually government or insurance money, the officials responsible for doling it out still behave as if it is undeserved and grudgingly given. When a man goes on the dole, the first luxury he must learn to give up is his self-respect. Some men and women simply will not do it.

And in this case, the woman could probably have claimed some sort of widow's benefit. But, can you imagine having to answer the question, 'How did your husband die?' with 'He hanged himself'. And since self-slaughter is against the law, she might even have thought she might somehow be blamed and be taken off to prison.

It is a puzzle. I have done what I can to alert the Chaundler Fund people to the problems of widows, and they say they know where the problems lie. They agree with me that the solution would be a network of advisers, independent of church and state, who would have access to funds if they were urgently needed, but more importantly, be able to guide widows and orphans over the many hurdles, emotional as well as bureaucratic, that stand in their way and which force so many of them into prostitution or – worse – the desperation of that poor woman in Derby.

But, all that aside, the thing that is burnt in my mind is that, on the wall of that terrible room where we found the woman and the dead babies were written the words – the letters were faded, but quite legible

– 'CHRIST IS THE HEAD OF THIS HOUSE, THE GUEST AT EVERY MEAL, THE SILENT LISTENER TO EVERY CONVERSATION'.

Did Christ listen to the pleas of the poor woman, to the whimpering of her starving children, to the last breaths of her dying babies?

I have never entertained doubt. But I no longer know what to think.

You, dear cousin, have never had faith in God and live your life as an agnostic, or an atheist even. All these years, my faith has been my rock and my foundation. But to cling to it simply out of habit, for the comfort it affords, would be the action of a hypocrite and liar.

I do not know what to do. I cannot talk about these matters even to Norah. I am ashamed and frightened.

Please help me.

Alan had signed the letter in his usual way, 'I am ever yours faithfully in the joy of Jesus', but then crossed it out and replaced it with a simple, 'I wish you all the best, Alan.'

Edgar came in as Skelton was finishing the letter.

'Letter from your cousin?' he asked. 'How is he?'

'He's not very well. He's losing his faith.'

'In Jesus? Well, there's a turn up.'

'I think I am a bit, too.'

'I didn't think …'

'Not in Jesus. I think I'm losing my faith in everything.

In the stuff we do. In knickerbockers and lavatories and "The Man Who Refuses to Lose" and … everything.'

'I thought you thought the knickerbockers and lavatories were fun.'

'Compared with Anglo-American Abrasives cleaning out your toe-jam's fun. And anyway, as I told Glazier, it's not supposed to be fun. Did you see McCardie's rant in the paper?'

Edgar nodded. Mr Justice McCardie, delivering the annual Maudsley lecture to the British Medical Association had said that perjury had become a matter of course in criminal and civil trials. The solemn oath to tell the truth was routinely disregarded and, though lying in court was undoubtedly a grave offence, there were few prosecutions. 'I think perjury in the law courts,' he'd said, 'is in some degree encouraged and increased by the low standard of frankness and honesty so widely and unhappily shown in our party-political system.'

Skelton mooched over to the window. At the end of Foxton Row, he saw a man walking along hand in hand with an ape of some sort, then realised it wasn't an ape at all but a particularly unprepossessing child.

'The thing is,' he said. 'People – and I mean me as much as anybody else – just treat the courts as a game. A joke. So, you think "I might just as well have a laugh". But the fun stuff. The daft stuff. It's not what I should be doing, is it?'

There was an unfamiliar tone of desperation in Skelton's voice. Edgar spoke quietly. 'Of course, it isn't. You're Honest Arthur from Leeds.'

Skelton turned. Was Edgar making fun of him? 'Well, don't you get fed up of it all?'

'Not in the same way, no. But then I was never Honest Edgar from Stepney.'

'What do you mean?'

'I've never drawn an honest breath in my life, have I? I was a thief, and I've never stopped thieving.'

'I don't—'

'The way I talk, the things I talk about, the things I like, the way I dress … everything … I stole from posh people, didn't I? I go to first nights at the opera in white tie. I've no right to be there, have I? I'm Edgar from Stepney. I'm nicking an experience.'

'Strange way of looking at things.'

'Don't you ever feel a fraud?'

'Of course I do. All the time. I felt a fraud at Cambridge, and I've felt a fraud ever since.'

'Stealing something that isn't yours by right.'

'Mila would say it is my right.'

'When we all live in a Communist world, that may well be the case, but we don't. You nicked an education and I nicked a whole person with refined manners and exquisite taste in modern interior design.'

'So, what can we do about it?'

'Stop worrying. Enjoy the rich pickings of your thieving. Revel in the swag.'

'I can't. I'm Honest Arthur from Leeds.'

Thursday, 4th December 1930

Rose and Vernon had breakfast at the cafe near Universitätsplatz then wandered around the old town, looking in shops. Rose wanted to buy presents for Joan and Mrs Westing, and perhaps Mr Duncan and Mr Hobbes but all the specifically German things, pipes, tankards, toys and books could only end up as embarrassing ornaments, and most other things she saw you could buy just as easily in London. At a gallery she was tempted by some watercolours of local views, but once she had bought – at great expense – a watercolour to give to her dad when she was camping in Wales, so she knew that such things quickly lose their charm once they've spent time in a knapsack or suitcase.

She wasn't much of a shopper, and she'd never known

a boy who was any sort of shopper at all. With Vernon it was different. They pointed at things in windows and made jokes, not clever jokes or even particularly funny, just things like, pointing at a hat and saying, 'I can just see Mr Duncan wearing a thing like that.' Twice they said exactly the same thing at the same time, as if they were both thinking the exact same thoughts.

Back at the hotel there was a message waiting. Rather earlier than anticipated, Professor Forsch had finished his work on the head.

Rose and Vernon practically ran to the university.

The written report was short, but it came with a sheaf of drawings, some very plain, just outlines, full face and two profiles, others more like proper paintings.

'The line drawings are probably more accurate. The others are, of course, somewhat fanciful, being based on a certain amount of conjecture as well as measurement. There were a few strands of hair attached, which may or may not have belonged to our man, but cross-contamination is always a problem – from the murderer, the police, maybe even the pathologist. We have done our best.'

Rose looked but had no way of knowing whether the drawings were accurate. They were certainly well done inasmuch as they looked like a person, somebody you could meet in the street.

She didn't think the telegraph apparatus would be able to send the coloured drawings, and even if it could, the newspaper wouldn't be able to print them, but the line drawings, she supposed, would be fine.

'They are excellent,' she said. 'Thank you.' She reached into her satchel for the folder of German money. 'Do I have to pay you or …?'

'The payment is all arranged with the *Daily Graphic*,' the professor said.

'Good. They said they want these as soon as possible and I might be able to telegraph them from the offices of the *Heidelberger Tageblatt*.'

'You've arranged that?' the professor said.

'I went to see them yesterday morning.'

Vernon looked impressed. The professor looked concerned.

'It's only a five-minute walk from here,' Rose said.

'I know,' the professor said. There was something he wasn't saying. He handed her the hatbox. 'Here. Don't forget your head.'

They could hear music almost as soon as they left the university. There were police on Hauptsrasse, and a crowd, some of them in Brownshirt uniform, marching to the sound of a band.

Rose, who, as always, had studied her map until she knew it by heart, led Vernon off the main road up a side street. A couple of left turns brought them on to the north end of Brunnengasse. The march, meanwhile, had also turned off the main road and was now coming towards them, led by trumpets, drums and a tuba all played by Brownshirts.

They played better and were better turned out than any Boy Scout band that Rose had ever seen. Two men at the front were carrying banners displaying the same Nazi emblem, the cross with bent arms, as the men's brassards.

Vernon said something else, but Rose couldn't hear him. The marchers had started chanting.

They had stopped outside the offices of the *Heidelberger Tageblatt*, which seemed to be the focus of their discontent.

Vernon pulled Rose back the way they'd come. 'Isn't there anywhere else that could send the stuff?' he asked.

'I don't know. I don't think so. It needs special equipment. What's going on?'

'It's getting worse and worse. I think the *Tageblatt* printed something in support of Emil Gumbel, the mathematics professor who was forced to resign.'

'And the Brownshirts don't like him?'

'It was the Nazis who forced his resignation. He's a pacifist and a Jew.'

The band stopped playing and the chanting grew more insistent. Somebody threw a stone at one of the windows. Others followed.

'Should we get the police?'

'The police won't get involved. Half of them are Nazi sympathisers anyway.'

'Doesn't anybody stand up against them?'

'Only the Communists. They'll probably show up in a bit. Then it'll be outright warfare. Come on. We should get out of here.'

'But this isn't right. People—'

'Come on, Rose.'

Through the bodies, she could see the Brownshirts had invaded the building and were dragging people out. One of them wore a green suit. He fell to the ground. The Brownshirts kicked him.

'It's Willy.'

'What?'

'It's Willy Brechenmacher, the man who helped me yesterday.'

Vernon grabbed Rose and forcibly turned her. 'There's nothing we can do, Rose.'

The crowd had spread the length of the street. Somebody thrust a leaflet into Vernon's hand. He gave it a glance, crumpled it into a ball and threw it to the ground. The man looked from the paper and back at Vernon.

Smiling, the man pressed another leaflet against Vernon's chest. Vernon backed away. Behind him, two other men, one of them in uniform, were moving in.

The men formed a threatening circle around Vernon.

One of them threw a punch but, before it could connect, they were all distracted by Rose, doing a war dance, chanting the Guide Promise in a voice loud enough to be heard a mile away and, most effectively, waving the charred head. One of the assailants moved towards her and, quite inadvertently, Rose's flailing fists caught the side of his head, near the eye. Furious he grabbed her arm and shouted at her.

A moment later, as if Rose had summoned it, a typewriter,

thrown from one of the windows, landed at their feet with a terrific crash, scattering the tormentors.

Rose saw her opportunity, shouted to Vernon and, still swinging the head, ran. Vernon was close behind. The tormentors came after them.

Rose ran west, with the vague idea of getting back to the safety of her hotel, but by now, too many roads were blocked by people, cars, horses and trams, so she turned south and ran for a while and then saw an alleyway where they could perhaps hide while the Brownshirts ran past. It was a dead end. A fence divided the alley from a mess of railway lines and points. Rose gave the fence a shake. Chain link, perhaps seven feet high. Solidly built. She and Vernon exchanged a nod. Rose carefully placed the head, only a little worse for wear, back into the hatbox, passed it to Vernon, and began to climb. At the top she did the sort of vault you'd do over a five-bar gate and dropped to her feet at the other side. Vernon climbed to a point where he could throw over the hatbox and Rose's satchel then followed.

They found a concrete coal bunker, nearly empty, open where it faced the line, and cowered together, listening to the sounds of their pursuers shouting to each other.

After a while, the sounds died down.

Rose could feel Vernon's breath on her cheek.

'That was …' Vernon said.

'Exhilarating.'

'Actually, I was going to say "terrifying".'

Rose smiled.

Vernon smiled back. 'Do you think they've gone now?'

'Best stay here a couple more minutes, be on the safe side.'

It was very cold.

A train approached and passed, thunderously close.

When it had gone, Vernon emerged from the bunker and looked up and down the line. His clothes were already filthy with coal dust.

He returned to the bunker and seemed about to say something, then didn't, walked away, and back again.

'I know this is a daft thing to talk about now, but it's not unlikely that we're both going to be either beaten to death by Brownshirts or run over by a train quite soon, so I'd better say it.' He was talking very fast. 'Only I don't know what you think of me, really. I've never met anybody like you. And, the thing is, the first time I met you, I thought you were very nice and since then my … admiration has grown.' He was looking at the sky now, as if casually wondering whether it was going to rain. 'Because you're clever and funny and you speak like an ordinary intelligent person, which makes a refreshing change from Clarissa.'

'Who's Clarissa?' Rose said.

Another train was approaching. Vernon ducked back into the bunker. The driver saw him and shouted something from the footplate.

'We should move soon,' Vernon said, but didn't. On the other side of the fence they heard more running footsteps and shouts.

'The thing is, when I got the chance to come over here to study, I didn't have to think about it very hard – it was a wonderful opportunity and, after all, there was nothing to keep me in London.'

'Not even Clarissa?' Rose immediately felt awful for saying that, worse because an unfamiliar spikiness had infected her voice.

'I'm not doing this very well, am I?'

'To be perfectly honest, I'm not sure what it is you're doing.'

Vernon stood up took a look through the fence. Everything seemed to be quiet. He knelt down in front of Rose. Another train went past, so some time went by before he could speak.

'The thing is, I've given the matter a lot of thought and … I'm not sure I want you to be my girlfriend and I'm not sure I want to be your boyfriend.'

'Oh,' Rose said.

'No, I mean. Because … boyfriend, girlfriend feels silly and it's only a stage on the way to something else, so I was thinking perhaps we could go straight on to the something else.'

'Oh.'

Vernon cleared his throat and ducked back into the coal bunker. 'The thing is, if you were to live to be a hundred, I would want to live to a hundred minus one day so I wouldn't ever have to live without you.'

'That's Winnie the Pooh, isn't it?'

'Sort of. I thought it might be …'

'Well – it isn't. And anyway, you're nearly two years older than me, so if you died a day before your hundredth birthday, I would have to be a widow for over a year.'

'Is that a "yes"?'

'I didn't know you'd asked a question.'

'Well, I have.'

'Right,' Rose was trying hard to remain sensible. In these situations, she knew, people get overexcited and say silly things.

'You do know it's polite to give an answer either way,' Vernon said. 'Quite quickly. Put a chap out of his misery.'

'Are you sure it's not just the excitement?'

'I'm sure.'

She didn't want to be sensible any more.

'Then, yes it would be very nice to marry you, Vernon, and thank you very much for asking and now I think we should do some kissing, if that's all right.'

They kissed.

Another train went by.

Over Vernon's shoulder, Rose caught sight of the hatbox and imagined the head inside watching them. She thought of Alma Dent, Girl Reporter.

'Missing a deadline is probably the worst thing a journalist can do,' she said.

'Good thing you're not a journalist, then.'

They kissed again.

'Is that the station down there?'

Vernon looked. A little further down the line there were lights and shadows. 'Probably.'

Rose stood. 'Come on,' she said.

'Where are we going?'

'I've had an idea.'

Friday, 5th December 1930

It was just after midnight. Rose and Vernon had been parked near a radiator at the offices of the *Daily Graphic*, in the hope that the hot pipes, together with cocoa and sandwiches might coax some warmth back into their aching, shaking bones. Their clothes were smeared with coal dust, they smelt of sick and were stone deaf.

They had had an adventure.

At Heidelberg Station, Rose had checked the timetables and discovered there was a through train to Frankfurt in twelve minutes.

'Why are we going to Frankfurt?' Vernon asked, as they joined the queue at the ticket office.

'Airmail. There's only one service on a Thursday from

Heidelberg that leaves from Mannheim airport at eleven in the morning and there's no service on a Friday. But then I remembered, when I was looking into it, the one from Frankfurt airport leaves at six o'clock in the afternoon. The train gets in at five twenty-two.'

'And how far is it from the station to the airport?'

'I don't know. Perhaps you could ask the man in the ticket office if he knows.'

Vernon's German was rudimentary, but he managed, '*Wo ist der Flughafen in Frankfurt?*', then, while the queue behind him grew increasingly impatient, had to get the ticket seller to repeat his answer several times, more slowly and using simpler words.

'He kept saying Beckenheim.'

'What does that mean?'

'I don't know. And it's either ten or fifteen minutes or half an hour or longer with a bus.'

'We'll ask a taxi driver when we get there.'

In the Alma Dent story, Alma had had a dramatic race against time to get her 'copy' in before the paper was 'put to bed'. Some of this was on horseback while she was being pursued by members of the criminal gang she was in the process of unmasking and who were shooting at her from a fast car. Luckily for Alma, even the fastest car cannot jump fences. Then she had had an altercation with an interfering but well-meaning fellow reporter, male, who had a crush on her and who didn't want her to file her copy because he knew the criminal gang would seek revenge, hunt her down to the ends of the earth and murder her horribly. Alma had had to deal with him, albeit reluctantly, with a single right hook to the jaw – for her dad, who always wanted a son, had insisted she take boxing lessons.

In comparison, Rose and Vernon's race to meet the deadline had been humdrum. The train had arrived in Frankfurt station a couple of minutes early. There was no queue at the taxi rank and, despite their clothes still being covered in coal dust, the taxi driver agreed to take them. He knew the aerodrome well and the roads were clear all the way. The driver took them right to the door of the *Luftpost* office. Even at this late hour, the *Luftpost* agent was happy to make sure that their envelope was included in the mailbags, on receipt, of course, of two Reichsmarks for the stamp. He assured them that, winds and weather being favourable, the plane would land at Croydon aerodrome shortly after ten o'clock.

Rose then wanted to know whether it would be all right if she arranged for a courier to be sent from the *Daily Graphic* to pick up the letter from Croydon. This proved something of a challenge to Vernon's German, the agent's English and Rose's phrase book, but eventually it was established that a single letter could not be removed from the bag and, though a special messenger service was sometimes available, it could not be obtained at such short notice, and certainly not on this particular flight. The envelope, once it reached Croydon, would be sent onward to its ultimate destination by ordinary post.

Rose, it seemed, had lost. '*What*,' she wondered, '*would Alma Dent do?*' Alma, she was fairly sure, would run out on to the runway, steal an aeroplane and fly it herself, possibly even low enough down Fleet Street to throw the envelope through a window to her grateful editor. She would have been taught to fly by her father, an ex-RFC man who had always wanted a boy. Rose's father had been a Birmingham solicitor who was perfectly happy she was a girl and had never been up in an aeroplane or, indeed, higher than the Lickey Hills.

The agent was saying something. Vernon listened carefully and translated. 'I think he's saying that it is possible for us to accompany the letter and take it ourselves from Croydon to the *Daily Graphic*.'

'What, you mean, go on the aeroplane? As passengers?'

Vernon and the agent spoke German. 'He says there is room for four passengers. Two of the seats are already taken, but the other two are free and they cost two hundred Reichsmarks – more than ten pounds. That's a ridiculous amount of money.'

Rose was already burrowing in her satchel and counting out banknotes.

'It's *Daily Graphic* money,' she said. 'Is that two hundred each?'

'I can't come,' Vernon said.

'You must come.'

'I've got nothing to do with the *Graphic*.'

'Without you none of this could have happened.'

Rose piled the money onto the counter and the man issued her with tickets.

Vernon always carried his passport as required by law, and checked to make sure it was there, nestling in his inside pocket. 'You've left all your things at the hotel,' he said.

'I can have them sent on,' Rose said. 'People do that, don't they? I've read it in books.'

'Or … I'll have to come back on Monday, anyway. I'll have to send wires to Ben and Matt to cover for me over the weekend, but I'm sure when I tell them I've got engaged they'll understand.'

It was the first time either had used the word 'engaged' and it made them smile. It was, as Vernon had so ineptly explained, much more grown-up than 'boyfriend' or 'girlfriend'.

'*Du musst dich beeilen*,' the agent said.

They ran out to the aeroplane, the pilot showed them where to sit and issued them with enamelled bedpans to be sick into.

Their fellow passengers were two businessmen, one English and one German. Both were dressed for extreme cold in thick, fur-lined, coats. The Englishman also had a deerstalker with the earflaps down.

Rose just had her ginger coat and woolly hat. Vernon a thin overcoat and battered black trilby.

'First time?' the Englishman asked.

Rose and Vernon said it was.

'It's horrible. The noise is deafening, you'll freeze to death, get chucked about all at sixes and sevens and your stomach'll swap places with your tongue.'

They returned his grim smile.

'They didn't ask for our passports,' Rose said.

'No,' the Englishman said. 'I don't think they count us as human beings. Just parcels wrapped in skin.'

She clutched the parcel wrapped in skin that was to be her husband.

Then the noise began.

They had crawled into a taxi at Croydon and, still deafened by the plane's engine, huddled together for warmth.

In Fleet Street they had half fallen into the *Daily Graphic* building. A commissionaire approached, saying, 'You've no business in here, clear off the pair of you,' at which Rose, with difficulty, stretched to her full height and announced, as loudly as she could and in her poshest voice 'My name is Rose Critchlow, I have flown here on the mail plane from Frankfurt in Germany. Please inform the powers that be, the duty officer, the night editor and anyone else who might be interested that I have the report from Professor Forsch which reveals the identity of the Mystery Blazing Corpse.'

The man at the reception desk was already on the telephone, jabbering excitedly. Within seconds people filled the entrance hall. One examined the drawings and handed them over to some other people who ran off with them to do who knows what. Somebody else, having had a brief conversation with a very senior-looking gent who smoked a cigar, picked up a telephone and shouted into it what Rose later learnt are generally regarded as the most exciting words in journalism.

'Stop the presses! We're making up a whole new front page.'

A lady arrived and scribbled in a notebook while a man with a hat but no jacket, cigarette dangling, dictated the new front page. Another lady ushered Rose and Vernon into an office, sat them, luxuriously, by the radiator, brought them coffee and offered them whisky, which they refused. Gradually the awful roar, the throb and the clatter of that terrible aeroplane abated, and they could hear as well as see the people around them, all of whom seemed to be screaming at each other and into telephones.

'Should we tell them we just got engaged?' Vernon asked.

'God, no,' Rose said. 'They might put it on the front page.'

Vernon nodded. 'I haven't told my mum and dad, yet.' He looked up at Rose as if he'd just said something terrible. 'Sorry,' he said.

'What for?'

'You haven't got a mum and dad to tell.'

'I'll tell Mrs Westing and Mr Hobbes. Although I am a bit worried the excitement might kill them. Oh, lord.'

'What?'

Chester Monroe was bearing down on them, looking fresh as a daisy. His suit was a shade of light brown that could best be described as orange. His shirt was blue and his tie red with white spots. He wore a white hat, with a brim slightly narrower than one was used to, on the back of his head and was snapping a Lucky Strike cigarette out of its soft packet.

'Hello there, Miss Rose,' he said. 'And you must be Mr Vernon Goodyear. I believe you two have got quite something of a story to tell me.'

He fired questions at them about Professor Forsch and their flight from Frankfurt. They answered politely, volunteering as little information as possible.

'Now, a little bird told me that you two are … well, let's say a bit closer than casual colleagues?'

Rose and Vernon's faces turned to stone. Who was the little bird? Who could possibly know, or even guess? Was he just fishing?

'No,' Vernon said. And Rose, only slightly worried that he meant it, echoed, 'No.'

Chester looked from one to the other as if inviting them to say more.

'Well, if that's the way you want to play it …' he said.

The faces remained stone. Chester gave up that line of enquiry and instead said, 'Now, tell me about the riots in Heidelberg. Who was doing the rioting and what were they rioting about?'

And thus, Chester ended up with not one but two scoops for the *Daily Graphic*.

The headline, BLAZING CORPSE – MYSTERY REVEALED, together with one of Professor Forsch's pictures, filled the front page of Friday morning's *Graphic* – the London edition, anyway. The early northern and Scottish editions had to make do with the original front page, which was mostly about Mr Winston Churchill's demands that Gandhi and the other 'extremists of the Indian independence movement' had to be 'crushed'.

Inside was the full – and mostly inaccurate story – of how Skelton, 'The Man Who Refuses To Lose', determined to find the true identity of the burning corpse, had approached the *Daily Graphic* with the scheme of sending the head of the corpse to Germany, where, he had heard, an egghead scientist by the name of Forsch had worked out his elaborate and very precise scheme for recreating an identity from a skull. Though, to many, the scheme seemed madcap, the *Graphic* thought it was worth investigating so put up funds 'in excess of £2,000' to finance the enterprise. Skelton, man of the hour, had arranged for his assistant and 'envoyette', Rose Critchlow, to carry the skull to the Prof. and liaise with the Prof.'s genius British collaborator, Vernon Goodyear, who supervised the work. It also told of how, to get the results of the Prof.'s investigation back to the *Graphic,* the 'envoyette' and the collaborator had chartered an aeroplane and flown through the night – a terrifying journey through wind, rain, thunder and lightning (full story on page 4). The piece was liberally illustrated with pictures of Rose and Vernon, both still covered in coal dust, and of 'The Man Who Refuses to Lose', a map of Germany, and an artist's impression of an aeroplane flying through a storm.

The story made excellent copy, there was no doubt about that. It stirred the senses and, when the figures came in, was proved to have added 12.7 per cent to the *Graphic's* circulation.

The only disappointment was Professor Forsch's drawings. Nobody doubted their accuracy, but it was such a very ordinary face with nothing in the way of distinguishing features. Some people said it looked like Stanley Baldwin, the former prime minister, others that it was the spit and image of Captain Scott, the explorer. Most people had an uncle who looked just like that.

The calls started coming in not long after the paper had arrived at the newsagents.

'He's a chap I used to see in the Nag's Head in Walthamstow. I was wondering what had happened to him.'

'He's Mr Williams, who said he was going to live in Swindon, but nobody's heard from him since.'

'He's a chap used to work at Taylor's the chemist in Peckham. Ran off with £12. 17s. 4d. out of the till and was never seen again.'

By mid-afternoon, the *Graphic* had designated six members of staff to deal with the calls and, with help from the police, sort out the possibles from the duds. The deluge came with the post on Saturday morning. Six bags all from people who were absolutely certain they had the right bloke.

'All sewn up, then?' Aubrey said. He was balanced between his heels – legs stretched out halfway across the room – and a quarter of an inch of buttock, which was just in contact with Skelton's desk.

'From my point of view, yes, it is,' Skelton said.

'I heard a rumour that the *Graphic* was paying you two thousand quid.'

'That was for finding the identity of the corpse. All we have at the moment is Professor Forsch's sketches, which I had nothing to do with. In the unlikely event that the *Graphic* agrees to pay up, I'd have thought Rose should get a sizeable chunk of that cash and Vernon could probably make good use of another sizeable chunk. I'll be happy with my fifteen guineas.'

'Fifteen guineas?'

'One of those Poor Person's Defence thingummies,' Edgar said.

'Oh, those. Three weeks' work for the price of a pair of socks.'

'Where the bloody hell are you buying your socks?' Skelton said.

Aubrey bounced acrobatically off his buttocks and heels and stood without a single teeter. 'I thought we should have a word about the Beck business.'

'Ah, yes.'

'I've arranged a meeting with Edward first thing on Monday morning.' Edward was Sir Edward Atkinson, the Director of Public Prosecutions. 'I thought we'd better show him the photographs. See what he makes of it all.'

'Are you sure that's the right way to proceed?' Edgar asked.

'Well, we have no credible defence and it would seem a little unfair if Beck was to spend the rest of his life in prison for killing Mrs Roberts with his machines when we know for a fact that she never went near the machines. But the only way we can prove that is to produce the photographs.'

'All the same,' Edgar said.

'You don't think we might be overestimating the danger presented by Mr Lazell, do you?' Aubrey said.

'No. If Lord Rosthwaite is willing to pay a thousand pounds in hush money, Norris Lazell is prepared to slit throats.'

'I'd have thought if throats were going to be slit, they'd most likely have been slit already,' Aubrey said. 'Rosthwaite, after all, offered his bribe as soon as he knew Beck was being investigated. Anybody involved would know it would only be a matter of time before we found out about the Special Treatments.'

From the rack on his desk, Skelton selected a pipe – a billiard with cherrywood bowl and ceramic stem that he hadn't used for a while. He took it apart, ready for cleaning.

'Did you read about Phil Kirkpatrick?' Edgar said.

'Was he the chap they found nailed to the timbers in the West India Docks?'

'Wife and kids had their throats slit as well.'

Skelton looked up from his pipe. 'Wife and kids?'

'Phil Kirkpatrick had stolen half the loot from some job, hadn't he?' Aubrey said. 'It was a matter of pride'

'Whereas people seeing Lazell dressed up as a baby with

a dummy in his mouth wouldn't damage his pride at all? Is that what you're saying?' Edgar said.

Skelton heard a crack and looked down, surprised to discover he'd snapped the pipe stem in two. 'I didn't know about the wife and kids,' he said.

Saturday, 6th December 1930

Lawrence had found a new way of torturing his family. The grammar school's junior choir had recruited him as a second treble. This meant that, for the Christmas concert, he had to master the harmony parts of a selection of well-loved Christmas carols. There was nothing wrong with his voice. If he'd been singing the actual tunes it might even have been pleasant. But harmony parts out of context just sound wrong. Worst were those that started off with the right tunes but then veered off in an entirely different direction. 'It Came Upon a Midnight Clear', for instance, stayed with the tune for the whole of the first verse, lulling you into a false sense of security, before flying off at a distressing tangent with ups and downs that made no sense at all.

'I wonder, whether you might like to do that in the front room,' Skelton said as he scraped a bit of abandoned marmalade off the cloth and ate it from his knife.

Lawrence skulked into the front room and, instead of singing, practised scales on the piano as loudly as he could.

'Oh,' Elizabeth said, '*he's* a *very* merry old soul.'

It was her response to everything these days and usually got a laugh from her dad. But not today.

'Are you all right?' Mila asked.

'Yes. Fine. I've just got rather a lot on my mind. Work things.'

On his walk, Skelton reduced the problem to two essential questions. First, should he tell them that at any moment Norris Lazell's henchmen might turn up and kill them: and second, if he did tell them, how should he go about it?

There was a lot to consider. 'Oh, by the way, some bruisers might come to the house and kill you all,' would be sure to spread panic and dismay. Worse, it would send Mila to the gun shop in Reading to acquire whatever she deemed necessary for the defence of hearth and home. She'd buy at least one gun. More likely, she'd buy four and try to teach the children and Mrs Bartram how to use them, with inevitably fatal consequences.

On the other hand, not telling them would leave them totally unprepared. They'd be sitting ducks.

Solemnly, he mooched back home.

An unfamiliar car, a Riley, was parked on the green outside his house and two men, big men in dark hats and overcoats were standing in the front garden.

This was it, then.

Skelton kept his distance. A shot, he reckoned, would alert the neighbours. They'd spot the car and the police would give chase. No, it would be the eight-inch hunting knife or maybe a stiletto. Probably the smaller of the two men had a selection of weapons in the briefcase he was carrying.

He held his ground near the front gate.

'Hello, can I help you?'

The men turned and said something, but the words were carried away by the wind. They seemed friendly enough, but that, of course, is exactly what they'd want him to think.

Skelton looked at his wristwatch. At any moment, Mila would arrive home from her archery class carrying her bow and arrow. At fifty yards, even with the wind, she'd have a reasonable chance of a kill. At twenty-five yards it'd be a dead cert. The only problem was finding some way he could alert her that these men presented a threat and needed killing.

The men approached, smiling. Skelton backed off. Perhaps he could take cover behind the car and call for help from the neighbours, although he was at a loss to know what Mr and Mrs Meadows could do. They were both in their seventies and Mr Meadows was a martyr to rheumatism. They weren't even on the telephone.

'We've come about the sewers.'

They'd come about the sewers. This made a sort of sense. A year or so before, a lot of new houses had been built in the valley behind Skelton's house. They were all connected to the

339

main sewer. There had been a promise at the time that the rest of the village, which made do with often defective tank arrangements and soakaways, would also be connected.

Competent bruisers would do their research. They'd know how to gain your trust in order to get close enough to slice the jugular.

On the other hand, if they really had come about the sewers they must not, under any circumstances, be discouraged or turned away.

Few people in history have been called upon to weigh the risk of being stabbed against the chance of effective plumbing. Skelton came down uneasily on the side of the plumbing.

'You'd better come in, then.'

With astute doorstep choreography, he managed to get his key in the door and open it without ever turning his back on the sewer men/bruisers.

There was a cricket bat in the hallstand. If needed, he could use it as a weapon. Skelton pulled it out and said, 'Oh, there it is. Been meaning to oil it up before the season. Go through.'

'It's your back garden we'd really like to see,' the smaller of the two bruisers said. He wore glasses. Killers can have optical troubles the same as anybody else. 'That's where the line would be running.'

Mr Nailham, the gardener, was in the kitchen, finishing off a plate of lamb chops with spuds, cauliflower and gravy. He looked up and nodded when Skelton entered.

'Brought over a couple of cotoneasters need heeling in before the bad frosts come,' he said.

'Cotoneasters' and 'heeling in' were as much a mystery to Skelton as 'Syrie Maugham' and 'Czech cubism' but he had learnt early on not to question anything that Mr Nailham said or did. It only led to upset.

'These two gentlemen have come about the sewers,' Skelton said. 'They'd like to have a look at the back garden. I wonder if you could show them around?' He turned to the killers and explained, 'Mr Nailham knows far more about the garden than I do.'

The gardener finished his last spud and, still chewing, led the killers out.

'His wife's sister in Hungerford has been taken poorly,' Mrs Bartram explained, when he'd gone, 'so his wife's been up there all week. I asked him, "Who's cooking your dinner, then?" and he said he'd been having jam sandwiches. Well, I couldn't let him starve, could I?'

'No. Of course not. Are those the lamb chops we were going to have for dinner tonight?'

'Yes, they are. But I was planning to do something with a tin of corned beef instead.'

From the window he could see Mr Nailham talking to the two gents. They were pointing at flower beds and shrubs but, as far as he could see, nobody was being stabbed. The man with the glasses took a notebook from his briefcase and began to write things. The cover of the book bore the arms of Royal Berkshire County Council.

'Why have you got the cricket bat out?' Mrs Bartram said.

'Oh, I was going to oil it,' Skelton said. 'I'll go to the butcher's, shall I? See if Neville's got some more lamb chops.'

He went back to the hall, returned the cricket bat to the stand, put on his hat, and checked to make sure he had his keys. He could have sworn he'd put them in his trouser pocket when he let the men in, but they weren't there. Once or twice, he'd left them in the front door, but they weren't there either.

'Did I leave my keys in here?' he said, rummaging through the cooking debris on the kitchen table.

'Did you leave them on the hallstand?' Mrs Bartram asked.

'No. And I looked to see if they'd fallen down the back.'

'Or in the door?'

'No. I looked there, too.'

'Have you been through all your pockets?'

Skelton began to pile the table with pencils, handkerchiefs, wallet, baccy, pipe and accessories, used train tickets, more baccy, string, loose change, vital reminders and – puzzling until he remembered – the comfrey leaves.

There was a hole in the overcoat pocket. The keys had slipped through the hole and were lodged in the lining. He wrestled for a while with the skirts of his overcoat.

Mr Nailham came back in, watched the wrestling then spotted the comfrey leaves. Tentatively, he picked them up and sniffed them.

'What you doing with these?'

'Comfrey leaves. Somebody's maid gave them to me. Said if I brewed them into a tea it would be good for my hip. Comfrey's supposed to work wonders for bones.'

'Them's not comfrey.'

'Really? The maid seemed to think ...'

'Where she get 'em?'

'She said a lad picked them on some wasteland somewhere.'

'Well, you should tell her to find a lad who can tell the difference between *symphytum officinale* and *digitalis purpurea*. Comfrey ain't got the spiky bits there on the leaves.'

'Hasn't it?'

'You make tea with that you'll know about it.'

'What d'you mean?' Skelton asked.

'You'll be poorly.'

'Really?'

'Foxglove, isn't it? It's poison. Make you sick, give you the runs, make your heart go ten to the dozen.'

'Really?'

Skelton went into the front room and found *The Home Doctor*. It told him that foxgloves were poisonous and that the chemical derived from them, digitalis, could, in very small doses be used to revive a heart patient, but in larger doses could kill.

Monday, 8th December 1930

The *Graphic*'s headline read, BLAZING CORPSE REVEALED. The letter and telephone call sorters, it seemed, had by Saturday night narrowed the field down to three contenders. On the Sunday, house calls made by stringers and local police had discounted two of the three.

Remaining was Walter Gale, a 32-year-old unemployed miner from a pit village near Mansfield in Nottinghamshire, married with two small children. His story could have been that of a thousand other miners. When it had become apparent that the pit might never re-open, in order to keep his family fed and decent, he had decided to travel south, take whatever work he could find, and send the proceeds home.

A farmer somewhere near Leicester said that he had taken him on in early October to lift sugar beet. Later in the month, another farmer had taken him on as a labourer to help with repairing a barn and renovating a track.

Most telling of all was a report from a commercial traveller in Biggleswade who said that Gale had approached him as he was getting into his car, wondering if he was going anywhere near Ampthill in Bedfordshire, and if so, could he have a lift. When the commercial told him he was going north, he had seen Gale approach another man with the same request.

On the Sunday afternoon, the Nottinghamshire Constabulary had sent a man out to see Gale's wife. She had not seen the *Graphic*. They showed her the pictures. She confirmed their resemblance to her husband and told them that she had not heard from him since the fifth of November. They broke the news. A kindly neighbour was summoned to look after her and make sure the children were all right.

It was not difficult to piece the whole thing together. Having taken out the £1,250 and decided somehow to fake his own death so as to escape from his various debts, paternity suits and the bigamy charge, Musgrave had, like the other commercials, been approached by poor Walter Gale, a man of similar size and build to his own. Offer him a lift, drive to a quiet spot, pretend you have engine trouble, take out a tyre iron or starter handle, deliver the fatal blow, douse everything liberally in petrol, strike a match, run for it.

What had subsequently become of Musgrave, remained a mystery. Did he walk the five or six miles through the rain back to Biggleswade and take a train south to London or north to Peterborough? Was he now being shielded by another of his 'harem', or had he fled the country?

It was the *Graphic*'s scoop. The other papers, Skelton noticed, led with news of riots in Spain that might have riveted the attention of the good people of Valencia as they munched their *desayuno* but did nothing at all for the toast-butterers of Clapham and Gateshead.

As soon as he got into Foxton Row, Skelton called Aubrey.

Aubrey cancelled his meeting with the Director of Public Prosecutions, got in touch with Evie, the maid who had given the leaves to Skelton, with Dr Edgar who had treated Mrs Roberts after the heart attack and signed the death certificate, and with the pathologist who had conducted the autopsy.

Evie agreed to make a sworn statement attesting to Mrs Roberts' intake of 'comfrey tea'. Dr Edgar acknowledged that he had tried to revive Mrs Roberts with an injection of digitalis – a standard procedure – not realising that he was, if anything, exacerbating the problem, the cure being also the cause. The pathologist confirmed that substantial amounts of digitalis had been detected in the corpse but this, they assumed, had come from Dr Edgar's injection.

'So, charges will be dropped,' Edgar said, as they sat over their morning tea.

'I can't see any reason why not, can you?'

'And Beck will walk free?'

'He will indeed.'

'What about the photographs?'

Skelton took the envelope from his desk drawer. 'What do you think?'

'Burn them?'

'You're sure?'

'What?'

'Well,' Skelton said, 'they would be rather crucial evidence if Beck were to be charged with living off immoral earnings.'

'Why would he be charged with anything of the sort?'

'Because …'

'Does the law specifically say that it's immoral to dress up as a teddy bear and be beaten by a woman in a leather mask? Or to dress up as a baby? Or put a saddle on your back and be ridden like a horse? We have no evidence that any sort of sexual congress took place between Mrs Roberts and her clients.'

Skelton stared at the ceiling for a bit, then said, 'Go on, then.'

'What?'

'Burn them.'

'Good. You've got an American-Abrasives meeting in twenty minutes.'

'Bugger.'

'Kemble's afterwards?'

'Oh, I think so.'

* * *

Kenneth, the proprietor of Kemble's, spotted Skelton getting out of the taxi and was at the door welcoming him. He took his coat, hat and scarf and even went so far as to give the shoulders of his suit a little whisk with a clothes brush. This, Skelton knew, was a service usually reserved for actors currently starring in West End shows and film stars.

'Can I just say it's absolutely marvellous what you did finding that poor man's identity,' Kenneth said.

'Well, in point of fact—' Skelton said, but Kenneth interrupted.

'And the clever way you did it, as well. I'd never have believed such things were possible. And though it must be terrible for the poor man's family, what happened to him, I suppose it's better than not knowing and forever wondering, isn't it? I'd have thought so, anyway. If somebody precious to me had just gone missing like that, I'd rather know, wouldn't you?'

Edgar hadn't arrived yet, so Kenneth showed Skelton to their usual table, pulled back a chair, noticed a slight tear in the seat cover and replaced it with another from the next table.

'I was just saying to Tony, it'd be a close-run thing to say who's the more famous these days, you or Yvonne Arnaud.'

Skelton had barely heard of Yvonne Arnaud. He studied the menu.

'You were all over the *Daily Graphic* this morning, although, if you don't mind me saying, the photos they used didn't show you off to your best. If you were to invest in some proper studio portraits it'd be money well spent, Mr Skelton. Sasha's very good. Have you seen his Reginald Denham? Did him full face but looking down so you barely notice the chin at all.'

Skelton had never heard of Sasha or Reginald Denham either, but did his best to smile and nod until Kenneth paused long enough to take his order. Egg and cress and macaroons with tea for two.

'And no brown macaroons,' Kenneth added remembering an occasion when a plate of all brown macaroons had had Edgar threatening to take his custom elsewhere.

The remaining sandwiches were curling slightly, and Skelton was on his third cup of tea by the time Edgar turned up.

In buoyant mood, he crossed the restaurant almost skipping on his toes, hailed Tony, the cloakroom attendant, as hearty as a rum-filled mariner, danced out of his coat and hat, and waltzed over to Skelton grinning so hard his face had turned red with the strain.

'You'll never guess,' he said as he sat down.

'What?'

'Rose was at Foxton Row and – you'll never guess.'

'Vernon's asked her to marry him.'

'You knew?'

'I just can't imagine anything else that would make you explode with pleasure like this.'

'I am exploding, aren't I? I'm exploding with pleasure. Isn't it wonderful? And the thing is …' He took out his hankie and gave his eyes a pre-emptive dab. 'She's asked me …' The fight to control the voice did not result in a conclusive victory. 'She's asked me to give her away.'

'That is wonderful. Congratulations, old chap. *In loco parentis,* father of the bride.'

Edgar buried his head in his hankie.

Over by the cloakroom, Skelton could see Kenneth and Tony looking their way and exchanging remarks, possibly wondering whether Edgar was still upset about the macaroons.

'Oh, God,' Edgar looked up in panic. 'I won't have to make a speech, will I?'

'It is customary for the father of the …' Seeing that this was about to set Edgar off again, Skelton amended the phrase to, 'certain members of the wedding party … to make speeches.'

'I couldn't possibly make a speech,' Edgar said. 'Can you imagine? Look at me now? I'd bluster three words, then drown everybody in a pool of tears. You'll have to make the speech. You're good at speeches. Of course, you are. It said so in *The Times.* "Master of forensic eloquence". It's what you do. You can do the speech. Promise me you'll do the speech.'

'Well, it's up to Rose and Vernon, isn't it?'

'They'll be pleased as punch. They'll be honoured. They'll jump at the chance.'

'Did he ask her when she was in Germany?' Skelton asked.

'I believe so, yes.'

'Church wedding?'

'Not decided yet. They're both staunch agnostics so I think on balance they'd prefer a register office do. But she understands that Vernon's parents might be disappointed – and to tell the truth, so would I. There is something very special about a …'

The hankie came into use again. Quick wipe of the cheeks and a blow.

'I'm very old-fashioned about these things,' he said. 'I tend to think of a register office do as a broomstick wedding.'

'That is very old fashioned. I don't think anybody's talked about "broomstick" weddings since the 1836 Marriage Act.'

On the way out they saw Chester Monroe and did their best to escape his attention but failed.

'Mr Skelton, Mr Hobbes, I've been looking for you. I came here on the off-chance and here you are. I've got something for you.'

He reached into the voluminous depths of his overcoat, pulled out an envelope embossed with the *Daily Graphic* crest and ceremoniously handed it to Skelton. A cheque, rather bigger than an ordinary cheque, made out to the sum of £2,000.

'Good lord,' Skelton said. 'I thought this was provisional on my finding the identity of the burnt man – which had almost nothing to do with me, by the way, despite what it said in your newspaper – and tracking down Musgrave, and since Musgrave has not been found …'

'Well, we've got every copper in the country tracking down Musgrave now, haven't we, Mr Skelton? He's killed again. News came in lunchtime on the wires. A Mrs Paterson in Battersea. He'd moved in with her, apparently. Same as before. Smashed the back of her skull in, then tried to burn the house down. Didn't make such a good job of the burning as he did before, though. Fire brigade say they've done easier chimney fires. Anyway, he's on the run, and the coppers say it's only a matter of time.'

Saturday, 13th December 1930

Edgar's flat was on the first floor. It was, Skelton was pleased to note, a well-kept building. The stair carpet had been recently brushed, the bannister polished and it didn't have the smell of cooking that you often find in the communal areas of even the most respectable mansion blocks.

Skelton rang the doorbell. Mila had wanted to bring flowers but Skelton, worried that even white roses might clash with Edgar's precise colour schemes, had suggested that chocolates might be a more suitable housewarming gift, so they bore a box of Charbonnel et Walker's lavender creams. Edgar's favourites.

Thirty seconds or so went by without a sound from the flat.

'You're sure he said three-thirty?' Mila asked.

'Yes, of course.' Skelton pressed the buzzer a second time and was immediately answered by Edgar's voice.

'Who is that?'

Skelton and Mila exchanged a puzzled glance. Had Edgar forgotten they were coming?

The door opened a crack and Edgar appeared, pulling wild faces and gesticulating with his head to indicate that all was not well inside.

'What is it, old chap?' Skelton asked.

Edgar opened the door a little wider to reveal that Harold Musgrave was standing behind him, holding a revolver.

'A very great pleasure to meet you, Mr Skelton,' Musgrave said. 'And Mrs Skelton, I believe. It's an honour. Do come in. Sorry about the gun but desperate times do call for desperate measures, don't they? Shall we go into the sitting room? This is your first visit, is it? Well, I'm sure you'll agree Mr Hobbes has done it up quite beautifully and very much in keeping with modern fashions in interior decoration.'

The sitting room, the only reception room, had to serve the dual functions of sitting and dining. It was desperately overfurnished. Edgar had grown too excited about more things than he had room for. The four of them had to weave their way carefully through the beige sofas and bleached oak side tables.

Though quite small, the dominant feature of the room was the Czech cubist cocktail cabinet. It was certainly arresting, anyway, and either, Skelton supposed, the height of exquisite taste or a disgusting monstrosity, depending on whether you were a keen *aficionado* of modern cocktail cabinet design.

'Perhaps you and Mrs Skelton would like to sit there.' Musgrave indicated two high-backed dining chairs. 'And if you wouldn't mind putting your hands behind the backs of the chairs. And Mr Hobbes, if I could ask you to take these …' he produced two thick Indiarubber bands from his pocket, 'and secure Mr and Mrs Skelton's hands to the chairs. Double the band over to make it tight but do be careful not to cut off the circulation.'

Edgar did as he was told.

'They're drive belts from an Auto-Vac-It 250,' Musgrave continued, 'in case you were wondering. Guaranteed for five years. It is, I agree, a horrible indignity to impose on a man of your standing, Mr Skelton, and a disgustingly unchivalrous thing to do to a lady, but it is terribly difficult to keep three people covered by a single pistol and the worry is that I might catch some sudden movement out of the corner of my eye and shoot instinctively before enquiring as to the nature and purpose of the movement. And I know you are something of a swordswoman, Mrs Skelton, and I saw you looking at that stick over there as you came in, wondering whether it could be pressed into service – what is it, by the way?'

'It's a yardstick,' Edgar said. 'The man who came to measure up for the blinds left it behind.'

Musgrave looked at the curtains and nodded. 'They are

357

somewhat out of keeping, aren't they? Lovely big windows. Roller or Venetian?'

'Well, shutters, really, but with Venetian style inserts.'

'I saw something like that once on a house near Leamington Spa,' Musgrave said. 'They looked very nice.'

Musgrave pulled out a third dining chair and placed it next to Skelton's. 'Perhaps you'd like to sit there, Mr Hobbes. I won't bind your hands, because I have things I need you to do for me in a moment.' He pulled out the fourth chair and positioned it to face the other three. 'And I'll sit here.'

He was silent, setting his thoughts in order. Then he wriggled his shoulders and leant forward.

'You see,' he said, 'before the war, I'm told I worked in a soap factory. I say, "I'm told" because I actually have very little memory of it and what memory I do have more than likely isn't really *memory* at all, just scraps I've assembled from things that people have told me. I had a mother and father. But I have no memory of them either. They died of the Spanish Flu just before Armistice Day. I probably have uncles and aunties and heaven knows who else, but I've never had a wish to find them, and I expect the lack of curiosity is reciprocated. Anyway, then I became a soldier and sometime after that, I became nobody. Because of this.'

He pointed to the lump at the side of his head. 'You've read all about that in my medical reports, haven't you? How they wrote me off for dead, but it turned out I wasn't. Well, that's a curious thing to happen to anybody, isn't it? To wake up a blank. I didn't know how to talk. Did it say that in the reports? I had to learn all over again. Then things came back, but patchy. I could remember my name, and how to read and write and count. Ask me to take away 17s. 11d. from £3. 14s. 6d. and I'd be on it like a shot – £2. 16s. 7d. Six sevens are forty-two. I suppose I must have gone to school and positively shone as a scholar. Spelling impeccable. L-I-B-R-A-R-Y. Funny how many people have trouble spelling a simple word like that. B-I-C-Y-C-L-E. A lot of people get the "I" and the "Y" the wrong way round. Hastings, 1066. Agincourt, 1415. Trafalgar, 1805. You see? All shipshape and Bristol fashion in the scholarship department. No slacking there. "Thirty days hath September …" I knew all the rhymes. "Remember, remember, the fifth of November, Gunpowder treason and plot, I see no reason why gunpowder treason, should ever be forgot." That's one that's taken on a weighty significance, hasn't it? Eh? That was supposed to be the date of my second imaginary death. Anyway, these doctors in these hospitals I was in, they seemed very keen on restoring my memory back to what it was. And I couldn't see any sense at all in that. What spirited human being could? Why would I want to remember working in a soap factory and being a soldier? How *boring* could that be, eh? How unremittingly *humdrum*. Enough to make a man ashamed. Why would I want to do a thing like that when I could have any memories I wanted? I could be anybody I wanted. So, each time I met one of these doctors in these hospitals, I'd tell them it was all coming back to me now. Before the war I was a skating policeman chasing criminals along the frozen canals of Amsterdam. "They're too fast for me," the Dutch bobbies would say. "Only one man could catch criminals that fast. Send for Musgrave." Or I was the Professor of Ancient Languages at the University of Bologna and could speak Chaldean, as well as any inhabitant of Ur. "Rishti minnie bracktoo oof simmi goot." There you are. I just said, "I hope I find you in good health."

'This confused the doctors for a while. Then it amused them. They let me go on like this for a few weeks, making up new stories until the day came when they let me go off into the outside world to seek my fortune. Electric vacuum cleaners were the coming thing, then, weren't they? After the war. And Auto-Vac-It was just starting up in Coventry, so I went to see them. Told them I'd had some success selling electric irons in Canada before the war, but then came home to do my duty. I told them I'd been a lieutenant in the Prince of Wales Dragoons. Well, for all I could remember I might well have been, and it does afford respect, doesn't it? Officer class. They had no reason to disbelieve me. Officer class is as officer class does.

'Then – this is where the story takes something of a turn – this chap approached me. I won't tell you his name. He caught me one day just as I was leaving the factory in Coventry and took me for a walk. Very commanding sort of chap, he was. Top drawer. And he told me that one of the doctors I'd been seeing had put him on to me as a chap who can spin a yarn and stick to it come what may. He asked me about how much I loved my country and my political affiliations and so on. And I told him I did love my country, but I didn't have any political affiliations and that seemed to suit him down to the ground. He told me he worked for Military Intelligence and they were looking for chaps like me to work undercover. I was chary at first, but when he reassured me about the money side of things, I agreed to sign up. Not that you sign anything. God forbid. Putting your actual name on a document would be mistake number one. Anyway, I've been involved in this secret work ever since. I can't tell you the exact nature of the work because that would be treason, but I can tell you that if it wasn't for me and my colleagues this country would now be in the hands of the Bolsheviks. But they were on to me, you see. The Russian Bolsheviks. So, I had to fake my own suicide. It was essential for the sake of national security. It was a great pity that the tramp had to die, but he was just another of the many thousands who have given their lives for their country in recent years. "At the going down of the sun and in the morning, we will remember them." You're barking up the wrong tree with Walter Gale, by the way. The man I set fire to was Sidney something. A tramp. Those pictures you got looked nothing like him. To be honest, I think that German professor might have pulled a fast one on you.

'I knew this lady called Mrs Paterson in Battersea. You might have read about her. Very nice lady. One of my favourite ladies in the world, to be honest. And I had it all arranged with her. With the £1,250 we were going to go away somewhere, start a new life. We might have done, too, except the Russian Bolsheviks were on to me in spades by this time. Then Mrs Paterson began to suspect I wasn't being absolutely straight with her about various things. Anyway, she threatened to call the police, so she had to sacrifice her life for King and Country, too. It's hard, I know, but this is essential work in which I am engaged, and I can assure you that the death of one tramp and one woman is as nothing when compared to the unendurable hardship this country would suffer under the Bolshevik yoke.'

Musgrave paused and looked slowly from Edgar, to Skelton to Mila. He smiled. 'Any questions, by the way, feel free to dive in.'

Skelton, Edgar and Mila exchanged glances; the way people do at the end of a lecture when the 'any questions' bit crops up.

Mila broke the silence. 'What exactly do you want from us?'

'That's simple. I read in the *Graphic* that you were generously rewarded for your efforts. I want the two thousand pounds the *Daily Graphic* gave you. I want your car and I want him.' He gestured with his gun towards Edgar.

'I don't see how I can get you the money,' Skelton said. 'The banks are closed and—'

'You write me a cheque.'

'But surely you realise that I could stop the cheque at—'

'That's why I want him. I'm going to … doesn't matter as long as it's civilised and remote enough so they can't come and get me. I'll just get the first boat that's sailing. And he's coming with me. Any funny business and he gets it.'

There was an astonished silence.

'Sorry,' Edgar said. 'I might have misunderstood. You want me to come with you to … where? … Rio de Janeiro or Shanghai … on a boat, a journey that could take weeks and you'll be holding me at gunpoint the whole time?'

'I might bind you and gag you and put you in a cabin trunk.'

'He gets sick in cars,' Skelton said. 'God knows what he'd be like on the high seas.'

'You couldn't leave me bound and gagged in a cabin trunk for weeks,' Edgar said.

'I'll think of something,' Musgrave said. 'I always think of something. It's my forte. Thinking on my feet, sizing up the situation, formulating a solution.'

'Why can't you ask MI5 or somebody to help you?'

'Because they would deny all knowledge of me. Of course they would. Secrecy is everything.'

'How did you find my address, anyway?' Edgar asked.

'Stroke of luck. Mrs Stewart – your housekeeper, I take it – filled in one of the forms in *Woman's Life* magazine, saying she wanted to take advantage of the two-week trial with no obligation to purchase we offer on the 250 and 260 models. Had to fill in the name and business of the head of household "Mr E. Hobbes, Barrister's Clerk". We only get three or four of those forms a week, and all the ones from the Midlands and the South-East come to me, and I was booked in for a visit. "Mr E. Hobbes, Barrister's Clerk."

Said in the paper that the "Man Who Refuses to Lose" had a clerk called Edgar Hobbes. Does Mrs Stewart do your trousers?'

Edgar looked down at the creases. Even in such trying circumstances, he found it impossible to dim the glow of pride. 'The knack is to pin them to the ironing board.'

'Is that how she manages it?'

'I think there's probably more to it than that,' Edgar said. 'Some fluid perhaps that stiffens the cloth.'

'How's she getting on with the Auto-Vac-It, by the way? It was a 260, wasn't it, with the disinfecting pad that charges the air with a germicidal fragrance. Does she like it?'

'No.'

Musgrave reeled back in his chair with a great show of horror and astonishment.

'She says it's all right on the carpets,' Edgar continued, 'but no good on the parquet.'

'She can't be using it right, then. Either that or the fools have delivered the 200 rather than the 260. Show me.'

'What?'

'Show me the vac.'

Musgrave stood and glanced over at Skelton and Mila. They'd be all right for a moment tied in their chairs. He repeated, 'Show me the vac.'

Edgar not quite able to believe that he was being forced at gunpoint to show a man the way to his broom cupboard, led the way into the hall.

When he was sure they were out of whisper range, Skelton

turned to Mila, said, 'Shhh!' and showed her his unbound hands.

'Mr Pilsudski had nothing but praise for my long, slim, pianist's fingers,' he said.

'Get me loose,' Mila said. Skelton did. 'And pass me that yardstick. I'll conceal it behind my back. If we pretend we're still bound, we'll have the element of surprise on our side and I'll have him disarmed and disabled before he knows what's hit him.'

'I was thinking I might just phone the police,' Skelton said.

'He'll hear.'

There came, from the hallway, the whine of the Auto-Vac-It 260. It was a noisy machine.

Skelton got through to the operator and asked to be put through to the police station, which, he knew, was just a few hundred yards away on the corner of Downshire Hill.

From the hallway, they heard Musgrave saying, or rather shouting over the noise of the 260, 'And this little lever disconnects the beater mechanism. Has your Mrs Stewart been disconnecting the beater mechanism?'

'I'm afraid I don't know.'

'Because if she hasn't, it's hardly surprising that its performance on the parquet has been disappointing.'

Skelton sat back in his chair. 'Mad, would you say?'

'Probably not asylum mad,' Mila said, 'but certainly flapping with the hinges very loose indeed.'

The vacuum cleaner was switched off. Skelton went back

to his chair, noticed that the Indiarubber bands were lying on the floor and whisked them into his pocket. Both he and Mila took up their helplessly bound positions.

Edgar and Musgrave came back. Edgar was carrying the Auto-Vac-It, now with a little brush on the end of a tube attached.

Musgrave held the gun steady. 'I did notice it as a matter of fact,' he said, 'and may I say what a striking piece it is.' They were standing one either side of the cocktail cabinet. 'But I can promise you that the upholstery brush will make short work of the dusting. Now, is there an electrical socket? Oh yes. Excellent.'

Supervised by Musgrave, Edgar began to dust the cocktail cabinet with the Auto-Vac-It's upholstery attachment.

'You see,' Musgrave said, 'every nook and cranny it just magics the dust away.'

It was true. Skelton noted that the deepest recesses were turning from a dingy grey to the beige of the bird's-eye maple and deep brown of the rosewood.

The door buzzer sounded.

'Switch it off,' Musgrave said, and before Edgar could find the switch, kicked at the wire dislodging the plug from the socket. 'Were you expecting anyone?'

'It might be the postman,' Edgar said.

Musgrave waggled the pistol to indicate that any funny business would result in a bullet to the heart.

Edgar called out with fairy-tale sweetness, 'Who is it?'

'It's the police.'

Musgrave whirled round. At the same moment, Mila disarmed him with the yard ruler. The gun went off as it fell to the ground and the bullet reduced a good-sized bit of the cocktail cabinet to splinters.

At the sound of the shot, the police abandoned restraint and started kicking at the door.

Mila, in Three Musketeers' pose, was repeatedly smacking Musgrave's head and shoulders and poking him with the ruler.

Musgrave edged over to the window, saw his chance, found the catch, flung it open and jumped out.

It wasn't much of a drop. They were on the first floor. All the same, he landed badly. From the window, Mila saw him try to stand and wince with pain as his ankle gave way. Two constables gently pushed him to the ground and got the handcuffs out.

'They've got him,' Mila said.

Edgar was examining the shattered cocktail cabinet.

'At the very moment,' he said, 'that one learnt of its dustability …this.'

EPILOGUE

Saturday, 21st March 1931

Skelton and Edgar had had sherry before the meal, wine with it and champagne with the toasts. Now they sat reflectively to one side, watching the comings and goings.

It had been a church wedding, after all. Rose and Vernon hadn't really minded one way or the other, as long as they were married, so when Vernon's parents had expressed a vague preference they'd gone and seen the vicar and said all the right things.

It was a pretty church, in one of the villages near Wolverton, Vernon's hometown. Parts of it were supposed to be Saxon and a general who was famous for doing something brave in the War of Jenkin's Ear was buried there. People sometimes came to do brass rubbings of his coat of arms.

Rose had worn a dress of white georgette trimmed with pearls and sequins and a bridal veil with a coronet of orange blossom. She carried a sheaf of Madonna lilies and wore a string of pearls – a gift from Skelton and Mila. She looked, in the nicest possible way, like a dog's breakfast.

Edgar, his chest visibly heaving with sobs, had walked her up the aisle. Four people, as he passed, had made a whispered remark to their neighbour about the creases in his trousers.

Rose was attended by Joan, who lived in Edgar's old rooms at Mrs Westing's in Swiss Cottage, and Muriel, an old friend from school and Girl Guides. They came out of the church beneath an arch of staves held by members of the 1st Wolverton Boy Scouts, Vernon's old troop.

Vernon's side of the church was filled with his uncles, aunts and cousins. He had hundreds of them.

Rose's sole remaining uncle and aunt, in Birmingham, were too unwell to come, but there was a fair turn out of friends from Birmingham, including Beth Tyrell, her old patrol leader, as well as Skelton and his family, Aubrey and three or four people from the office, and Mrs Westing.

The reception was in the upstairs function room of the local pub. They'd done a lovely spread with soup, chicken, trifle and the cake.

Edgar had done his best to make a speech but had collapsed in tears after a couple of sentences and Skelton had had to take over. The guests all agreed that Rose and Vernon must be very special indeed if they'd got Arthur Skelton, the 'Man Who Refuses to Lose', to speak at their wedding.

Afterwards, Rose had done the rounds, exchanging a few words with everyone, and had ended up having an altercation with Mila about the future of the German Nazi party. Mila was of the opinion that either the party would be made illegal – there had already been moves along these lines in Prussia – or that the Brownshirt tactics would bring the entire country to violent revolution from which the Communists, with backing from Russia and from the worldwide party membership, would emerge triumphant. Rose, who had had first-hand experience and been chased by Brownshirts, feared that Mila was living in a dreamworld and pointed out that on the one hand it might be a mistake for the Communists to look to Russia for support and on the other that Hitler had the big German industrialists on his side, men who were prepared to pay handsomely to keep the reds at bay.

Later, Mila had noticed a park nearby, and had taken all the children off – they had been growing a little boisterous – and organised a game of rounders, which she was winning.

Skelton and Edgar, in their quiet corner, smoked and watched Mrs Westing who, having had one too many milk stouts, was demonstrating the Highland fling to Vernon's Auntie Brenda and Uncle Ralph.

'Did you see the letter from the chap in Bedford?' Edgar asked.

'Holland? Yes, I did.'

The letter had contained the news that Tommy Prosser

had thrown himself from a bridge under the wheels of a passing train. He'd been killed instantly.

'Did you speak to Holland on the telephone?' Skelton asked.

'Briefly.'

'Any news of the train driver?'

'He said he'd make enquiries.'

It was a conversation that the two friends had had many times before. When people end their lives by throwing themselves under trains or buses, nobody ever gives a thought to the drivers, who will, no doubt, spend the rest of their lives reliving the moment in great distress.

'Ask him to get in touch. See if there's anything we can do.'

Aubrey, over the other side of the room, talking with a chap Skelton didn't recognise, let out a sudden barking laugh.

'How's your cousin Alan?' Edgar asked.

'Oh, I had the usual letter on Wednesday. His faith in God, you'll be glad to know, has been restored by a miracle.'

'Yes?'

'An anonymous banker's order for two-thousand five-hundred pounds for the Chaundler Fund's widows and orphans charity.'

'I thought the Chester Monroe money was two thousand.'

'I gave half of that to Rose and Vernon. Their money, anyway. They earned it. Give them a decent start. Buy a house, furnish it, get herself a new overcoat.'

'So where did the …?'

'I had the thousand from Lord Rosthwaite.'

'He paid up, did he?'

'And I felt obliged to give that to charity. And then the other five hundred came from Denison Beck because I told him that since he'd been very lucky to escape prison a substantial donation to charity was the very least he could do.'

'Immoral earnings, then. And possibly the last earnings you'll ever see.'

Skelton had signed up to do two evenings a week as a Poor Man's Lawyer in a settlement off the Mile End Road. Preparation and possible court appearances would mean he would be spending less time on Foxton Row business. 'You disapprove, don't you?' he said. 'It's all right for you to say it, you know.'

'Of course I don't disapprove. It is a fine and noble thing you're doing.'

'Clarendon-Gow disapproves.'

'Because you'll be spending less time at Foxton Row and it'll cost him money.'

'It'll cost you money, too.'

'I'm sure I'll be able to make it up elsewhere. Oh, I meant to mention, *Rex versus Thornborough*.'

'Which one's that?'

'The man who stabbed his wife with a cricket stump.'

'Yes, what about it?'

'It's at the Warwick assizes, isn't it?'

'Yes.'

'And Stratford-upon-Avon is on the way to Warwick, isn't it? If one were to drive.'

'Why would I drive to Warwick?'

'There's this cocktail cabinet. This one is definitely the work of Pavel Janák, rather less severe than the previous one and entirely in bleached oak.'

'More like the Syrie Maugham one at the Yellow House, then?'

'You're catching on.'

AUTHOR'S NOTE

This book is dedicated to Marc Beeby.

He was a man of remarkable talent who, with just one or two exceptions, produced all the BBC radio dramas and comedy series that Caroline and I wrote over a period of about twenty years, including the two series of plays about Norman Birkett, the barrister on whom Skelton is very loosely based.

He died at the end of 2020.

Marc was blessed with rare insight. He understood not just how writers work, but intuitively how *we* worked, and it was the same with actors. After a particularly bad take, while Caroline and I were hoping he'd seriously consider recasting at least a couple of the parts, Marc would be thinking. Then he'd pop into the studio and, full of encouragement, put everything right. Often his remarks to the cast seemed to have little to do with what, it seemed to us, was going wrong. But Marc understood the psychology of acting, the insecurities and other troubles that can bind talent. He knew exactly how to calm, chivvy or coax. Often the difference between take one and take two was the miraculous equivalent of turning water into wine.

Though sometimes in the pub afterwards, he would confess to wanting to murder this or that member of the cast – and at times I'm fairly sure he wanted to murder us – I never once saw him lose his rag in the studio.

He was erudite and very funny.

I don't think we'll be writing for radio any more. It wouldn't be the same without Marc. We miss him.

Nearly all the stories in the book – main plots and minor subplots – are based in some measure on real events.

The annoying thing about true stories is that they're usually too complicated or too simple to make a decent narrative. The protagonists learn of the twist in the tale too early or too late, or they come upon it too easily; or there is no twist and one has to be manufactured. Events are often too bizarre for plausibility or too mundane to be interesting. And, in real life, people often do things apparently for no reason – again an unacceptable trait in what usually passes as a decent story (although Shakespeare flirted with the idea in *Hamlet*).

The burning car mystery dominated the headlines at the end of 1930. The names and many of the incidents have been changed in this heavily fictionalised version but many of the details – even some of the stranger ones – are based in fact. I won't mention which ones because, if you're working backwards and reading this before embarking on the book itself, it might give the game away.

The medical electrician subplot too, is based on a real case, again heavily fictionalised, this time largely because the real events were downright distressing and would have added notes of dread and gloom where they would have been inappropriate.

Trawling though old newspapers is a wonderful way of avoiding the pain of actual writing and can happily fill days and weeks. I try to convince myself it's something more than procrastination—that all the time I'm reading about the Heysham Ramblers' Club Annual Picnic in *The Morecambe Guardian* or studying the five-a-side football results in the *Linlithgowshire Gazette,* the book is forming itself magically in my head. But this is a glaring delusion.

Having said that, though the book's never going to get written this way, one does now and then turn up nuggets of pure gold that make the hours spent prospecting spuriously worthwhile.

The events at the Lord Mayor's show – which are all true (you can even watch some of the parade on YouTube) were a delightful discovery and came in useful, as did the incident with the eels. Both contributed to the bubbling of doubts that, in the end, leads Skelton to reassess the course of his career.

The 'knickerbocker/plus fours' case probably fits into the category of 'too bizarre to be plausible' but it did indeed happen at the Eastbourne County Court in August 1930, and, unlike the plus fours in question, needed very little alteration to be a good fit for Skelton.

The inept safe-cracker story is almost entirely true, as is case of the sweating policeman and – with the dates shifted by a few months – many of the things Rose and Vernon witness in Heidelberg.

Oh, and if your appetite for Czech cubist furniture has been whetted, you'll be glad to know there's a permanent exhibition displaying some fine examples at the Museum of Decorative Arts in Prague.

David Stafford 28/06/2022

ACKNOWLEDGEMENTS

Acknowledgements must start with Caroline.

Caroline and I have been married for thirty years and writing partners for twenty-five. The original inspiration for the Skelton novels – the radio series we did together based on the casebook of Norman Birkett – was her discovery and her idea. For all three Skelton books, she has put endless patient hours into discussions of plot and character. Her involvement in the creation of *Skelton's Guide to Blazing Corpses* became all the greater when, half-way through its writing, I had to take time off for illness. The German chapters in this book are mostly her work.

* * *

The British Library had limited access in times of Covid, so much of the research for *Blazing Corpses* relied on other libraries, generous gifts ('I've got some 1928 tram timetables if you think they might help') and lucky finds. A list of every website and publication consulted would run to several pages, so here's just a few of the sources that were particularly useful.

The British Newspaper Archive provided companionship, entertainment and work-avoidance potential as well as information about, for instance, how much British people would have known about Brownshirts in 1930, what you might expect to pay in those days for a hot gravy dinner with custard pudding, and attitudes in general towards cake, cabbages and Kings.

As always A. E. Bowker's *Behind The Bar* supplied endless insights into the day-to-day life of barristers and their clerks in the first half of the twentieth century, and H. Montgomery Hyde's *Norman Birkett*, which was where the idea came from in the first place, continues to entertain and enlighten.

Nigel Gray's *The Worst of Times, an Oral History of the Great Depression* was the source of some of Alan and Norah's experiences. Walter Greenwood's *Love on The Dole* gives a flavour of the times as does *The Long Weekend* by Robert Graves and Alan Hodge. And for historical detail, style and its celebration of the ordinary, I keep going back to (and would highly recommend) R. C. Sherriff's *A Fortnight in September*.

Then there are the many people who have given help and support, practical, moral, spiritual and physical. They include, with apologies for any I've left out: every librarian and archivist in the world (may they thrive and prosper for theirs is the most noble of professions), Bill and Jen Baker, Jon Rust, Warren Sherman, Carol Reyes, Alexei and Linda Sayle, Keith and Rebecca Erskine, Stephanie Moran-Watson, Bill and Laura Oddie, Dion Morton, Charlie Dore, Tom Climpson, Nigel and Roberta Planer, James Wilson, Ellie Richards, Sue and John Thompson, Ben and Clementine Kelly, lots of Staffords – Michael, Edna, John, Connie, Georgia, Cosmo the dog, and most of all you, dear reader, without whom …

DAVID STAFFORD began his career in theatre. He has written countless dramas, comedies and documentaries including two TV films with Alexei Sayle, *Dread Poets Society* with Benjamin Zephaniah, and, with his wife, Caroline, a string of radio plays and comedies including *The Brothers*, *The Day the Planes Came* and *The Year They Invented Sex* as well as five biographies of musicians and showbusiness personalities. *Fings Ain't Wot They Use T'Be – The Life of Lionel Bart* was chosen as Radio 4 Book of the Week and made into a BBC Four TV documentary.

dcstafford.com   @dstaffordwriter